Hoping to escape a trail of blood and death, Peaches arrives in Florida only to discover that the death toll had just begun. The Argots and the Heathens suddenly find themselves pitted against one another in a vicious drug war, forcing Peaches to fight to save her beloved club. Now, in order to survive she must tame a powerful Columbian Drug Lord, and out fox an F.B.I. and D.E.A. Task Force.

The Wee Hours III: Florida Snow

FLORIDA SNOW

THE WEE HOURS III

W.D. BURNS

Bad Ass Outlaw Publications

BAD ASS OUTLAW PUBLICATIONS
4216 Riverview Lane
Lorian, OH 44055
www.badassoutlawpublications.com

This book is an original publication of Bad Ass Outlaw Publications.

William Daniel Burns
FLORIDA SNOW: THE WEE HOURS III
Library of Congress
Copyright 2010 TX
u001889306
revised 2015

Editing, typesetting and cover design by J.D. Williams
(www.behance.net/jdwilliams)

ISBN: 978-0-9962651-2-6

Printed in The United States of America

10 9 8 7 6 5 4 3 2 1

FLORIDA SNOW: THE WEE HOURS III

INDEX

Dedication

To my mother and father, for without their love I would not have the gift of life. And to our heavenly father for without his wisdom, guidance, understanding, and patience, there would be nothing.

Acknowledgements

Special thanks to Colleen Brown, for without her assistance this book would not have been possible. Props to my Editor in Chief and friend, Ronnie Jones.

CHAPTER ONE
FLORIDA SNOW

"Good morning Miami. Susan Lichtman of WTVJ reporting. Early this morning F.B.I. and D.E.A. agents raided the Heathens clubhouses throughout central Florida arresting more than two hundred outlaw bikers. In Altamonte Springs, a house was raided and automatic weapons and hand grenades seized. Johnny Rowe and Richard Allen Doyle, members of the Argot outlaw biker gang were charged with federal firearms violations, murder, attempted murder, and conspiracy to commit murder. A gold Lincoln Towncar was seen leaving the residence a half hour before the pre- dawn raid. Let's go to Richard Bower, reporting live from the scene in Altamonte Springs. Richard, what can you tell us?"

"Susan, the raids stem from and ongoing war between the two biker gangs that have left thirteen dead. State and Federal agencies have joined forces to end the mayhem. Agencies throughout Florida have been told to arrest any biker wearing the Heathens or Argots patch."

"Thank you, Richard. WTVJ will continue updates as information is received. On the other side of the news, powerboat designer Don Aronow, the winner of the 1969 Bahamas 500, announced his company Apache Performance has reached an agreement to build powerful Catamarans for the U.S. Customs Service. The Dade County weather service reports blue skies today and tomorrow. Sunny, in the high 80's with possible showers towards late evening. It's a great day to spend at the beach. Pitch your umbrella in the sand and relax. Have a great day Miami. Susan Lichtman for WTVJ, Channel 4."

* * *

"We are forming a task force. I want anyone who is remotely associated with this investigation here to answer questions. That means every agency. The Argot motorcycle gang is believed to be responsible for several murders occurring in the State of Maryland. I want detectives from Maryland and Pennsylvania in the conference room at nine o'clock in the morning," Special Agent H. Thomas Moore barked.

Moore had been with the F.B.I. for 15 years, and he was a seasoned investigator graduating with honors after his 18-months of rigorous training at Quantico, Virginia. Every morning before breakfast, Moore dressed in a jogging suit or shorts and began his day with a five mile run. He stood six feet one, weighing a firm 185 pounds. He was clean cut and well groomed, his hair graying slightly around the ears.

"Yes Sir!" F.B.I. Agent John Sweeny snapped. Always quick to please, Sweeny had been Moore's sidekick for the past five years. His attitude made up for his short stature.

"Also invite D.E.A. Agent Pete Elliot to the meeting." Moore added. The first call was made to Detective Daniel Marks of the Baltimore City

Homicide Division. Marks supplied the names of two known associates of the Argot motorcycle gang, Charlie and Nicole Redman. Charlie's current address was in Millersville, Maryland which was in the jurisdiction of the Anne Arundel County Sheriff's Department.

The second call was placed to Detective Sergeant Hill of the Anne Arundel County Sheriff's Department.

A third call was placed to Detective Ralph Criswell of the City of Harrisburg, Pennsylvania's Police Department.

The final call was to D.E.A. Agent Pete Elliot. Since he was assigned to the Orlando Office, there would be no need to do more than notify him of the meeting and request his participation.

F.B.I. Agent Sweeny made reservations at the Hilton Hotel in downtown Orlando, with separate rooms for Detectives Marks, Betty Crawford, Sergeant Hill, and Criswell. Within an hour, Special Agent Sweeny called to give them their flight itinerary, and reservations. They were already keenly aware of the meeting to be held at the F.B.I.

Headquarters at 9 a.m. The detectives were in a quandary wondering why they were being to called the meeting.

* * *

After spending several hours in the drunk tank at the Orlando County Jail, Ramrod was banging on the steel bars shouting. "I know my Rights. I'm entitled to a phone call!"

One hour later, the jailer allowed him to make a five minute call. Ramrod called attorney Harold Glazer.

"You boys are making a lot of noise down there," Harold reported. The news of the biker wars had gone nationwide.

"The feds raided the house where we were staying early this morning, Bulldog and myself are charged with federal firearms violations, murder, attempted murder, and conspiracy to commit murder. We are scheduled to appear before a magistrate for a bond hearing at ten o'clock tomorrow morning. Is it possible for you to be there?"

"My license doesn't allow me to practice law outside of the state of Maryland. However, if you retain local counsel, the law allows me to act as co-counsel."

"I don't know any local attorneys and I'm only permitted one five minute call."

"Are you authorizing me to act on your behalf?"

"Of course."

"Good, I thought you might, so I've already made inquiries. I was referred to a local attorney, Harry Swogel. As we speak, my secretary is placing a call to his office."

"That's why you're the best, Harold. You are always thinking ahead.I'll see you in the morning."

"I'll be there," Harold promised.

Bulldog used his five minutes to call The Pink Pussycat. Charlotte answered on the first ring. "Hello."

"Hi Sugar. Your man used his five minute call to call an attorney." Bulldog grinned, looking at Ramrod for a reaction.

"Are you guys okay? Nobody has heard from Nicole. And, Charlie is still missing. I don't know what to do. When are visiting hours?"

"We're fine. Harold Glazer will be here in the morning for our bond hearing at ten o'clock along with a local attorney. This shit is driving me nuts. You will have to call the jail to find out what the visiting hours are. If you hear from Nicole, tell her that I love her."

"How sweet." Ramrod chuckled.

"Tell Ramrod that I said he's an asshole."

"C'mon guys," The jailer interrupted. "Playtime is over. You're being moved upstairs. Grab a blanket. Rolled up inside the blanket are linens, a bar of soap, and a towel. When the gates break at four o'clock, the showers are at the end of the hall. After you shower, you will be issued a fresh pair of coveralls and a clean towel. Any questions?"

"I specifically asked for a room with a view," Bulldog joked.

The cell-block housed twenty men, mostly black. There were two vacant bunks, at opposite ends of the cell-block. Ramrod and Bulldog made their beds, then sat off to themselves to discuss their situation.

"Did Harold mention a possibility of our being granted bail?" Bulldog asked in a whisper.

"Nope, but there's always a possibility." Ramrod grinned, thinking there was a better chance of eight inches of snow in Florida.

Both men were looking forward to a hot shower and a meal. When the gate opened, Ramrod and Bulldog followed the other men. As Bulldog lathered, a huge black man patted him on the ass and whispered in his ear, "Nice butt."

Bulldog grinned, then whispered in the big man's ear, "You would have a nice one too, if you kept the dicks out of it."

It was the start of a vicious brawl. It was pretty much a free for all, two against ten ending with a few black eyes and missing teeth, the floor of the shower covered in a spray of blood.

"Well, I guess there went any chance of our getting a bond." Ramrod snarled, as they were handcuffed and dragged off to the hole. Seeing the small glass window in the door, Ramrod chuckled. "But you're getting a room with a view."

* * *

Hours earlier, Nicole was standing on the back of the powerboat wrapped in chicken wire with cinder blocks tied to her feet. She offered her kidnappers five hundred thousand dollars each if they spared her life. When they grinned and grabbed the chicken wire wrapped tightly around her, she cursed them. "Fuck all you bitches!" In her fury, she failed to see the rouge wave rise up to slam into the side of the boat. One of the men screamed in agonizing pain as the chicken wire sliced into his fingers like razor blades. "Shit!" The older of the two cursed as he ran to a compartment below the steering wheel, returning seconds later with an emergency medical kit. First, with the help of the injured man, Nicole was lowered down into the bottom of the boat. The older of the two poured peroxide over his cuts, then began wrapping his fingers with gauze. "I've done many bad things in my life, but I have never killed a woman. I've never killed anyone," he explained. The second his hand was wrapped the younger man grabbed a pair of wire cutters from inside the cabin and cut away the chicken wire from around Nicole's body. Peaches lay on her side shivering motivating the younger man to grab a blanket and gently place it around her. He smiled.

Peaches returned the smile. "Thank you for saving my life."

"My name is Raul and that is my older brother, Tony."

Raul pointed with a motion of his head. Blood was soaking through the gauze on Tony's hand. So Peaches gently removed the blood soaked gauze and rebandaged his hand.

"If John Leder finds out that you're still alive, we will all be searching for Davy Jones' locker," Tony declared, in a heavy accent.

"He will think something is wrong if we do not collect the payment he promised us," Raul added.

"The first thing we need to do is to get you to a hospital. Then I want you to return to the island to collect the money John Leder owes you. He will have no reason to be suspicious and that will give me enough time to figure things out," Peaches promised.

Raul started the engines and raced for the dock in Miami.

The nearest hospital was five miles inland and two of Tony's fingers were sliced to the bone and in need of stitches.

After docking the boat, Tony drove his brother Raul and Peaches off at a nearby Holiday Inn. Peaches had no money, no identification, and no change of clothes. Tony opened his wallet and handed Raul two hundred and fifty dollars instructing him to rent a room, buy some clothes for Peaches, and for him to buy them something to eat. "Don't let her leave the room until I get back!" he added.

Tony drove himself to the hospital. As his fingers were being stitched, his thoughts wandered to his returning to the island. He hoped that Leder wouldn't ask questions, but that was probably wishful thinking. He could anticipate at least three questions. Did everything go alright? What happened to his hand? And, where was his brother Raul?

Nicole turned on the TV, then sat on the edge of the bed waiting for the morning news to come on.

"Good morning, Miami. Susan Lichtman of WTVJ Channel 4 reporting. Early this morning the F.B.I. and D.E.A. raided Heathen clubhouses throughout central Florida arresting more than two hundred bikers. A house in Altamonte Springs was raided and automatic weapons and hand grenades seized. Two men were arrested. Johnny Rowe and Richard Allen Doyle were charged with federal firearms violations, murder, attempted murder, and conspiracy to commit murder. While being housed in the Orange County Jail the two outlaw bikers sent six men to the infirmary and they are now being housed in segregation." The news anchor repeated the earlier report.

Peaches cupped her hands covering her face, and sobbed.

"What's wrong?" Raul asked. "I've made a mess of everything."

The look on Raul's face was one of awe. He had no idea what she was talking about.

"The two men arrested in Altamonte Springs are my family!" Peaches sobbed, reaching to turn the knob on the TV to see if there were any other news reports.

"Tony is the only family that I have," Raul offered. "Our parents were killed in an automobile accident when I was eight years old. We were taken in by relatives, but they never really wanted us. After school, we had to work in the fields until dark to help pay for our keep. Tony quit school when he was sixteen. When he started making money selling drugs, we moved out in search of a better life. I don't understand you. You don't make sense."

"What do you mean?"

"Well, you do not cry when we kidnapped you from your place. You never shed a single tear when you were wrapped in chicken wire. Now, you sit on a nice comfortable bed crying your eyes out."

"Love will make you do things that are often out of character." Peaches sighed, forcing herself to smile.

Raul and Tony were both deeply tanned with black hair and brown eyes. Raul was five feet ten, two inches taller than his brother. Both men were lean, and unshaved.

"You are beautiful." Raul announced, admiring her Platinum blonde hair.

"Oh yeah!" she replied, sarcastically.

"No, I really mean it. You are a very beautiful woman. What is your true name?"

"Nicole Redman. If I told you my middle name, I'd have to kill you. Peaches is my stage name. How did you and your brother get mixed up with the likes of John Leder?"

"We drive the boat," Raul explained. "Small airplanes fly from Bogota, Columbia to an island near Norman's Cay. The airplane lands.

We unload it, then race across the ocean in the darkness of the night to Boco Raton without using running lights. When we dock, the cocaine is unloaded and carted off to a waiting van. I don't know where it's taken, probably to a nearby warehouse. From there, it's distributed all over the country. I'm hungry. Would you like to order something?"

"How can you eat? Aren't you worried about your brother?"

"If Tony was hungry, he would eat." Raul grinned

"I'm more concerned with a shower, a change of clothes, a toothbrush, toothpaste, deodorant, and a hair dryer would be nice."

"I know a girl. Tell me exactly what you want and I will call her. Maria will bring whatever you need."

An hour later, Peaches showered, then dressed in a short white mini- skirt, a pink white-stripped halter top, and on her feet she was wearing a pair of multi-colored flip-flops.

"I love these flip-flops," Peaches announced. "Where did you get them?"

The young Cuban girl told her the name of the store and where it was located, then opened the door to the motel room, and left.

"I'm starved. Now, can we get something to eat?" Raul asked.

"When is Tony coming back? It's driving me nuts not to be able to make any calls."

"He should be back soon." Raul replied, feeling badly for her.

* * *

Nuni pleaded with Sugar to stay at his house, but she insisted in staying at the club. If Nicole called, she needed to be there for her. She asked Nuni to open and close the club. It would be business as usual, She was certain it was how her sister would want it.

CHAPTER TWO
FEVER IN THE FUNKHOUSE

Peaches heard the closing of a car door, then a moment later a knock sounded on the hotel room door. Raul cautiously peeked through the curtains, smiled, and unlocked the door.

Nicole felt the love as the brothers embraced and patted each other on the back.

Tony dumped a brown paper shopping bag filled with money on the bed. It was more money than Raul had ever seen in his young life. The money failed to impress Peaches, but she shared in the joy of her captor's. "It took long enough," Peaches declared. It was now 4 o'clock in the moning.

"I was at the hospital for three hours."

"How many stitches did you get?" Raul asked.

"Twenty-four. Thirteen on one finger and eleven on the other."

"What happened when you went to see John Leder?" Peaches asked.

"I told him that your last words were, 'Fuck all you bitches!'" Tony laughed. "He said that's one bitch that won't be causing me any more problems."

Peaches giggled, then retorted. "He hasn't seen the last of this bitch."

"Did he ask where I was?" Raul wanted to know.

"I told him you stayed behind to look for a better place for us to live. He laughed and asked what was wrong with his private island. I believe he referred to it as a tropical paradise."

"Have you made any calls?" Tony asked, directing the question at Peaches.

"No. You told me not to, but it's been driving me crazy. My old man and the president of the Argot motorcycle club have been arrested and charged with federal firearms violations, murder, attempted murder, and conspiracy to commit murder. Plus they got into a fight in the

Orange County jail where they are being detained, they sent six men to the infirmary, and now they're in segregation."

"How do you know this?"

"It's been all over the news," Raul explained. "Why does El Jefe want you dead?"

"El who?" Peaches asked, unsure who Tony was referring to.

"El Jefe in Spanish is 'the boss'. That's what we call John Leder." Toni explained.

"From what I know, he gave my ex husband the east coast to distribute cocaine. When he wanted Charlie to sell larger amounts, it was my idea for the Argots to open a Chapter in Orlando. The Heathens motorcycle club claimed Florida as their territory and a war broke out. I was never told that Charlie was given a specific territory, Besides that, the east coast is from Maine to Florida."

"How much cocaine were you distributing?"

"At first, fifty kilos a month. That was a little over a year ago. Before all of this started, between Maryland, Pennsylvania, and Florida, three hundred kilos. I made John Leder a lot of money."

"There are many police everywhere, in my country the police always mean great trouble."

"What are we to do?" Raul asked.

"When we are paid by Peaches, we shall change our names and move far away from this place," Tony replied.

"Running is your solution?" Peaches laughed. "What else can we do?"

"If El Jefe finds out that I'm alive, he will use all of his money and connections to hunt you down. I'm sure he will take great pleasure in having you tortured before he kills you. Right now he thinks me to be dead, giving us the element of surprise. I think we should deal with the problem."

"I told you that we have never killed anyone," Tony snapped.

"I'm not asking you to!" Peaches snapped back, "How much do you know about the island, Norman's Cay?"

"I know every square inch of the island. We lived there for a year before we were given the job of driving the boat."

"How many men are on the island?"

"Counting the Jefe, there are five men. The bungalow has three rooms. There's a small bungalow across from his with four bunk beds. It has only one door."

Raul was lost in thought. He had not heard a single word spoken between Tony and Peaches. Out of nowhere, he spat his bitterness. "Paradise my ass! There's no electricity. The only fresh water is drawn from a well, There's a crude make-shift shower with a wooden planked floor. There's no faucet to turn the water on or off, we had to fill a bucket with water. Sometimes we could not shower for days. We, my brother and I, named the bungalow 'the funkhouse'."

"Can you draw a map of the island showing where the bungalows are located?"

"With my eyes closed." Tony boasted.

"You can not imagine how badly it smelled living in that small, enclosed dump." Raul recalled.

Tony looked around the room. There was a desk with a chair, a color television mounted on the wall, a bathroom with a sink, toilet, and combination tub and shower. A queen sized bed was centered in the room with a nightstand and lamp on each side, A telephone rested unused on the bedside table.

"You should have got more than one bed." Tony looked over at Peaches, then frowned at his brother.

"I never thought about that," Raul answered with a shrug.

"Well, I'm exhausted." Tony said, his face suddenly looking haggard. "Let's get a few hours sleep. By the way, when I asked for a week off, he asked me to make the run to Boco Raton Wednesday night. I told him it would not be a problem," he explained, then added for Nicole's benefit. "That's where we deliver the drugs for distribution."

As Tony emptied his pockets onto the nightstand, he pulled out an ounce cocaine. At the information concerning Boco Raton, Nicole felt the wheels begin to turn in her head. Raul busied himself counting money, placing it back in the grocery bag as he finished each stack.

"Mind if I do some of that?" Peaches asked, staring at the baggy filled with powder.

"Help yourself."

"Make me a couple lines," Raul requested.

"I just want some sleep," Tony yawned and stretched out across the welcoming bed.

Peaches laid out four lines, grabbing a fifty dollar bill from the money on the bed, rolled it up and snorted a line into each nostril. She titled her head back and sniffed hard before passing the rolled up bill to Raul, who quickly snorted his lines.

"I needed that," Peaches said as Raul continued counting the money. Within minutes Tony was snoring: quick, short, continuous snorts.

Peaches giggled, then whispered to Raul. "Let's sit on the floor and talk so we don't disturb your brother."

Raul followed her to the far corner of the room. They sat facing each other with their legs crossed like Indians.

"How many kilos do you deliver to Boco Raton?"

"A lot. Never less than three hundred. Sometimes more."

"Do you have any idea where the warehouse is?"

"No."

"Do the men who meet you at the dock carry any guns?"

"I've never seen any. We unload at a big house that has a private dock area."

"Are there any houses close to the dock?"

"Not really. Why?"

Peaches paused a brief second before asking. "Has a shipment ever been ripped off?"

"Not that I know of." Raul laughed softly, careful not to awaken his brother. "You know what would be really crazy?"

"No, what?" Peaches smiled her encouragement,

"They never lock the van and I am sure the keys are left in the vehicle. There is a line of bushes next to where we park. Someone could sneak up to drive off while the other men are down at the docks getting the last load."

Despite his accent, Peaches was able to understand him perfectly. "How would someone know it was the last load?"

"I could set a red gas can on the dock as we prepare to leave."

"That could work perfectly. I would love to see the bastard's face when someone told him his shipment was stolen," Peaches stated coldly.

"The only problem would be if my brother and I were to tell El Jefe. He would shoot us on the spot."

"Well, that pretty much shoots that idea all to hell. But it was a great thought," Peaches yawned.

Raul stood up to go over to the night table to lay out four more lines of cocaine, he motioned for Peaches to join him. She performed her normal ritual and Raul joined her. They returned to their corner seats.

"What if we load the boat but never show up at the dock in Boco Raton?"

"That's it!" Peaches announced excitedly. "You could unload at a place of our choosing. This is not going to be without risk, but I would give you and your brother a third of the load. With the fifty thousand John Leder gave you, and the five hundred thousand from me, you guys should be set for the rest of your lives."

"What about El Jefe?"

"I wouldn't be worried about him. He told me that he was my worst nightmare. I plan on being his."

"What are you going to do to him?" Raul asked in concern for himself and his brother in case she failed in her plans.

"I haven't decided yet. But I'm going to return to the island with some of my own men. We will capture the men in the bunkhouse and

I will personally wake up John Leder."

"Are you serious?" Raul said in wonder. "For a woman you have more balls than a mighty bull."

"Do you think you can get us onto the island undetected?"

"This I think is easy. You must know that there will be a man awake guarding El Jefe's bungalow. I can get everyone on the island. How do you take the guard by surprise? That will not be so easy."

Peaches ignored his concern. "Do you think they will go along with my plan?" she asked instead.

"I do not know this. It is risky. Tony's forever a cautious man."

"It's better than looking over your shoulder for the rest of your lives. Risky? You and Tony have weathered storms at sea to deliver shipments of drugs. You even kidnapped me from my club. These things were filled with risks. Taking over the island should be simple in comparison."

"Maybe this is so." Raul replied, deep in thought. "Do you have a girlfriend?"

"What?" Raul asked, unsure if he heard her correctly. "Do you have a girlfriend?" she repeated.

"No." Raul smiled cautiously. This Peaches was a great danger, and if his brother had been awake, he would have warned him to be careful. He glanced over at the bed, but his brother was sleeping soundly.

"Have you ever been with a girl?" she asked bluntly.

Raul blushed. "What kind of question is this you ask of me?"

"Answer me." Peaches demanded in a commanding voice. "Once. I have been with only one girl," Raul lied.

Peaches' eyes went to his crotch. Through his pants she could see a bulge slowly growing. It made her horny. Maybe it was the stress or even the cocaine. Whatever it was, she yearned to feel his hard dick pressed deep inside of her warmth.

"Would you like to get lucky?" she whispered, already hiking up her mini skirt. She pulled her white G-string to the side, exposing her well trimmed bush. Before Raul could answer, she reached forward grabbing hold of his hard boner. Unzipping his pants she pulled out his dick to suck him into her mouth, making him moan softly in pleasure. She gently ran her tongue over it before deep throating the entire shaft. Raul grabbed her ass and slid her closer, moving her legs apart to at her moist slit. At the touch of his fingers against her pussy, he snatched the G-string off and quickly mounted her. As he entered her in one long jerk, Peaches thought that his size made up for his lack of experience. They both bucked and moaned quietly, trying desperately not to wake up the sleeping Tony. It was Raul's first time and that made it even better. They climaxed together, then laid on the carpet breathing heavily, and gazing into each other eyes.

"I'll never forget seeing you on the back of the boat tied in the wire. My people call this a wire cage," Raul said with a little grin.

"It's a time I would rather not be reminded of," she replied coldly, not believing he would dare to find her pain amusing. The mere thought of it made her livid. How could he bring something like that up after she had just fucked him. If he would talk about it now, then he would surely talk about it at a later date. Oh no, he wouldn't! She would make sure of that.

Peaches grabbed her g-string from the floor, stood up, and slowly walked to the bathroom, closing the door behind her. She took a hot shower washing away Raul's manly body odor. Afterwards, she stood looking at herself in the frosted mirror.

Her hair was wet and stringy. Dark circles appeared around her eyes. She sat on the edge of the bath tub, cupped her hands to cover her face, and finally broke down and cried. What was wrong with her? What made her do such foolish things on the spur of the moment? She knew that her heart belonged to Bulldog, but when he wasn't around she made some very bad decisions. Or, maybe she was simply over sexed. She compared her life to a roller coaster. One minute she was on top of the world; the next she was at the bottom crying her eyes out. Thoughts of John Leder snapped her back to reality. He was going to feel her wrath! She had only known him for five minutes, yet she despised him with every breath she took. Peaches dried her eyes and ran her fingers through her hair before returning to the main room of the motel. She walked to the window, pulled back the curtains, and peeked out into the quiet parking lot. The sun was coming over the horizon and it had a gorgeous pink glow.

"What time is it?" She asked.

"Six-thirty." Raul replied, having a hard time meeting her eyes.

"What time are you going to wake Tony up?" she asked.

"I'm awake." Tony growled.

Raul blushed, and Peaches smiled. Neither had paid attention to his not snoring.

"The two of you could wake the dead with all your moaning and grunting," he said, then rolled over.

Within a few quiet minutes, Tony was back to sleep and snoring. Peaches and Raul sat back down in the corner and continued to talk about Norman's Cay. Peaches mind was ice cold, yet spinning with a million different thoughts at once. One minute she was scheming, planning, and plotting her revenge against John Leder. Moments later, she was thinking about her baby sister Charlotte Lynn, her beloved Bulldog, and Charlie. Her worries were multiplied by the presence of the F.B.I. and D.E.A. She would have to tread carefully around a minefield of law enforcement and a very dangerous drug lord.

CHAPTER THREE
IN ALL FAIRNESS

The phone began ringing at seven o'clock in the morning and rang continuously until Betty Crawford snatched up the receiver.

"Good morning! This is your wake up call."

Betty recognized the voice of the front clerk receptionist. "Thank you," she said, and the line went dead in her hand.

Betty returned the receiver to its cradle with a yawn, stretching her arms out wide, while slowly crawling out of the narrow hotel bed. She was feeling the effects of jet lag. Wiping the sleep from her eyes, she wondered if her boss, Detective Marks, was awake, and how long it would be before he called.

The meeting at the downtown Federal building was scheduled to happen at 9 a.m. Surely they would stop somewhere for breakfast. With this in mind, she rushed to take a shower.

By 7:30, she was dressed with her hair wrapped into a conservative bun. She wore black rimmed glasses, making her look like a school teacher. Detective Marks often teased her about her fair, almost pale skin, claiming that her make-up bag consisted of nothing more than tube of lip gloss. Beneath her clothing Marks often thought that she might have been hiding a fantastic body, but seriously doubted that she was sharing it with anyone. By 8 o'clock, Detective Marks was sitting in the hotel dining room, sipping a cup of coffee and enjoying the hotel's free continental breakfast. He was reading the local newspaper, the The Orlando Sentinel, when Detective Sergeant Hill approached the table.

"Good morning. The receptionist pointed you out and said that you were from Baltimore, Maryland. My guess is we are both here for the same meeting. I'm Detective Sergeant Hill from the Anne Arundel County Sheriffs Department."

"Good Guess." Marks nodded.

"I'm Detective Daniel Marks from the Baltimore City Homicide

Division. Try the cream puffs. They are filled with coconut cream and are extremely delicious."

The two sat across from each other devouring donuts, sipping coffee and making idle conversation. Neither knew exactly why they were here, but agreed that the climate was terrific.

* * *

Harold Glazer flew in the night before Ramrod and Bulldog were to appear in court. He rented a new metallic blue Cadillac Coupe Deville at the Orlando International airport and drove to the Holiday Inn downtown, which was adjacent to a golf course. He had reserved a suite and thoughtfully brought along his golf clubs hoping to get in eighteen holes before returning to Maryland. Harold was in his early forties, fifty pounds overweight, with well groomed dark brown curly hair. He was always immaculately dressed and he was well known for his courtroom mannerism and theatrics. In court, he was a master showman. His rosy red cheeks were soon forgotten as he showed his brilliance regarding matters of the law. Harold was articulate and he could read a juror's body language like an open book. It was as though he knew what they were thinking.

By eight o'clock Harold was sitting in the Country Kitchen restaurant sipping on a fresh cup of coffee, reading the morning edition of the Sentinel, and waiting for Harry Swogel to arrive. They had spoken briefly the night before, by phone. Harry graciously agreed to accept a ten thousand dollar retainer to act as lead counsel for Johnny Rowe and Richard Doyle. He offered to visit his new clients at the jail, but Harold suggested he wait and they enter their appearances at the hearing. He wanted the element of surprise to tip things in their favor. After all, this was certainly not his first rodeo. Harry walked inside the restaurant, smiled, and introduced himself. They shook hands then ordered breakfast. Harold ordered three eggs sunny side up, with side orders of bacon and ham, two slices of toast, and a cup of coffee with cream and sugar.

Harry Swogel was in his late sixties, thin with a pot belly, gray hair, and spoke with a thick southern accent. He was dressed in a well worn gray pin-striped suit, white dress shirt, and a solid red tie.

Harold opened his suit jacket, grabbed an envelope containing ten thousand dollars in cash from an inside pocket, passing it across the table with a smile.

Harry looked inside the envelope, quickly placed it in the inside pocket of his jacket and said, "this is not normally how we do business here in Florida."

"Is there a problem? If you prefer, I can write you a check."

"No! No! Cash is fine."

"I'm not filing your taxes," Harold grinned. "You can claim whatever you want."

Harry Swogel smiled. He liked Harold and they were off to a great start.

* * *

Special Agent H. Thomas Moore and Agent Sweeny were at F.B.I. Headquarters by eight o'clock discussing strategy. The building was exactly a quarter of a mile from the courthouse.

"Did everyone make their flight?" Moore asked Sweeny. "Yes. Everyone should be present for the meeting."

"Good. We only have forty-five minutes before we have to be at the courthouse, the bond hearing is at ten o' clock, Is there anything else that I need to be made aware of?" Moore asked, smiling. Sweeny knew that he hated last minute surprises.

"Did you watch the news last night?"

"If you are referring to the fight at the jail. Yes, I saw that."

"Johnny Rowe and Richard Doyle beat the holy shit out of six prisoners sending them all to the infirmary."

"Who initiated the fight?"

"The jailer says that Doyle was making racial slurs. When questioned, both Rowe and Doyle invoked their 5th Amendment Right. They told the jail investigator to talk to their attorney."

"Who is their attorney?"

"No one has entered an appearance in their behalf. Do you want me to ask for a copy of the report and statements from the jail administrator?"

"No, that's of no interest to me." Special Agent Moore replied looking at the clock on the wall. It was 8 o'clock.

* * *

The jailer opened the slots on the metal doors and began passing out brown plastic rectangular trays with clear plastic lids. Next to the tray he placed a pint of Milk.

Ramrod peered through the slot into the narrow hallway, looking in both directions, then shouted, "Bulldog!"

"Yeah." Bulldog hollered back thought he open slot of his cell door. "You okay?"

"I think I broke a knuckle. My shit is pretty swollen. How about you?"

"I'm tired. Having this fuckin' concrete slab for a bed sucks. I'm fucking exhausted."

After serving the trays the jailer walked back down the hall slamming the trap doors shut.

Ramrod sat down to inspect his breakfast. There was a handful of cornflakes, two sugar packs, two burnt slices of toast, two butter patties, two small containers of grape jelly, and a plastic spoon.

Bulldog looked around his cell. There was a combination stainless steel sink and toilet, a raised concrete slab for a bed, and an enclosed light above the sink that was stained yellow and provided very little illumination.

* * *

"Would you please ring Betty Crawford's room and tell her I'm waiting in the hotel lobby for her?" Detective Marks asked the receptionist at the front desk.

"Yes, sir. I gave her a wake up call this morning," the receptionist smiled. "But I will gladly ring her again."

A few minutes later, Betty joined Marks and Hill in the dining area. "Did you oversleep?" Marks demanded of her.

"No! I've been expecting your call. I thought we would be stopping somewhere for breakfast."

"You just missed the hotel's free continental breakfast." Detective Marks announced, looking at his watch. "We've got a meeting to attend, so we'd better get moving."

Hill stood up. "Hi, I'm Detective Hill from the Anne Arundel County Sheriffs Department. I will be attending the meeting, also."

"Betty Crawford." She shook his offered hand, then looked at her boss and curled her lip, knowing that there would be no breakfast for her.

"It's five blocks to the courthouse and it's a nice day for a walk." Detective Marks pretty much ordered.

Betty glared at him. The audacity of the man. He would not be walking if he were wearing the high heels she presently had on her tiny feet. Her exposed toes were painted a bright red. He had given her the nickname "Twinkle Toes" because of her well manicured and polished nails. As they walked she sized up Detective Hill. He was handsome; probably in his early thirties, well dressed and very polite. He seemed to be the kind of man she could actually like.

Detective Marks bore a strong resemblance to Jackie Gleason. They were the same size, similar features, and they both smoked terrible smelling cigars. The one huge difference was that Detective Marks had no sense of humor. Today he was wearing his tan hat with the brim turned slightly down, a plain brown suit, and a beige overcoat. As he walked he puffed on yet another God awful smelling cigar, leaving clouds of smoke in his wake. She hated his nasty cigars with a passion.

* * *

"Wake up, Tony! It's eight forty-five. Peaches needs to make some phone calls." Raul shook his brother awake.

"Some?" Tony replied, wiping the sleep from his eyes.

"That's right, and I need for you to trust me," Peaches snapped. "If John Leder finds out that I'm alive, he will have us hunted down and killed. I'm quite sure the F.B.I. has a tap on the phone at the club. There's a lot of heat on anyone associated with the Argots, and I've got to be extremely careful. I know someone who lives in Miami. If I can reach him, I can set everything in motion. I will need for him to come here."

"What would you tell this person about us?" Tony wanted to know.

"I was kidnapped from the club and taken to Norman's Cay. John Leder ordered me caged and thrown into the sea. The two of you saved my life. For that I'm giving you five hundred thousand. In return you will be helping me seek my revenge."

"Help you? Help you how?"

"While you were asleep I talked to Raul and I have a plan. After you make your delivery on Wednesday night what do you normally do?"

"Return to the island to report that everything went smoothly."

"What time do you return?"

"Between four and five in the morning."

"What does the guard do when he hears the boat approaching?"

"He walks down to the dock to make sure it's us and not an intruder."

"Look at this map." Peaches produced a rough drawing that Raul had made of the island. Tony spared his brother a brief glare.

"If a boat pulled up to the far side of the island ten minutes before you arrived, those men could be in position to spring into action. You and Raul could capture the guard. If you have to, shoot him. Four men will capture the men sleeping in the bunkhouse while myself and one other person sneaks into John Leder's bungalow. He's in for a rude awakening."

"Your plan could certainly work." Tony nodded, looking down at the detailed map.

"By the way, instead of making the delivery to Boco Raton you will drop the load off at another location. A hundred kilos will be for you and Raul."

"You can make this happen"

"I can." Peaches promised.

"Make your calls," Tony stated flatly.

Peaches picked up the phone and dialed information.

"Operator, I would like the phone number for Chris Delgado on Seventh Street."

Tony walked to the bathroom, closed the door, and turned on the shower as she dialed Chris' number.

"This better be good." Chris snapped, looking at the time on the clock next to his bed.

"Chris?"

"Peaches?" Chris replied, shocked to hear her voice. "Everyone has been looking for you."

"I need your help."

"What do you need?"

"I need to talk to you in person. Can you come to the Holiday Inn on Ocean Drive, room fourteen."

"I'll be there in a half hour. Are you okay?"

"Yes, I'm fine. But don't tell anyone that you have heard from me and I'm sure the feds have the phone tapped and it's extremely important that I stay off their radar. I will explain everything when you get here."

"Okay." Chris replied, but his gut was telling him that something was terribly wrong.

* * *

"Welcome to Florida, ladies and gentlemen. My name is Special Agent H. Thomas Moore and this is Agent Sweeny." Moore gestured to the man standing at his right side. "I am in charge of this task force. Agent Sweeny is second in command. You were called here to assist the Federal Bureau of Investigation with any information you may have in regards to two rival biker gangs. More specifically, the Argots and the Heathens. You are each a unique and integral part of this task force. In less than one hour we have a bond hearing to attend for Johnny Rowe and Richard Doyle. Some of you might know them better by their biker names, Ramrod and Bulldog. This meeting will be brief. Does anyone have any information that would support a request for these men to be denied bond?"

"Yes. My name is Detective Ralph Criswell and I'm from the Harrisburg City Police Department in Pennsylvania. The Argot motorcycle club owns a cabin that sits on a hundred acres. When we raided the club's cabin we found evidence of a meth lab. We also have reason to believe this outlaw biker gang has strong ties to organized crime."

"I would like to add to that," Detective Marks spoke up.

"My name is Detective Daniel Marks and I am from the Baltimore City Homicide Division in Maryland. We are investigating two murders that we have reason to believe were committed by Johnny Rowe and Richard Allen Doyle."

"Could you be more specific?" Moore asked.

"An informant named Roger Pickett cooperated against one of the Argots' associates, a man known as Charlie Redman. Pickard was found tied to his bed with an apple in his mouth. He had been burned alive." The big man looked at Betty Crawford, raised his eyebrows, and anxiously waited for her input.

"My name is Detective Betty Crawford, and I'm also with the Baltimore City Homicide Division. Ryan 'Dollar' Porter, a known member of the Argots, was discovered in the underground parking lot of a luxury high rise apartment building called the Regency Towers, shot twice, once in the stomach, the second bullet right between the eyes. It was an execution- styled murder. Two forty-five caliber casings were found near the body. Nicole 'Peaches' Redman resides in that building," she explains, looking around the conference table.

"Anything else?" Special Agent Moore asked.

"Yes. My name is Detective Sergeant Hill. I'm with the Anne Arundel County Sheriffs Department. I know very little about Charlie Redman. I met Nicole Redman when I investigated the death of her six year old daughter, Charlotte. She was hit by a stolen vehicle believed to be linked to an assault in an adjacent neighborhood. I'm not sure why I'm here, or what value I can be."

"We're very much aware of her history," Agent Sweeney added. "Nicole Redman goes by the nickname of Peaches. She danced topless at the Blue Onion on Howard Street. She performs burlesque at the Two O'Clock Club, both of the bars are in Baltimore, Maryland. Now she owns a club named The Pink Pussycat in Downtown Orlando."

"I would like for everyone to attend the bond hearing this morning. We had better get on our way if we're to be on time," Agent Moore added.

* * *

Chris Delgado quickly dressed in blue Bermuda shorts, a colorful short sleeve Hawaiian shirt, brown sandals, and Ray Ban sunglasses. His shirt was un-tucked, and in the small of his back he carried a chrome plated pearl handle Colt .45 caliber automatic pistol. He parked his Corvette convertible in the parking lot of the Holiday Inn, walked down the sidewalk to room 14 and knocked lightly on the door.

"Hi!" Peaches answered the door with a smile. "It's good to see you," she said, then invited him inside.

Chris' eyes ran from one end of the room to the other, coming to focus on the two men who were sitting on the bed. He could cut the sudden tension in the room with a knife.

"Everyone thinks you were kidnapped by the Heathens."

"I was kidnapped, but not by them. This is Tony and Raul Rivera. They are responsible for saving my life."

The tension instantly left the room as Chris offered his hand in friendship. "It's nice to meet you."

"I need your help."

"You said that. I'm here, what's up?" Chris grinned.

* * *

A crowd gathered outside the courtroom. On one side was the defendants' counsel. On the other, the prosecution. They nodded to acknowledge each other's prescence. Detective Marks grinned and told Agent Moore that he was in for a treat.

"The defendants have retained the best criminal defense attorney that I've ever known, Harold Glazer. He's from Baltimore."

"Good morning," the young prosecutor introduced himself to Harry Swogel and Harold Glazer. "My name is David Dart Queen," he said, extending his hand.

Harold guessed Queen to be in his late twenties. he had coal black hair, was well mannered, and wore a modest blue suit.

Queen continued. "In all fairness you should prepare for my requesting that your clients be denied bail."

Harold grinned as the prosecutor turned and walked away, chuckling quietly to himself. He looked over at Harry, and said, "In all fairness? I like that."

CHAPTER FOUR
SHADES OF GLORY

Chris listened to Peaches and followed her instructions to the letter. When he left the motel he stopped at a pay phone and called his friend Ulises 'Nuni' Alverado.

"Hello?" Nuni answered on the third ring.

"Don't mention my name. Go to a pay phone and call my house in twenty minutes. It's urgent!" Chris lived in an apartment, not a house. His intention was to throw anyone listening a curve ball if Nuni's phone was being monitored.

"I gotcha, baby boy." Nuni knew not to ask any questions.

This wasn't the first time someone called and asked him to call them back from a pay phone.

"Twenty minutes." Chris repeated urging Nuni to get a move on it.

Twenty minutes later Nuni called from a pay phone outside of a neighborhood grocery store. The phone was in a booth, the booth reeking of day old urine. It was 10 o'clock in the morning and the day was getting hotter by the minute. The fan in the booth failed to come on so Nuni left the accordion sliding glass door open in the hopes of catching a breeze.

"What's up." Nuni asked the second Chris picked up the phone.

"Peaches is alive."

Nuni immediately felt his pulse quicken with excitement. He had fallen in love with her from the moment he had laid eyes on her. "How do you know that? Where is she? Did the Heathens hurt her?" Nuni was firing questions one after another, not giving Chris an opportunity to respond.

"She's fine, but she needs some help."

"Whatever the fuck she needs I got her," Nuni stated coldly.

"I have to tell Sugar."

"You can't tell her," Chris cautioned.

"Whatcha mean I can't tell her…"

"Just that!" Chris cut him off. "You can't tell anyone. Peaches' life may depend on it. She was kidnapped from the Pink Pussycat to be killed. The person responsible thinks she's dead and it's very important that he continues to think so. Your Lincoln was described leaving the house in Altamonte Springs twenty minutes before it was raided. I'd expect that the Feds have already made a connection between the club, Peaches, the Lincoln and you."

"So what? I don't know shit."

Chris laughed. "Do you know three solid guys you can trust with your life?"

There was a long pause, then Nuni retorted. "I don't trust nobody with my life!"

"Peaches needs three trustworthy men, not including yourself. And, bring some guns. Let the guys know that this could get dangerous and meet me at my apartment tomorrow afternoon. I will take you to see Peaches."

"I'll be there!"

As an afterthought, Chris added. "Drive a different vehicle and make sure that you aren't followed."

"I won't return to my house just in case there's a bug on my phone. The F. B. I. won't get a chance to set-up any kind of surveillance."

Chris chuckled, knowing Big Nuni, could be one crazy mother fucker, On the other end of the phone, Nuni was filled with excitement. Just knowing that Peaches was alive was a huge burden off his mind, but he was anxious to find out exactly what had happened. He vowed that some mother fucker was about to have a really bad day.

"Tell my baby that daddy is coming and he's bringing the Calvary." Nuni said before hanging up the phone.

* * *

"Bailiff, before the hearing we would like to request five minutes with our clients." Harry Swogel addressed the burly bailiff.

"They're en-route from the Orange County jail and should be here any minute," the bailiff offered in response.

It was 8 o'clock in the morning, and the courtroom was quickly filling up with willing spectators. Special Agent Moore was seated at the prosecutions table with David Dart Queen. Behind them in the first row sat Agent Sweeny, Pete Elliot, Detective Marks, Betty Crawford, Sergeant Hill, Detective Criswell, and the Jail Administrator, Keith Salis.

"My apologies for not making this mornings meeting," Agent Elliot whispered to his colleges. "Did I miss anything?"

"Nope," Agent Moore smiled. "There was no coffee and donuts this morning."

Harry Swogel and Harold Glazer were seated at the defense table with open briefcases and yellow pads at the ready.

"All rise!" The bailiff shouted. "The Honorable United States Magistrate Judge Rudolph McCallister presiding."

"Court is in session. You may be seated. I believe we are scheduled for a bond hearing this morning, but it appears that we are missing the defendants." The Judge announced, glancing at the empty chairs at the defense table.

"The defendants are en-route, your honor," the bailiff reported.

"If it pleases the court, my colleague and I would like to take this time to enter our appearances on behalf of our clients, who are obviously missing from the courtroom. Our clients names are Johnny Rowe and Richard Allen Doyle." Harry Swogel stated for the record.

"Any objections?"

"No, your honor." Queen replied.

"My name is Harry Swogel, S-W-O-G-E-L. A copy of my certification and license to practice law in the State of Florida is currently on file with the clerk of this court. I will be acting as lead counsel for the defendants. My colleague, Harold Glazer will introduce himself and act as co-counsel in this case. Thank you."

"Good morning, your honor." Harold began. He stood up,

shuffled through some papers, then continued. "My name is Harold Glazer, G-L-A-Z-E-R. I have a copy of my law degree from Harvard University and a copy of my license to practice law in the State of Maryland that I would like to present to the court for filing with the clerk at this time."

The prosecutor was very young which meant one thing to Harold; he lacked experience. But a jury would love how he appeared. David Queen was clean cut, well dressed, articulate, and well mannered.

Following Harold, the governments attorney stood and introduced himself. "David Dart Queen, Q-U-E-E-N on behalf of the Untied States. My certification is on file with the clerk of the court, your honor."

"Well then, are we ready to proceed gentlemen?"

"The defendants are still en-route," the bailiff replied. No sooner had he reported that the defendants were still en-route they were escorted into the courtroom through a side door dressed in orange coveralls and wearing blue slip-on tennis shoes. They were handcuffed to a chain that was wrapped around their waist and leg irons prevented them from taking normal steps. As they entered the courtroom they shuffled their feet like two baby penguins. It was somewhat amusing to watch, but a pathetic sight. Their hair was uncombed and they were noticeably unshaven, and their eyes were bloodshot from the lack of sleep. But the moment they saw Harold they both felt a sense of relief and grinned. Ramrod sat on one side of Harold, Bulldog on the other.

"I'm glad to see the two of you could join us," the judge remarked. "Your honor, the State requests that the defendants be considered a flight risk and that they be denied bail as they are not residents of the state. We have no reason to believe they would return for trial," the U.S. Attorney explained.

"Excuse me, your honor. But the State has offered nothing in support of such an absurd request. It's unwarranted, baseless, and unconstitutional." Harry Swogel protested.

"The Constitution provides that every citizen of the United States should be afforded a reasonable bond," Glazer added.

"Providing that person doesn't pose a serious threat to the community." Queen retorted.

"Absolutely." Harold agreed, adding. "The government has offered no evidence that my clients pose a threat to anyone."

"The government intends to offer testimony from police officers in two other states, specifically Pennsylvania and Maryland. Their testimony will support the request for a denial of bail."

"Ok," Ramrod interrupted. "I have never met or spoken with any police agency!"

"Your honor, we requested five minutes to confer with our clients before this hearing started. May we have that time now?" Harold requested.

"Court is in recess for fifteen minutes," Judge McCallister declared.

Two guards from the jail escorted Ramrod and Bulldog to the jury chambers. Harry Swogel and Harold Glazer followed. As the door closed behind them, Harold asked Ramrod if he would like to defend himself? Ramrod frowned.

"Then let me do my job. If I need your help I'll ask for it. Now, tell me what happened at the jail yesterday? How did the fight start?"

"We were showering. Some black guy whispered in Bulldog's ear that he had a nice ass. Bulldog whispered in his ear that he would have a nice one too if he kept the dicks out of it. I guess he didn't like that. Like an idiot, he took a swing at Bulldog."

Harold and Harry could not contain themselves. They both laughed heartily.

"I think I broke my finger," Bulldog growled, showing Harold his crooked finger.

"Didn't they take you to the infirmary?" Harry asked.

"Hell no! They took us straight to the hole!" Ramrod declared.

"They claimed that everything was pending an investigation," Bulldog added.

"When the jail administrator tried to question us, we told him to talk to our attorney."

For fifteen minutes Harold asked questions and made notes. The door to the jury room opened and the bailiff informed them that the judge was on his way back into the courtroom.

Within a matter of seconds all parties returned to the courtroom. "All rise," the bailiff ordered.

The black robed judge entered the courtroom. Once seated, he told everyone in attendance that they could be seated, called court in session, and asked the counselors. "Are we ready to proceed?"

"Yes, your honor." Swogel replied.

"Yes, your honor." Queen spoke up.

"Very well. Is there any objection to the government presenting witnesses?"

"No, your honor." Swogel replied for the defense. "You may call your first witness, Mr. Queen."

"The government calls Detective Ralph Criswell. He is a detective for the city of Harrisburg, Pennsylvania."

"Detective Criswell, are you very familiar with the Argot motorcycle gang?"

"Objection, your honor!" Swogel shouted coming to his feet. "Withdrawn." Queen grinned. He was simply testing his opposition. He rephrased the question. "Are you familiar with the Argot motorcycle club?"

"Were you present when their cabin was raided in Pennsylvania the night before last?"

"Yes. The Harrisburg police department along with the Sheriff's department assisted the F.B.I. and D.E.A. It was a predawn raid coordinated with raids throughout Florida."

"To clarify your participation, is it correct to say that you have no personal knowledge or involvement with raids conducted in Florida?"

"That's correct. My only involvement was on the raid of the cabin just outside of Harrisburg."

"Do you know what was seized?"

"Lab equipment used for cooking crystal meth."

"Was there any resistance?"

"No."

"How many arrests were made?"

"None. There was no one at the cabin."

David Queen immediately wished that he could take the question back. It reminded him of the first thing he learned in law school. Never ask a question that you do not already know the answer to.

Ramrod and Bulldog looked at each other and grinned.

"Has your department investigated the Argots motorcycle club before this?"

"Many times."

"How many, two... three?"

"Since the late sixties, more than a hundred."

"Would you consider the Argot motorcycle club to be of good moral character?"

"Not hardly."

Harold wrote a note, passing it down the table to Harry. As Harry read the note, he smiled. Then, he nodded his head signaling his agreement. Harold had a game plan in mind.

"No further questions." Queen concluded. "Cross examination?" the judge offered.

"Not at this time, but we would like to reserve the right to recall this witness," Swogel replied.

"Any objections?"

"No, your honor," Queen replied.

"Very well, you may call your next witness."

"The government calls Detective Daniel Marks to the stand." As he was seated, Queen continued. "Please state your name, occupation, and place of employment for the record."

"Detective Daniel Marks. I have been assigned to the Baltimore City Homicide Division for more than ten years."

"Detective Marks, can you tell this court about the two murders that you are currently investigating?"

"Yes. A confidential informant cooperated against a known drug dealer, Charlie Redman. The local police raided his residence at five eight-one Gunpowder road in White Marsh, Maryland. As a result of the raid Charlie Redman was charged with possession of cocaine with intent to distribute. The informant was later discovered burned to death in his home. In a second investigation, Ryan Porter was found in the basement garage of Regency Towers, a high-rise apartment building. He was shot twice, once in the stomach and once right between the eyes. Through further investigation we learned that a Nicole 'Peaches' Redman, Charlie Redman's ex-wife, lived in an apartment in the same building."

"Was Ryan Porter a member of any motorcycle gang that you're aware of?"

"Objection!" Harry Swogel screamed, pounding his fist on the defense table.

"Withdrawn." David Queen smiled, rephrasing the question. "Was Ryan Porter a member of any known biker club?"

"Yes. He was a member of the Argot motorcycle club and his biker name was, Dollar..."

Harold was writing at an amazing speed. As the government's attorney announced that he had no further questions, he passed a second note to Harry.

"Cross examination?" the judge offered.

"No questions at this time, your honor. But we would like to reserve the right to recall this witness."

"Any objections?"

"No, your honor." Queen replied. "You may call your next witness."

"The government calls Keith Salis to the stand."

"Objection. Counsel was only made aware of two witnesses." Swogel protested.

"Your honor, Keith Salis is the investigator for the Orange County City Jail. The governments' position is we believe the fight at the jail is relevant in determining the defendants' violent behavior which poses a threat to the community at large. If counsel needs additional time in which to prepare to confer with their clients we will certainly not oppose their request."

Harold leaned to his left and whispered something to Harry. "Objection withdrawn." Harry announced.

Keith Salis walked to the witness stand and seated himself. "For the record, please state your name and official capacity."

"Keith Salis. I am the investigator for the Orange County City Jail."

Queen continued. "Did you investigate a fight that occurred at the jail yesterday afternoon?"

"Yes, I did."

"And can you tell this court what took place?"

"The defendants…"

Queen interrupted. "By the defendants, you are referring to Johnny Rowe and Richard Allen Doyle?"

"That's correct. Prisoner Willie Brown and the defendants were showering when prisoner Doyle instigated a fight by calling prisoner brown a nigger."

"What happened then?"

"It turned into an all out brawl. Six men were taken to the infirmary, two of them with missing teeth. I believe one had a broken arm, but I haven't received the full medical report yet. Instead of taking a shower, it turned into a blood bath!"

"Do you have reason to believe that Willie Brown's version of what happened is the truth?"

"Yes. Besides his statement, we have supporting statements of prisoners Laurel and Richard Greene."

"Objection, your honor. This is an ambush, a total surprise to the defense. We have been provided with no statements which makes it impossible for us to adequately prepare our clients' defense." Harry Swogel explained to the judge.

The judge waived an impatient hand. "This is a bond hearing, not a trial. It is not subject to disclosure, but the defendants do have a right to due process and equal protection of the law. This court is unprepared to make a ruling at this time. After reviewing applicable case law, I will render my decision."

"Did you attempt to question Johnny Rowe and Richard Doyle?" Queen continued.

"Yes. They refused to cooperate."

"Would you consider the defendants dangerous men?"

"Extremely."

"No further questions."

"Cross examination?" the judge offered.

"Not at this time. But we would like to reserve the right to recall this witness," Swogel replied.

"Any objections?"

"No, your honor," Queen replied. "The government calls Richard Allen Doyle to the stand."

"Objection, your honor!" Harry screamed, jumping to his feet. "First, the government was calling just two witnesses. Now, it's more surprises. Not to mention the fact that my clients cannot be compelled to give testimony against themselves.

"The defendants are free to invoke their Fifth Amendment right, if they wish to do so," David Queen offered.

"You are treading on thin ice counselor," the judge cautioned.

Queen countered, "Not only does the government have a right to call the defendants to the witness stand, it has a clear duty to inquire about criminal acts that support bail being denied."

The stage was set, and Harold wondered if Queen had any other surprises left in his bag of tricks. Harold smiled to himself at the thought of his own surprises yet to come.

"This court is adjourned for lunch. In fairness the court, as well as defense counsel, needs time to digest this request. Court will resume at one o'clock."

"Thank you, your honor." Harold Glazer spoke for the first time as he looked at his watch. It was 11:15 a.m.

* * *

"Good morning, Harold Glazer's office. How may I help you?" The receptionist answered the phone.

"Is Harold in?"

"No, I'm sorry, he's not. May I take a message?"

"No, thank you. When will he be in?" Peaches asked.

"Mr. Glazer is in Florida and isn't expected back until sometime next week."

"Thank you," Peaches replied. She hung up the phone. "Shit!" She cursed.

"What's wrong?" Tony asked.

"My fucking attorney is out of town for a week. He's in Florida, so hopefully he's defending Ramrod and Bulldog. I can't get money from my trust until he returns."

"Does that mean we aren't going to get our money?" Raul demanded.

"I will stay with you until you are paid in full. But never tell anyone that you kidnapped me. That could get you killed. Our story is you worked for John Leder. He ordered me killed, and you saved my life. That's all that anyone ever needs to know."

Tony and Raul smiled. Peaches picked up the phone and dialed another number. On the third ring she heard a familiar voice.

"Hello?"

"Hi, baby," she laughed softly.

"Nicole!" Manny's excited voice came over the line. "I was just thinking about you and Marsha."

"I hope they were pleasant thoughts."

"They always are! Will I be enjoying your company Wednesday?"

"I'm sorry, but I'm not going to be able to make it until next week. I called because I need a huge favor."

"What do you need sweetheart?"

"I desperately need to borrow five hundred thousand dollars for two weeks."

"Are you in some kind of trouble?"

"No, I'm fine. Can you loan me the money?"

"Sure, no problem. But that's a lot of money. Are you sure that everything is alright?"

"I swear to you that I'm fine. I need the money now, but I intend to give it back sometime next week."

"The money isn't a problem. I'll call my bank right away. Where do you want me to send it?"

Peaches covered the phone with her left hand. "Do either of you have a bank account?" she whispered.

"I do," Tony replied. He pulled a blank check from a very battered wallet and handed it to her proudly. The bank account had only been open for a few weeks, but it was the first real American thing he had accomplished since entering the country.

"Wire transfer the money from your account to this one," Nicole explained to Manny. She quickly read off the name, bank, and account number from the check.

"It should be there within an hour," Manny assured her. "Thank you, baby. I will give you a call this weekend."

"I'll be looking forward to it," he replied, the concern still on his voice. Nicole slowly replaced the receiver in its cradle, wishing that she could've said something to make him feel better. She turned her attention to Tony and his younger brother.

"Okay guys. My friend is wiring five hundred thousand dollars to Tony's account within the hour. Fair enough?"

"Sounds fair to me," Tony smiled. Raul smiled, giving his brother a happy little nod.

"Okay, now let's focus on finishing the job," She said coldly. She turned on the televison just in time to catch the news at noon. An attractive blonde news reporter was busy reporting the latest news on the outlaw biker war taking place in Florida.

"Good aftenoon. I'm Susan Lichtman of WYVJ. Our man in the steets Richard Bower reports from the scene of this mornings bond hearing for outlaw bikers Johnny Rowe and Richard Allen Doyle."

At that point the broadcast switched over to show a handsome middle aged man standing in front of the downtown courthouse. "Thank you, Susan." He smiled, holding a microphone to his mouth. "The governments attorney, David Dart Queen, has had a field day presenting undisputed testimony of horrendous murders and assaults in support that the defendants be held without bail…"

"Fuckin' assholes!" Peaches cursed at the television.

"…In a shocking move, Queen called Richard Allen Doyle to the stand. Defense counsel Harry Swogel argued that to compel the defendants to testify would violate their constitutional rights. Judge Rudolph McCallister cautioned the government's attorney that he's treading on thin ice. At that point the session was immediately adjourned for lunch. Court is to reconvene at one o'clock."

"Thank you for the report Richard. Now for the weather. The forecast for today is clear skies, sunny, with a heat index in the high eighties. Have a great day Miami! Susan Lichtman of WTVJ Channnel four reporting."

"Where in the fuck is Harold?" Peaches cursed again. She was disappointed that the news failed to report anything more on the fight at the jail. It would be a big relief for her to know that neither Bulldog or Ramrod were seriously injured.

* * *

"I have some things I need to do," Harold informed Harry Swogel. "Why don't you go to lunch and I will meet you in the courtroom at one o'clock."

As Harry walked down the sidewalk and crossed the street, Harold stopped another attorney and asked for directions to the office of the clerk of the court.

* * *

At precisely one o'clock the bailiff announced. "All rise."

Judge McCallister entered the courtroom. After seating himself, he told those in attendance that they may be seated.

The judge cleared his throat before beginning. "First, I've made a decision in regard to defense counsel's objection. The substance of the statements made by inmates housed in the county jail are limited to the jail investigators reason to believe that Willie Brown's version of the events were truthful.

"The defense can adequately cross examine Keith Salis..."

"I withdraw my objection," Harry Swogel interrupted. It was obvious, at least to him, the decision was not going to be favorable.

With the formalities out of the way, the Assistant U.S. Attorney called Richard Allen Doyle to the stand.

Bulldog stood, shuffled his feet to the witness stand and seated himself. "Do you understand that you are under oath, that you are required by law to testify truthfully, and that the penalty for perjury carries a maximum sentence of five years?"

"Yes Sir, your honor." Bulldog smiled, on his very best behavior.

"Have you had the opportunity to consult with counsel and do you understand that you cannot be compelled to testify against yourself?" the judge questioned.

"Yes Sir."

"Do you wish to waive those rights and give testimony in this case?"

"Yes, sir."

Harry Swogel drew in a deep breath, questioning what had

just happened. He had anticipated his clients invoking their Fifth Amendment Right not to testify. Harold offered a quick grin, signaling that it was no surprise to him.

"You may proceed," the judge instructed Queen.

Queen approached the defendant. "Mr. Doyle, I believe you also go by the nickname, Bulldog. Is that correct?"

"Yes."

"I see that you've been arrested a number of times."

"Objection, your honor. I believe the court should only be considering prior convictions." Swogel argued.

"Sustained. Do not use arrest, unless they resulted in convictions," the judge ordered.

"In 1968, were you arrested, tried, and convicted for an assault?"

"Yes."

"Did that result in the victim having to be placed in intensive care? In fact, the victim went from being on life support to remaining in a coma for three months."

"He deserved it!" Bulldog declared.

"He deserved it?" Queen repeated, adding, "So, you think it's alright to dispense your own justice?"

"That's not what I said. The asshole raped my thirteen year old sister. I went crazy. If my club brothers hadn't stopped me, I probably would have killed the guy."

"Do you dislike black men?" Queen quickly changed the subject, seeing the slight smirk on the judge's face.

"No."

"So, you just sent six black men to the infirmary for kicks?"

"Objection, your honor." Harry Swogel shouted. "Sustained."

"No further questions." David Queen walked to his table. He took a seat satisfied with his examination.

"Does the defense wish to cross examine this witness?"

"Yes, your honor." Harold Glazer spoke for the second time since the hearing began. He stood up, pacing back and forth in front of the defense table. "Mr. Doyle, just so the court is clear on this, you have only one conviction for assault, and that occurred under unusual circumstances."

"That's correct."

"Did you go to trial?"

"No, sir. I pled guilty. I never made any bones about it. I did it."

"Did you start the fight at the jail?"

"No sir."

"How did the fight start?"

"We were taking a shower when a big black guy that everyone called

'Willie' whispered in my ear that I had a nice ass."

"What did you do?"

"I whispered in his ear that he'd have a nice one too if he kept the dicks out of it."

There were chuckles throughout the courtroom. Judge McCallister bit his lower lip to maintain his dignity and professionalism.

Bulldog continued. "....Willie Brown hit me first. From that point, things got crazy and he sure had a lot of friends that jumped in."

"Did you receive any injuries?"

"I think my finger's broken." Bulldog said, holding his crooked finger up for everyone to see.

"Were you taken to the infirmary?"

"No sir. Ramrod and myself went directly to segregation."

"No further questions," Harold said flatly.

"Redirect?" The judge asked Queen.

"Nothing further."

"You may call your next witness."

"The government calls Johnny Rowe to the stand."

Bulldog stepped down from the witness chair. Ramrod stood, and he and Bulldog shuffled their feet as they passed one another. They shared a quick smile in passing, and within a minute Ramrod was seated in the witness chair.

"Do you understand that you are under oath, that you are required by law to testify truthfully, and the penalty for perjury is a maximum of five years?" the judge explained.

"Yes, sir."

"Do you understand that you have the right to invoke your Fifth Amendment Right to remain silent and not give testimony at this hearing?"

"Yes. But I have nothing to hide."

"You may proceed," the judge instructed attorney Queen. "Mr Rowe, do you also go by the nickname, Ramrod?"

"Yes."

"Are you the president of the Argot motorcycle club?"

"Yes, I am."

"Are you familiar with everything that's going-on with the club and its members?"

"No sir, many of the members have personal lives. Wives and kids."

"Do you know how many members have criminal records?"

"Objection, your honor. The government's attorney is on a witch hunt, and the members' criminal history merits absolutely no consideration for the purpose of this bond hearing."

"Sustained," the judge sighed his disgust.

"In 1967, were you convicted of assault?"

"Yes."

"Did you plead guilty to that charge?"

"No sir, I was convicted by a jury."

"No further questions." Queen smiled his pleasure.

"Cross examination?" the judge offered the defense.

"Yes." Harold Glazer replied, rising to his feet. "Mr. Rowe, did you serve in the Armed Services?"

"Yes sir."

"Which branch?"

"The United States Army."

"Did you serve in any particular unit?"

"Yes. I did." Ramrod spoke in the same polite differential voice that he had once used in the military when dealing with superiors. "After extensive training, I qualified and was assigned to a Special Forces unit, the Green Berets. During my commission, I volunteered for two tours of duty in Vietnam, each lasting thirteen months."

"You are a Vietnam veteran?"

"Yes sir."

"Were you awarded any honors?"

"Yes sir, two bronze stars and a purple heart."

"What did you expect when you returned stateside?"

"A hero's welcome with a marching band and possibly a parade."

"Did you receive one?"

"Objection. Relevance?" Queen shouted.

"Your honor, I believe this shows a more complete and adequate picture of my client's character."

"Overruled. You may proceed."

"Did you receive a hero's welcome?"

"No sir. We stepped off the airplane to be confronted by protesters. Some carried signs calling us murderers. A protester attempted to rub a rotten egg in my face and I reacted by breaking his arm. I was trained to react when threatened. I felt threatened."

"What happened next?"

"Just as I broke the protesters arm a photographer snapped a photo and I was charged with assault. I refused all of the plea agreements that were offered. My argument was that I was acting in self defense. The jury didn't agree."

"Who founded the Argot motorcycle club?"

"It was founded by myself and another Vietnam veteran, Rodney Anderson in nineteen sixty-seven. We called him Rod for short. Returning stateside we didn't fit in with the norms of society, so we rented a cabin that sits on a hundred acres in Pennsylvania. As our membership reflects, we obviously weren't the only ones who didn't fit in with the norms of society. Riding motorcycles gives us a sense of feeling free. I believe Rod started calling us Argots."

"What happened to Rodney Anderson?"

"He met a girl, got married, moved to Alaska and had a couple kids."

"Objection, as to relevance."

"Sustained."

"Do you consider yourself an outlaw?"

"No sir. The American flag flies proudly in front of the cabin. Below that a P.O.W. flag. We will always honor and never forget our brothers left behind."

"How did the fight at the jail start?"

"All I saw was a black guy take a swing at Bulldog. A second guy jumped on his back and I intervened to help my brother. It was two on one."

"Your brother?"

"In the club we are all brothers."

"What happened after the fight?"

"Bulldog and myself were taken to segregation."

"Were the other men involved in the brawl taken to segregation?"

"Not to my knowledge."

"Were you taken to the infirmary?"

"No sir."

"Did you receive any medical attention?"

"No sir."

"Why did you come to Florida? Was it on business or pleasure?"

"We came to attend the funeral of twelve of my brothers who were brutally murdered."

"Do you own a house in Altamonte Springs?"

"No sir."

"No further questions," Harold Glazer announced.

"Redirect?" the judge questioned.

"One second, your honor." Attorney Queen spoke briefly with the

Jail Administrator, Keith Salis. Then replied, "No further questions."

"You may call your next witness," the judge instructed.

"The government rests, your honor."

"Very well, does the defense intend to call any witnesses?" the judge offered.

"Yes, we do. The defense recalls Detective Ralph Criswell to the stand," Harold said with a slight smile.

In the front row, Detective Marks perked up, giving Betty Crawford a knowing look. Years of experience had taught him that Harold Glazer was not to be underestimated in any courtroom.

Moments later Detective Criswell seated himself in the witness chair and lowered the microphone to a more comfortable position.

"Have you personally met either of the defendants before today?" Harold asked, not bothering to leave his standing position from behind the witness table.

"No, I can't say that I have."

"I believe that its been established that you were present at the cabin in Pennsylvania when it was raided?"

"Yes, that's right."

"Can you tell this court what equipment was seized that is used to manufacture crystal meth?"

"That is not my expertise."

"Is it your testimony that in over a hundred investigations you have never met, or interviewed, either of the defendants?"

"That is correct."

"And, in regards to the lab equipment seized at the cabin, you aren't sure that it was used to manufacture crystal meth. You simply offered your personal opinion."

"I guess so."

"No further questions."

"Redirect?" Judge McCallister asked.

"No, your honor." Queen replied, with a deep sigh of disappointment. "You may call your next witness."

"The defense recalls Detective Daniel Marks to the stand."

"You are still under oath," the judge reminded him as Marks seated himself.

"Yes, your honor."

Harold Glazer smiled, and began with. "Nice weather, isn't it?"

"Objection!" Queen growled.

"Grounds?"

"Withdrawn," Harold snickered. "Detective Marks, I believe you testified in regards to two separate murders."

"That's correct."

"Have you ever questioned Johnny Rowe or Richard Doyle in regard to either murder?"

"No." Marks answered flatly, knowing that with Harold Glazer the worst thing anyone could do was tell a lie.

"Have you ever attempted to question either of the defendants in regard to any crime?"

"No."

"Were you impressed by Johnny Rowe's service record?" Harold asked, anticipating an objection would be coming. Here it comes, he thought, smiling to himself.

"Objection." Queen snarled.

"Sustained." The judge sighed, his irritation growing.

Glazer restrained his laughter. "Do you have a witness who claims that either defendant was involved in either murder?"

"No."

"Do you have a thread from a piece of clothing? Is there anything that would give you a reason to suspect that the defendants were involved in either homicide?"

"We have our suspicion."

"There is no evidence, is there?"

"There is no strong or solid evidence at this time," Detective Marks concluded.

"No further questions," Harold Glazer announced. "Redirect?"

"No, your honor." Queen sighed his disgust.

"The witness is excused," The judge said, a frown darkening his brow. "You may call your next witness."

"The defense recalls Keith Salis to the stand."

As Keith Salis sat down in the witness chair, the judge reminded him that he was still under oath.

"Mr. Salis, why were the defendants taken directly to segregation and not to the infirmary?"

"I'm not sure."

"When did you begin interviewing the prisoners?"

"Within thirty minutes after the assault toolk place."

"Were any of the other prisoners taken to segregation?"

"Not to my knowledge."

"While everyone else was having lunch, I spent my time investigating a few things. First, there's Willie Brown. What can you tell me about him. Did you check his prior criminal history?"

"No, I didn't."

"Well, Willie has twelve prior felony convictions and he is currently charged for first degree criminal sexual conduct. His prison record reflects that he is a known sexual predator. Knowing this, would you consider Willie Brown to be of good moral character?"

"No sir, I guess not."

"Prisoner Joe Laurel has five felony convictions. He is charged and waiting trial for felony assault on a police officer. Were you aware of this?"

"No, I wasn't."

"Do you know anything regarding inmate Richard Green?"

"No sir, but I have a feeling that you do."

"I do." Harold beamed. "Mr. Green's criminal history spans a decade. It begins with armed robbery and ends with first degree murder. He has an extensive juvenile history and nine prior felony convictions. He is housed ln the Orange County City jail pending a new trial. It appears that the time of his arrest he wasn't read his

Miranda warnings and the Court of Appeals overturned his conviction. In your opinion, would you consider prisoner Joe Laurel to be of good moral character?"

"No."

"In your opinion, do you feel the defendants have been treated fairly?"

"Objection, counsel is asking the witness to draw a conclusion." Queen shouted, his face blushed.

"No, I'm not. Allow me to clarify. I am asking the jail's investigator for his professional opinion."

"Overruled. the witness is instructed to answer the question."

"The defendants should have been taking to the infirmary first, then placed in segregation pending a detailed investigation."

"No further questions," Harold smirked. "Redirect?"

"Yes." Queen climbed to his feet. "Mr. Salis, do you feel that you did a good job in your official capacity as the jail's investigator?"

"Based on the statements provided, I acted appropriately. The defendants chose not to be interviewed. It was necessary to separate the defendants from the other men."

"Nothing further, your honor."

"The defense rests." Harold said, pleased with himself. "The witness is excused," Judge McCallister announced.

"Your honor, may we have a side bar?" Attorney Queen requested. "Approach the bench, counselors," the judge ordered.

"Your honor, the government has a witness in protective custody who is an eye-witness to the murder of Bobby Sands. Sands was the president of the Heathens motorcycle club. The Argots raided their clubhouse, tied Bobby 'Big Moose' Sands to the rear bumper of a stolen white Ford van, and dragged him to his death in broad daylight. I intend to call this witness at the defendant's preliminary hearing on Friday."

"That's all fine and dandy, but the government is asking this court to deny my clients a reasonable bail and there's been no evidence or testimony to support the request of their being denied bail. My clients have been subjected to what amounts to cruel and unusual punishment and denied medical attention."

"I've heard enough. Return to your tables, counselors," the judge ordered in a firm voice.

The attorneys returned to their tables and sat down.

The judge began, "I am going to order the Orange County Jail to provide the defendants with adequate and immediate medical attention." The judge spoke loud enough for those in the rear of the courtroom to hear his every word. "The defendants are to be escorted from this court to the Orange County Memorial Hospital for medical attention and assessment. In addition, the defendants are to be housed together, but separate from the general population and afforded equal privilages which includes the use of a telephone. Bail is denied, but I will reconsider the motion for bond at the conclusion of Friday's preliminary hearing. Gentlemen, normally a bond hearing takes no longer than fifteen to twenty minutes. This court does not expect Friday's preliminary hearing to become another mini-trial. Hopefully, I've made myself clear. Court is adjourned."

"Thank you, your honor." David Queen smiled his pleasure at the defendants being denied bail.

Ramrod and Bulldog were escorted from the courtroom and taken to a holding cell.

"Would you care to join me in a round of golf tomorrow morning." Harold asked Harry. "I'm staying at the Holiday Inn on the course."

"I have a club membership. What time would you like to tee off?"

"Is ten o'clock good for you?"

"I'll call and reserve a golf cart."

"I don't suppose you would care to place a small wager on the game, to make things interesting." Harold suggested with a grin.

"How about One Hundred dollars, and the loser pays for everything, including lunch."

"Sounds good to me." Harold replied, quickly accepting the

wager. Harold and Harry gathered their notes and briefcases, left the courtroom, and walked to the holding cell to speak with their clients before leaving the courthouse.

"You did good." Ramrod grinned, thanking Harold.

"Call me tonight, sometime after eight o'clock. I will instruct the clerk at the desk to forward all calls to my room. I'm staying at the Holiday Inn downtown." Harold wrote the phone number on the back of one of his business cards and passed it through the iron bars to Ramrod.

"There's a good chance the judge will grant a reasonable bond Friday," Harry added.

"Yeah, right," Bulldog said seriously doubting that. "If it wasn't for bad luck, we wouldn't have any luck."

"I'm just looking forward to a warm shower, a hot meal, and a good night's sleep." Ramrod sighed.

"Time to go!" the guard announced.

"Thanks!" Ramrod and Bulldog said in unison as they shuffled their feet and waddled away. Harry and Harold grimaced. Their clients were such a pathetic sight.

CHAPTER FIVE
GOOD MORNING

Chris Delgado returned to the Holiday Inn at three o' clock in the afternoon and reported on his conversation with Nuni Alvarado. "Nuni told me to tell his baby that he will be here tomorrow and he's bringing the cavalry."

"That's what he said, huh?" Peaches laughed, closing the door to the room.

"His exact words." Chris smiled. "I told him to bring three trustwrothy men with guns."

Tony and Raul watched closely from across the room, letting Peaches run the show.

"Come here, I want to show you something." Peaches motioned for Chris to follow her. She unfolded a hand drawn map that Raul had drawn and placed it on the glass top table next to the bed. "This is where the island Norman's Cay is located in relation to Miami and the island of Great Exuma. Here's the dock." She pointed. "John Leder's bungalow is here. The men's bungalow has four bunk beds and a table. When Tony and Raul return to the island after making the delivery, the guard at the bungalow walks to the dock to meet them. Raul assures me the guard always does that. The second boat carrying five armed men will dock here…" She marked the map with and x. "When the guard walks down the dock, Tony and Raul will capture him by surprise. At the same time, three men will rush into the men's quarters and capture the sleeping men. Nuni and myself will capture Leder. He's in for a rude awakening. If everything goes as planned, not a shot will be fired. By the way, Tony and Raul are expected to deliver the three hundred kilos of cocaine to a private dock in Boco Raton, then return to Norman's Cay. We're going to hijack the delivery as a bonus."

Chris chuckled at the thought of taking the delivery too. Peaches continued. "We are going to need a place near Boco Raton where

Tony and Raul can drop off the cocaine. The hijacked delivery will be divided three ways between you, me, and a third for Tony and Raul," Peaches concluded.

Chris quickly offered to pay Nuni and the other three men from his share of the loot. "I have a perfect place to unload the boat. I have a friend who owns a gorgeous home on the water, less that a mile from Boco Raton. It's perfect because the dock is before Boco Raton. Billy Bear is in Wisconsin attending a wedding. My brother has keys to his house, if we need it. There's a private boat ramp in the backyard with a thirty foot planked wooden pier and it's secluded."

"Problem solved." Peaches smiled, sitting down on the edge of the bed.

Chris left the motel room, promising to check-in later that evening around ten o'clock.

Tony left the motel, drove to his bank, walked inside and cashed a check for two hundred dollars. Before leaving, he asked the teller for the balance of his account.

"It's five hundred one thousand, six hundred and fifty-three dollars, and sixty-five cents," she replied smiling.

Tony found it difficult to keep his composure, especially when he felt like jumping for joy. "Thank you." He smiled, then walked calmly from the bank. Once outside, he grinned from ear to ear. He stopped at a Kentucky Fried Chicken and purchased two buckets of chicken, a large serving of mash potatoes with gravy and two six packs of Coca-Cola before returning to the motel.

"The money was there." Tony reported, with a huge grin.

"Did you think it wouldn't be?" Peaches questioned.

At six o'clock Peaches turned on the television and sat down on the edge of the bed to watch the news.

* * *

"Good evening, Miami. Susan Lichtman of WTVJ Channel four

news reporting. First, we will go to our man on the scene, Richard Bower, reporting earlier this afternoon from the steps of the federal courthouse in Orlando for an up-to-date report on today's bond hearing for outlaw bikers Johnny Rowe and Richard Allen Doyle."

"Thank you, Susan. Today's bond hearing was expected to last no longer than twenty minutes, but it lasted five hours. This morning Assistant U.S. Attorney David Queen called two out of state detectives to the stand who clearly portrayed the defendants as nefarious outlaw bikers responsible for two homicides in the State of Maryland. A detective from Pennsylvania testified that he was present when the F.B.I. and D.E.A. raided the clubs cabin seizing lab equipment used to manufacture crystal meth. The court recessed for lunch. When the court reconvened, Queen called the Orange County Jail Investigator, Keith Salis, to the stand. He testified the fight at the jail involving the defendants sent six prisoners to the infirmary. Perhaps the most shocking event of the day was when the governments attorney called the defendant, Richard Doyle, to the stand. Both of the defendants waived their right to remain silent. Richard Doyle freely admitted that he beat a man severely which resulted in his being in a coma for six weeks. Defendant Johnny Rowe admitted that he had been convicted for assaulting a man and breaking his arm. Under cross examination, the defendants' attorney, Harold Glazer, turned the tables on Assistant U.S. Attorney, David Queen. Defendant Doyle explained that he pled guilty, taking full responsibility for his actions. He expressed no regret for beating the man responsible for raping his thirteen year old baby sister. Defendant Johnny Rowe served eight years in the Army. He was a member of the Green Beret's and served two tours of duty in Vietnam ..."

Peaches could barely contain her happiness in knowing that Harold was on the job. Peaches sensed there was something special about Ramrod. She said, more to herself, with her eyes and ears glued to the news report.

"...For his service in Vietnam Johnny Rowe was awarded two

bronze stars and a purple heart." One after another, Glazer recalled the Government witnesses. Detective Daniel Marks from Baltimore, Maryland admitted there was no evidence to link either Defendant to any homicide. Detective Ralph Criswell from Pennsylvania testified earlier that he had been involved in more than a hundred investigations regarding the Argots. Under cross examlnation he admitted that he had never personally met, or talked with, either defendant. Further, he admitted that he had no reason to believe either of the defendants were manufacturing meth. The defense made a mockery of the Jail Investigator, Keith Salis, when he was recalled to the stand ..."

"Yes!" Peaches shouted excitedly. She sat on the edge of the bed with her hands cupped covering her knees.

" ... Defense attorney Harold Glazer attacked the credibility of the three prison witnesses who had given statements in regards to the fight at the jail. Willie Brown has twelve felony convictions and is currently in jail charged with first degree criminal sexual conduct. Joe Laurel has five prior felony convictions. He's awaiting trial for assaulting a police officer. Richard Greene has nine felony convictions and he is in jail pending a retrial for first degree murder. Investigator Salis previously testified that based on the statements given, he considered the defendants the aggressors. After his being informed of the prisoners criminal histories, Glazer asked if he still felt the witnesses statements to be credible. Glazer questioned why all of the offenders weren't placed in segregation pending investigaton? Also, why were the defendants the only ones not given medical attention? Judge McCallister denied bond, but he ordered the defendants to be taken to the Orange County Memorial Hospital and given immediate medical attention. He further ordered they be housed together, separate from the general population, and given the same rights and privileges as afforded the other prisoners housed in the jail. The judge added that he will reconsider the motion for bail following Friday's preliminary hearing."

"Thank you for the update, Richard."

"You're welcome, Susan."

"Locally, our eye in the sky reports a three car accident on Ocean Drive, one block south of Mango's nightclub. Traffic is backed up for two blocks. The weather forecast for tomorrow is clear skies, sunny, with temperatures reaching the mid 90's before noon with mild breezes by early evening. Have a great night, Miami! Susan Lichtman of WTVJ news Channel 4 reporting."

* * *

Peaches gave a sigh of relief and quickly said. "Thank you sweet Jesus and thank you too Harold Glazer."

Charlotte Lynn watched the news from the the Pink Pussycat and she could hardly contain her joy. Tears streamed from her eyes. She felt guilty for not attending the hearing, but someone had to be at the club in case Peaches called. She called the jail to learn that the visiting hours were from ten in the morning until two in the afternoon Tuesday and Thursday. In the morning, she planned to be the first visitor through the door.

Nuni and three of his friends were en-route to Miami. He parked his Lincoln beneath the carport of a friend's house and rented a new Dodge customized van; black and silver with dark tinted windows. He dressed casually, wearing light blue dress slacks, a tailored short sleeve Hawaiian shirt, and soft black leather loafers with tassles. Nuni adjusted his Ray Ban sunglasses, rested his arm on the edge of the driver's door window, and set the cruise control.

"You guys are down with this, right?" Nuni asked, not wanting to be embarrassed later. Especially in front of Peaches.

"Of course, we've got your back. That's how we roll," the men assured him.

* * *

From the courthouse, Ramrod and Bulldog were taken to the emergency room at the Orange County Memorial Hospital. Bulldog's finger was broken. The doctor gave him a shot to numb the pain, reset it, then placed the finger in a splint. Ramrod's x-ray showed bruised and battered ribs, but no breaks. They did decide to wrap his ribs before sending him on his way. Returning to the jail, they were taken to a smaller cell block normally used to house female pisoners. The cell block consisted of eight bunks, a small black and white television, and a wall phone. They could not dial information and neither remembered the phone number to the club, the house in Altamonte springs, or Nuni's residence. Ramrod tried to call the cabin, then the Holiday Inn where Harold was staying. There was no answer. The guards brought dinner served on plastic trays. The trays had abnormally huge portions and they were each given two pints of milk instead of one.

"I could get used to this." Bulldog grinned, loving the prefered treatment.

"Not me." Ramrod sighed. His thoughts were on Sugar. He wondered how his woman was coping with all of the uncertainties. She had no experierice to draw from and without her sister to lean on, things had to be very difficult.

Bulldog thanked the guard for the extra food.

After showering, they watched the evening news.

"That's not how I remember the fight." Ramrod laughed, remembering Bulldog's only conviction.

Bulldog grinned. "Well, I ain't no fuckin' war hero."

* * *

As Peaches watched the evening news, she suddenly started laughing.

She laughed so hard, it hurt. "What's so funny?" Raul asked.

"Bulldog. It just now dawned on me, nobody raped his baby sister.

He doesn't have a sister!"

Raul and Tony laughed heartily and Peaches wondered if Harold Glazer was aware of Bulldog's lie.

* * *

"Has anyone heard from Nuni?" Sugar walked around the club asking. No one had. Barmaids busied themselves restocking shelves with liquor, filling empty bins with ice, and inspecting glasses to make sure they were spotlessly clean. Assured that their service areas were in order, they walked to the office and asked Charlotte for the money drawer for their cash registers. The club opened at noon, the shift change scheduled for 7 o'clock. By then the club would be filled to capacity.

Where in the fuck was Nuni, Sugar wondered. He was the club manager. It was his responsibility to organize the bouncers, to delegate responsibility, and to take care of the dancers. She did not think Peaches intended for her to be in charge. Whenever the girls had a disagreement amongst themselves, or felt threatened by a customer, Nuni was always there to intervene. The girls respected him. He was their protector. With Big Nuni in the house the girls felt a sense of security and none of the bouncers could fill his shoes.

At nine o'clock, Ramrod's call was put through to Harold Glazer. "Hello?"

"Hi yourself." Ramrod cheerfully replied.

"How are you boys doing? Are you being treated good?"

"The doctor took care of Bulldog's finger. It was broke. An x-ray showed I have a few bruised ribs, and I'm wrapped up like a mummy! Our accomodations are much nicer and the jailers are much friendlier. We are really thankful for your coming to our rescue. For a minute I thought there might not be a fair trial. I thought these southerners might take us long haired bikers out behind the jail and lynch us."

Harold chuckled at the thought.

"I hate to impose, but I need a favor."

"What can I do for you?"

"Call information and give me the number to The Pink Pussycat."

"I can do that. Isn't that Peaches' club?"

"Yes. Her sister Charlotte should be there. We call her Sugar. She's my woman."

"Woman?" Bulldog said in the background.

"Give me a call back in a few minutes."

"Will do. Thanks."

Five minutas later, Ramrod called back. Harold was giving him the phone number. Ramrod realized that he had nothing to write on, or with. He also had a very poor memory. For dinner they had been served hot dogs and baked beans, the trays were still sitting on top of the stainless steel table. Ramrod grabbed a packet of ketchup, bit the tip off, and wrote the number on the wall, above the phone in ketchup. After thanking Harold he hung up, and quickly dialed the number to the club.

Sugar was sitting in a high backed leather chair behind the desk in the office. She looked at the clock on the wall, it was nine-thirty. She was already exhausted, her body longing for sleep. Her heart felt so heavy she wanted to unleash a flood of tears and she was at a loss as to what to do next. When the phone rang, she jerked it from its cradle, desperately hoping that it would be Nicky or Big Nuni on the other end. "Hello?" She answered.

"Hi, baby! Do you miss me?"

"Ramrod!" She cried, bursting into tears of relief. "How...are you... baby? Are you...okay." She stammered through her tears.

"Stop crying." Ramrod smiled, happy to hear her voice. "I'm fine."

"I'm sorry I wasn't there for the hearing, but someone had to be here in case Nicky called."

"Has anyone heard from Nicole or Charlie?"

"No!" Charlotte spoke bitterly, wiping at her tears in frustration.

"And, now Nuni is missing. He was supposed to he here at six o'clock. There's no answer when I call his house. I'm exhausted. I haven't been to sleep all night."

"That makes two of us."

"I will be there to visit in the morning by ten o'clock. Is there anything you want me to do or bring?"

"No, I'm fine. There's a chance we will be granted bail Friday. I need you to get some sleep. You need to pull yourself together and stay strong until then. I also want; you to know I... love you." It was the first time that he let feelings for her be known.

"Ain't that sweet?" Bulldog chuckled.

Charlotte Lynn heard him and snapped. "Tell that asshole I said to shut the fuck up! He's ruining my moment." Then in a sweeter tone she said, "I love you too, baby!"

"Sugar told me to tell you to shut the fuck up, that you're ruining her moment." Ramrod told Bulldog.

"Tell her I was just teasing. Ask her if she's heard from Peaches."

"Not yet." Ramrod told him, feeling the sudden weight of Bulldog's concern. The three of them were stuck for anything to say, each of them secretly wondering what the Heathens might be doing to Nicole.

* * *

At ten o'clock that night, Chris decided to stop by the motel instead of calling to check in. He wanted to make sure there would be no misunderstandings about their agreement to split the hijacked cocaine three ways. That needed to be discussed now, so it would not be brought up later in the presence of Nuni and the other men.

Peaches heard the closing of the car door outside of motel room, then a sharp knock at the room door. She went to peer out through the room's curtains. Seeing it was Chris she opened the door with a smile.

"I have secured a second boat," Chris announced, stepping into the room and closing the door behind him. "It's fueled and docked at the pier behind Billy Bear's house. At the end of the dock there's a lighted blue beacon, so Tony and Raul should have no difficulty spotting it. My brother Swag will meet them at the dock with a van, help unload the boat, take the cocaine to his house, then call us at the motel. We will take two vehicles, meet Tony and Raul at the dock and follow them in the second boat to Norman's Cay."

"When do we get our share?" Tony asked.

"When this is over, the four of us will go to my brother's house and divide the load three ways while Nuni and his men to the motel and wait for us." Chris explained.

"Sounds good to me." Tony exclaimed, satisfied there should be no problems.

Peaches' thoughts were far away. She had felt hatred before. She hated the man responsible for killing her daughter, Domonic 'Crowbar' Coroza, but she hated John Leder even more. The look on his face was etched in her memory. His grisly grin. His saying that he was her worst fuckin' nightmare. His ordering her to be caged in chicken wire, then tossed into the ocean to search for Davey Jones' Locker, She thought of revenge constantly. John

Leder deserved to die a slow, agonizing death. She could cut off his dick, shove it in his mouth and watch him bleed to death. She giggled at the thought of him having a tiny dick. She could bury him in the sand up to his neck at the edge of the ocean, watch the crabs feast on him, and when the tide rises, waves would splash on his face as he gasps for air. The thought of his offering someone money to spare his life nixed that idea.

No! John Leder would not get the opportunity to seek revenge on her unless it was in an Afterlife.

* * *

Nuni stopped at the Holiday Inn on Ocean Drive and rented

adjacent rooms, rooms 24 and 25. After checking in, he called Chris, suggesting they meet at Mango's nightclub in a half hour. It was eleven o'clock. The night sky was filled with stars, the smell of the ocean thick and salty.

Nuni arrived at Mango's, spotting Chris sitting in a red leather half- moon booth with a girl on each side of him. Chris ordered the girls a drink, gave them each a kiss, and sent them on their way so he could discuss business in private. Nuni watched admiringly as the girls strolled away with their drinks in hand.

Chris stood to greet his friend. After exchanging half-hugs and slaps on the back, Nuni seated himself across from Chris. "What's up?" Nuni asked, anxiously waiting to hear more.

"We've got all day tomorrow to go over that." Chris replied flatly, motioning for the waitress to order drinks. "Did you bring three trustworthy guys?"

"Of course. I left them at the motel. Where's Peaches?"

"She's safe. You will be seeing her in the morning. Until then, I don't want her name mentioned again."

"Why?" Nuni demanded in bewilderment.

"I need for you to trust me on this one. This isn't the time or place to be discussing anything."

They drank, snorted lines of cocaine, and played with the girls until closing. As they walked to their vehicles Chris asked Nuni to give him a call when he woke up. On second thought, Chris added. "After nine o'clock."

It seemed like he had only been asleep for a very short time when Chris found himself awakened by the sound of the ringing phone.

"Good morning!" Nuni announced loudly, irritating a very tired and sobering Chris.

"Fuck you!" Chris yawned.

"It's nine-thirty. Time to rise and shine, baby boy."

"Where are you?"

"At the Holiday Inn on Ocean Drive. Room 25."

"I'll be there in a half hour." Chris laughed. After hanging up, he dialed the number for Peaches room.

She answered on the third ring. "Hello."

"Are you up, and dressed?"

"Yes, I am. I went to bed early and slept for ten hours straight."

"Nuni is in town, and he's anxious to see you. We'll be there in about thirty minutes."

"Is he with you now?" Peaches asked wanting to talk to him. "No, but he's close by." Chris chuckled.

Twenty-five minutes later, Chris parked his red Corvette in the rear parking lot of the Holiday Inn. He knocked on the door of room 25. Within seconds the door opened, and Nuni asked, "Where's Peaches?"

"She's not far away." Chris smiled, motioning for Nuni to follow him. They walked side by side beneath the covered sidewalk until Chris stopped at room 14. Chris knocked lightly on the door, three quick raps. The door swung open. Peaches stood there wearing a pair of skimpy shorts and a tank top.

"Good morning," Peaches said with a smile.

Nuni looked at Chris. "You're gonna pay for this one," he growled.

Chris laughed heartily.

Peaches threw her arms around Nuni's neck, hugging him tightly. "I'm sorry I didn't listen to you. Did you bring the calvary?"

"You think I didn't?" Nuni beamed, picking her up in the air.

She bent her knees and hugged him tighter. Nuni felt the warmth of her body against his, and his heart nearly jumped out of his chest.

CHAPTER SIX
BLACK AND WHITE

At nine o'clock Sugar began preparing herself to visit Ramrod. Her suitcase, still unpacked, was sitting on a chair in the corner of the office. She opened the suitcase and ruffled through her clothes, selecting a pair of black shorts and a white halter top. With the chosen outfit in hand, she walked from the office and down the hall to the private dressing room she shared with her sister, Nicky. Inside there was a shower, a sink, and a long vanity with a mirror. Above the mirror there was a row of low intensity bulbs. She bathed in the small shower stall, washing herself carefully from head to toe. After drying off and getting dressed, Sugar grabbed a brush and a hairdryer, sat down at the vanity, and began styling her hair. She puffed powder on her face, dabbed perfume behind her ears, and opened a fresh tube of red lipstick. She called for a taxi, stepped outside of the club and locked the front door behind her. The brighthess of the sun made her eyes squint, causing her to remove the sunglasses from her small hand bag.

* * *

At ten o'clock Harold met Harry in the lobby of the Holiday Inn. "This is an eighteen hole course designed by the world reknown Robert Trent. The grass is well maintained, the fairways long, and the sand traps are painfully difficult," Harry warned Harold.

At the rear of the building they loaded their golf clubs onto the back of a green golf cart, using it to reach the very first hole. Harold flipped a coin to see who would tee off first, giving Harry the option of calling heads or tails.

Less than a mile away, the Federal Task Force was gathering inside the conference room at F.B.I. Headquarters. Everyone seated themselves in the same seats where they had sat the previous morning.

It was eerily quiet when Special Agent Moore and Assistant U.S. Attorney Queen entered the room.

Special Agent Moore frowned as he stepped forward to begin talking.

"The reason that we involved out of state agencies was to help establish a pattern of violence on behalf of the Argot outlaw biker gang. We clearly missed our mark!"

Attorney Queen added. "After yesterday's disappointing hearing, I personally interviewed the governments surprise witness, Jimmy Redick. His version of what happened is that he was standing on a street corner at a bus stop across the street from the Heathens clubhouse when he observed a white Ford van pull up to the door. The side doors of the van opened, and six men wearing blue jeans and black leather jackets rushed inside carrying chains and baseball bats. He heard blood curdling screams, then watched as two men dragged a huge man outside and into the parking lot. Presumably, that was Robert 'Big Moose' Sands, the club president for the Heathens. One man tied a rope around Sands feet, while another tied the opposite end to the rear bumper of the van. A group of men then ran from the clubhouse, hopped into the back of the van, and closed the door. A cloud of dust filled the parking lot as the stolen van fled the scene dragging the club president. He was dragged down Highway four-forty-one towards Orange Blossom Trail. The van was found abandoned two miles from the clubhouse behind a empty warehouse. It was torched. Dosed with gasoline inside and out. There were no fingerprints and no physical evidence. Jimmy Redick accurately describes Johnny Rowe and Richard Doyle, but he could not identify either defendant from a photo lineup. To make matters worse, from across the street he could not read the words on the back of their leather jackets or identify the club colors. Unfortunately, what we have is a witness who can tell us what happened, but not who did it. Gentlemen, unless someone can give me something concrete, this case is in serious trouble."

"Does anyone have anything new they would like to share with us?" Agent Moore asked, his pleading eyes scanning the room.

Heads turned to look at one another, but no one spoke.

"It's crunch time! Time to put on your thinking caps. Call your informants; offer deals to known associates serving lengthy sentences. It's impossible for someone to drive a van down highway four-forty-one in broad daylight dragging a screaming man behind it and not one person sees it. When you return to this table in the morning please bring something besides yourselves!"

* * *

"Mr. Rowe, you have a visitor," The jailer announced, unlocking the cell block door.

Ramrod turned around and walked backwards towards the door, expecting his hands to be cuffed behind his back. After standing still for a minute, Ramrod asked. "No cuffs?"

"Do you need them?" the jailer asked.

"Nope." Ramrod quickly replied.

The jailer escorted him down the hall, stopping at a small door. He opened it and Ramrod stepped inside. Inside the room there was a round steel stool, placed before a solid sheet of glass with a black phone hanging from the wall to his left. Visitors entered the room on the opposite side of the glass, sat on much more comfortable chair, using a black wall phone to talk. A ruff looking man was already seated on the other side of the glass. A look of shock came across Ramrod's face. He moved over to sit down, carefully picking up the phone on his side of the glass.

"You look terrible!" Ramrod said, suddenly breaking into a wide smile.

"You don't look so hot yourself," came the gruff reply.

"How have you been?"

"I've been a whole lot better. After I left the club and moved to Alaska I went to work on a crab boat in Anchorage. It was seasonal work and a dangerous job, but the pay was good. While I was at sea my home caught fire in the middle of the night. I lost my wife and kids."

Ramrod put his hand to the glass and on his side of the window the man did the same. They shared a brief moment of silence before dropping their hands.

"I'm sorry, man."

"I started drinking heavily. A year later I went to the Veterans hospital to clean up my act. Leaving the club was one of the hardest things that I've ever done, but I never regretted it. When my daughter sat on my lap, wrapped her little arms around my neck and called me daddy, it was the greatest feeling in the world. Anyway, I saw your ugly mug on the news and figured you could use a friend." Rod grinned.

"The second you lost your family, why didn't you come back to the cabin?"

"I guess maybe I felt like I had run out on you guys."

"No you didn't, brother. You have always been in our hearts and minds. You're our brother! A.F.F.A. remember? Argots forever, forever Argots."

Rodney 'Rod' Anderson smiled for the first time in a very long time. "Where are you staying?"

"I don't know. I just got off the plane an hour ago."

"I could use your help." Ramrod grinned.

Rod chuckled. "I kinda figured that."

"My woman, Sugar, and her sister Peaches own a nightclub downtown called the Pink Pussycat. Peaches is Bulldog's old lady, and she was kidnapped from the club three nights ago. The club's manager and Peaches' ex-husband are also missing. I don't like Sugar staying at the club by herself. When you leave, if you see a young gorgeous brunette in the lobby, that will be Sugar. Will you look after her until I get out?"

"I will guard her with my life." Rod swore.

"Word of caution. Do not wear any colors."

"Everything I owned was lost in the fire, my colors were burned right along with my Harley."

"I'm really sorry to hear about the loss of your family." Ramrod spoke softly offering his condolences.

"Times up, Rowe! But you may as well stay seated, you have another visitor waiting."

"Good to see you, brother. I'll give you a call at the club later."

"Take care of yourself, my brother." Rodney said as he left the room. He stepped into the lobby, his eyes scanning the room. It was not hard for him to spot Sugar, she stood out in the crowd of visitors. He gave a quiet whistle. She was certainly a looker. He stepped outside to light a cigarette and wait for her to exit.

"Hi, baby." Ramrod grinned.

"Are you okay?" She demanded with a look of concern.

"You look beautiful!" He replied, ignoring her needless concern.

"The jailer made me wait. He said you had another visitor. Was it another woman?"

"No." Ramrod laughed at her jealousy. "It was a very good friend, Rodney Anderson."

"The guy that started the club with you." Sugar asked in surprise. "Yeah. He's had some hardship in his life. In fact he lost his entire family in a house fire a year ago. We're the only family he has left."

"That's horrible." The mere thought sent chills running down her spine.

She rubbed her arms to get rid of the goose bumps.

"He saw me and Bulldog on the news in Alaska. He caught the next flight. He's going to be with you day and night until I get out of here. Have you heard from Peaches or Charlie?"

Tears suddenly filled her eyes. "Not a word. I'm really worried about Nicky."

Ramrod smiled. "Don't worry, she's alright. Everything is going to work out," he told her not really believing his own words. He and

Bulldog knew that there was a chance that Peaches was dead by now. He could not tell Charlotte this. Instead he said, "When this is over, what do you think about settling down somewhere? Maybe have us a couple of rug rats?"

"Are you proposing to me?"

"I think maybe I am."

"Well, you can kiss my ass!" Sugar said, pretending to be upset. "I'm not accepting a fuckin' proposal from behind glass. I will wait for you no matter how long it takes, but I want a proper proposal with a ring and everything that goes with it. Until then I'm your old lady, the only bitch allowed in your bed or riding on the back of your Harley."

"Yes, darling." Ramrod said meekly, a smile parting his lips.

Sugar laughed, knowing that there was nothing meek about her man. "I love you, baby." She blew him a kiss.

"I love you too." Ramrod wondered how he had got to be so lucky.

As Sugar left the visiting room she was ecstatic with thoughts of her and Ramrod getting married. She envisioned herself walking down the aisle wearing a white gown. Standing at the alter waiting for her was Ramrod dressed in a black tuxedo. She stepped from the jail into the blinding light of the sun, opened her purse, grabbed her sunglasses and put them on. As she snapped her purse closed, she heard someone calling her name. She turned to her right, in the direction of the voice, smiled, and said. "You must be Rodney?"

"I am." He smiled, unsure of himself. It had been a long time since he had shared a conversation with such an attractive woman. Gathering his courage, he said. "What do you say we go somewhere, have lunch, and get acquainted?"

"Sounds good to me." Sugar replied, returning his smile with one of her own. "I'm always happy to meet family. And, I'm really hungry."

Rod laughed. "I'm starved!"

As they strolled down the street, Charlotte Lynn sized Rod up. He was less than six feet tall, thin, with sandy blonde hair and blue eyes. By the lines in his forehead, he was well into his thirties and he had a hard life. He was simply dressed in jeans, a white tee-shirt, and black motorcycle boots. His blue eyes were as cold as steel, and he had at least a three day growth of beard.

Back at the jail, Ramrod was in the process of being returned to the cell block.

"I thought the visits were only fifteen minutes." Bulldog questioned as Ramrod entered the cell block.

"I had two visits. Rodney's in town."

"Rod Anderson?"

"Yeah! He saw us on the local news in Anchorage, Alaska, and caught the next flight here. He's been through some pretty rough times. He lost his family in a house fire a year ago."

"Man, that's some heavy shit!" Bulldog shook his head.

"I proposed to Sugar." Ramrod blurted.

"You did what?"

"I proposed!"

"Are you serious?"

"I proposed and she turned me down. She said she wasn't going to accept a proposal from behind a glass. She wants a proper proposal with a ring and everything that goes with it."

"That's funny."

"What's funny about it?" Ramrod frowned.

"I don't know. It just kinda struck me as funny that you asked and she turned you down."

Ramrod gave him the finger and left to go lay on his bunk, hearing Bulldog's laughter ringing behind him.

Rod and Sugar had been walking side by side for some time in comfortable silence.

"Were you and Ramrod in Vietnam together?" Sugar broke the silence.

"You mean, did we chase little Vietnamese soldiers through the rice patties, take turns sleeping in rain filled trenches, and fight side by side?"

"Something like that," she smiled.

"Ramrod enlisted four years before me. He served two terms. We've slept together in rain filled trenches, seen things that sometimes cause nightmares, and eaten things that would make most men puke. But we survived. We bonded, learned to trust the other with his life. Ramrod had my back and I had his. We have a mutual love and respect for each other that few men will ever know or understand."

"So, you were a Green Beret?"

"Yes Ma'am. Did Ramrod tell you that he asked me to stay by your side, day and night until he gets out?"

"He said it, but I'm sleeping on the couch at the club. There's no place for you to sleep."

"I reckon that if I can sleep in a rain filled trench, the floor will do just fine. At least I'll be warm and dry."

Sugar smiled. She linked her arm through his, drawn to him through his deep bond to Ramrod. More importantly, she suddenly felt very safe with him being around.

* * *

"I gotta know. What happened after I left the club?" Nuni was in the process of asking Peaches. She sat beside him on the bed.

"There was a knock on the back door," she began explaining. "It happened minutes after you and Sugar left, so I thought you had locked yourself out, and left your keys in the office. When I unlocked the door two men grabbed me, tied my hands behind my back, threw me in the back seat of their car, and drove me to Miami. I was put on a speed boat and raced across the Atlantic Ocean to a small island in the Bahamas called Norman's Cay. The island belongs to a drug kingpin by the name of John Leder. He held me responsible for starting the war between the Heathens and Argots. Also, for the involvement of the F.B.I. and D.E.A. Leder said that he gave my ex-husband Charlie the East Coast. Maybe so, but no one ever told me about territories being marked out. I didn't even know who Charlie's source was. I had never heard of a fuckin' John Leder. Leder ordered his men to wrap me in chicken wire, take me three miles out to sea, and throw me overboard. Tony and his brother Raul saved my life."

"Everyone is blaming the Heathens for kidnapping you. I thought they were responsible. Per Ramrod's orders the other Argot members have gone into hiding until he gives the word for them to come out."

"Ramrod and Bulldog still hasn't heard from Charlie either." Chris added.

"Tomorrow night, we're returning to the island. John Leder picked the wrong bitch to fuck with!" Peaches declared.

"I brought three guys that I've known all of my life, and enough artillery to cut down a small forest."

"Take a look at this." Peaches said, showing Nuni the hand drawn map of the island. Her finger traced from one place to another, explaining her plan.

"I like it!" Nuni laughed, his eyes shining with anticipation.

* * *

For lunch, Rod ordered a hot roast beef sandwich with gravy on the French fries. Sugar ordered a BLT sandwich.

"Fill me in on what's happening." Rod said, sipping a hot cup of coffee.

"My sister's ex-husband, Charlie Redman, has a cocaine connection. Charlie was having a hard time moving any large quantity. My sister Peaches is Bulldog's old lady. She started selling to the club. To make a long story short, as Ramrod explained it to me, the club opened a chapter in Orlando hoping to expand the business. The Heathens weren't very happy with the club moving into their territory. When an Argot member named J.D. was riding down highway 17-92 three Heathens pulled up alongside of him. One stuck a metal rod into his rear wheel causing his Harley to slide under a car, the bumper crushed his skull killing him instantly. After the funeral, Ramrod, Bulldog, Tiny, Jammer, Rooster, and Kapote went to the Heathens clubhouse to avenge J.D.'s murder. If you watched the news, you pretty much know the rest of the story. The Heathens club president, Bobby Sands, was tied to the rear bumper of a stolen van and dragged to his death. Everyone thought it was over. But the Heathens retaliated by raiding our clubhouse. They beheaded twelve of our members, stacked their motorcycles one on top of another, then set the clubhouse and motorcycles on fire. That's when the F.B.I. and D.E.A. joined forces. Ramrod and Bulldog were arrested during a raid in Atamonte Springs at the club's rental house. Aside from that, Charlie and his Corvette are missing, and I haven't heard from the clubs manager, Nuni." She shook her head, then added. "The funeral for our fallen brothers is at one o'clock this afternoon."

"Do you know where the funeral is being held? I think we should pay our respects." Rod told her flatly.

"I know they are going to be buried in Greenlawn Cemetery, and that's where the eulogy will be given. It's the same cemetery where J.D. is buried." A tear formed and slowly trickled down Sugar's face. Rod reached across the table and wiped away the teardrop with his hand, and softly announced. "You and I are going to the funeral to pay our respects. After lunch, would you mind going shopping with me? In my rush to get to the airport on time the only stop I made was at the bank to withdraw money."

"Are you kidding me? I'm a girl! What girl doesn't love to shop?" She replied, giggling. It was a silly question, she thought.

Rod asked the waitress for the check, leaving a tip on the table. He stopped at the register to pay the cashier for their meal, then together they stepped outside. It was a beautiful day, the sun was bright and warm, a gentle breeze lightly tossing Sugar's hair.

"The Woodville Mall is only six blocks away. Would you like to walk or take a taxi," she asked.

"It's a nice day for a walk."

They walked, passing shops, making small talk along the busy street. Once they arrived at the Mall, Rod stopped at a Men's Apparel and purchased a couple pair of jeans, two short sleeve shirts, underwear and socks. Sugar entered a women's fashion store where she bought two new halter tops, a mini shirt, and several pairs of black mesh nylons. They stopped at a drug store and he paid for a number of hygiene items. He left the store with soap, deodorant, toothpaste, toothbrush, and razors.

With their purchases in hand Rod hailed a cab. Sugar slid into the back seat and moved over, making room for Rod to slide in behind her.

Sugar told the cab driver to take them to The Pink Pussycat. By now everyone in the surrounding area knew where the club was located. It was less than three miles away from their present location and in a short period of time had become the talk of the City. Unlike the club before it, The Pink Pussycat had very good reputation for high class entertainment and service. Peaches preferred to call her girls performers, never allowing them to advertise their wares in the nude. Nor were they allowed to hustle customers for drinks or run any type of sleezy games on the customers. Her girls had class, and Charlotte was determined to make sure the business was managed how Nicole wanted it.

As they neared the club Rod saw the huge pink neon outline of a girl sitting sideways on top of a blue neon letters that spelled THE PINK PUSSYCAT.

"Very nice." Rod reported, admiring the huge sign.

While he paid the taxi driver, Sugar fumbled through her purse for the keys to the door of the club. Her purse was always cluttered with useless items that should be left somewhere else, such as fingernail polish remover, Q-tips, and a can opener. Once inside the club, she led him to the private dressing room that she shared with her sister. Rod showered, shaved, and changed into a new set of clothes.

"You cleaned up pretty good." Sugar smiled approvingly, as he joined her in the office.

"If we're going to make the eulogy you better call us a cab." Rod suggested.

Ten minutes later they left the club and were en-route to Greenlawn Cemetery. The slain members were local men, so the funeral procession consisted of mostly family and friends. Rod told the cab driver to leave the meter running.

As Charlotte stepped from the taxi, she softly said. "This is so sad." Tears ran slowly down her cheeks.

After paying their respect and returning to the comfort of the waiting taxi, Rod gently rubbed Charlotte's back to comfort her, but said nothing. He figured there was nothing to say when you were surrounded by so much death. There was a time for everything, he thought, his heart growing cold. This was clearly a time for revenge.

* * *

"This place is well known for their steak sandwiches." Harry boasted, entering the sports bar at the Holiday Inn.

Following Harry's lead Harold ordered a cocktail and a steak sandwich with country fries.

"What do you think is going to happen at the preliminary hearing Friday?" Harry asked.

"It's going to be interesting, that's for sure. Queen isn't going to be nearly as easy the second time around. He's going to be prepared."

Twenty minutes later, Harry paid the food bill and handed Harold a crisp One Hundred dollar bill for his losing their golf bet.

* * *

Detective Hill dialed information and asked for the phone number for Nicole Redman at the Regency Towers in Baltimore, Maryland. The number was unlisted. He knew that he could ask for a Supervisor and get approval, but he would have to identify himself as a police officer and use his name and badge number. With such a massive investigation going on it would probably be wise for him not to do that. He wondered how much trouble she had gotten herself into this time. Deep down he would always have a soft spot for her. The torch was still burning.

* * *

Throughout the night, Ramrod and Bulldog called the club to talk with Sugar and Rod. Rod filled in for Nuni, the bouncers readily agreeing to take their orders from him. He personally watched over Sugar, the dancers, and the door. Sugar never asked for his help. She did not need to. Leadership was his strong suit, his natural instinct.

* * *

Wednesday morning at ten o'clock, the conference room at F.B.I. Headquarters was filled with sad, tired faces. No one had any good news to report. Special Agent Moore, Agent Sweeny, and D.E.A. Agent Elliot were no closer to finding new evidence than the state agencies. David Queen concluded that he needed to come up with something fast, in enough time for Friday's preliminary hearing.

"This Task Force is finished! Thank you for coming. You are all dismissed to return to your normal lives." Special Agent Moore reported disgusted.

It was mid-afternoon when Harold Glazer received an unexpected call from David Queen.

Harold quizzed. "You must have heard about my excellent golf game, and now you're calling to challenge me to a round."

"No. I would have been shocked if you had lost. Everybody beats Harry." Queen chuckled. "I have three offers to put on the table, but I need a decision today."

"I'm listening."

"Option one. We can proceed to the preliminary this Friday."

"That's scheduled, it's not an option!" Harold Glazer snapped, wondering what kind of game Queen was playing.

"Option two. All charges dismissed contingent your clients pled guilty to one weapons charge which carries a two year minimum sentence."

"What's the third option?"

"The government will dismiss all charges under the condition your clients sign a capias not to return to the State of Florida for a period of five years."

"I will need the offers in black and white. Put them on paper."

"I sent the written agreement to you by courier. It should be at the front desk within the next half hour."

"I'll get back to you after I talk to my clients."

Harold called Harry and asked if he could meet him at the Orange County Jail in one hour. "What's up?"

"We've got a deal to present to our clients."

"I'll be there." Harry promised. Presented with three multiple offers Ramrod and Bulldog looked at each other and smirked.

Ramrod was the first to speak, directing his attention to Bulldog. "We've got to make our own decision. I don't want my decision to influence yours one way, or another."

"Harry, you present Mr. Doyle with the three options and I will discuss the options with Mr. Rowe."

Harry and Bulldog went into another corner of the room to quietly discuss the situation. After presenting the options to Ramrod, he asked Harold. "How do you feel about this?"

"I'm not sure what evidence they have. We won't know that until after the case is bound over and discovery is granted. My gut feeling is that they don't have a very strong case. The house didn't belong to you. Your name wasn't on the search warrant. I seriously doubt there's enough evidence to convict you of the federal firearm violations."

"If you were me, what would you do?" Ramrod asked.

"Like you told Bulldog." Harold spoke honestly. "It's entirely your decision. Should you decide to accept the two years, with good time credit, you would serve fourteen months and ten days."

"I don't like it. Tell this David Queen that my answer is no deal!" Harold Glazer shook his head with a grin. "I'll tell him."

Bulldog was unsure what a capias was. Harry explained. "If you return to the State of Florida within the five year period, you would be subjected to arrest and the state could reinstate the charges."

After making their decisions, Ramrod and Bulldog were escorted back to their cell block.

"What was your decision." Bulldog asked. "No deals! What was yours?"

"I went with the capias."

Ramrod gave Bulldog a disgusted look.

"Hey dog, I thought you were going to take the deal, too!"

Twenty minutes later, the jailer returned and called out. "Pack up Doyle!

The Deputies are here to escort you to the airport."

CHAPTER SEVEN
FALLEN ANGELS

"Good evening, Miami. Susan Lichtman WTVJ reporting with the six o'clock news. One of the two men charged with the brutal murder of the Heathens club president, Bobby "Big Moose' Sands, was released from custody today. Richard Bower, our correspondent in Orlando, reported two Deputy Sheriffs escorted Richard Doyle from the Orange County Jail to the Orlando International Airport without restraints. Doyle was last seen boarding flight 268 with a one way ticket to Harrisburg, Pennsylvania. The Argots club president, Johnny Rowe, remains in custody. Sheriff Deputy Robert Bratten refused comment. In the local news, F. B. I. and

D.E.A. agents coordinated a predawn raid early this morning resulting in the arrests of three local men and the seizure of over a thousand kilos of cocaine, the largest seizure in Dade County this year. Arrest warrants were issued for Antonia Mendoza, Sal Munutto, and Sammy Sosa. The weather reports showers throughout the evening with highs in the mid 80's by noon tomorrow. Have a great evening, Miami. Susan Lichtman reporting for WTVJ Channel 4 news."

"Hell, yes, my baby is free!" Peaches shouted. In her excitement nothing else mattered.

"I wonder why they didn't release Ramrod?" Nuni said, pondering the thought.

"I hope Bulldog isn't being returned to Pennsylvania to be arraigned on more charges." Peaches worried.

"If that was the case, he wouldn't be on the airplane unescorted, and he would have been in leg irons and handcuffs." Chris offered his opinion. It was true, Peaches thought. Common sense should have told her that.

"I guess we will find out tomorrow." Nuni concluded, pleased that, for the moment, Bulldog was out of the picture.

"At least my baby is out." Peaches sighed her relief.

Time was passing quickly, and they were only hours away from their pre-dawn raid on Norman's Cay.

"Did you bring me a gun?" Peaches demanded of Nuni.

"Whatcha want, baby girl?" Nuni asked, not bothering to question her need for a gun.

"A forty-five automate."

"I gotcha!" Nuni beamed.

Peaches looked at Nuni and smiled her appreciation. Nuni returned her smile, happy to have pleased her.

* * *

Sugar and Rod watched the evening news together. "Why didn't they release Ramrod too?" Sugar asked. Her first thought was Bulldog made a deal to cooperate. It's not something Ramrod would ever do, not in a million years. She was sure of that.

Whatever Rod was thinking, he kept to himself. He already knew how stubborn Ramrod could be.

At seven o'clock Ramrod called the club. He told Rod about the deals that were offered and the decision Bulldog had made. Rod was livid. He immediately disowned Bulldog. In Rod's mind, Bulldog had shown his true colors, showing that he gave less than a fuck about his fallen brothers. Accepting the capias was a coward's way out. If he could not return to Florida for five years, then Bulldog had no intentions of seeking revenge for the brutal murder of his brothers.

"I was disappointed, but I told Bulldog that it was important he make his own decision. I didn't want mine to influence his one way, or another. For that reason I suggested he speak with Harry Swogel while I made my decision with Harold."

"When did you find out that he accepted the deal?"

"As we were returning to the cell block we discussed our decisions. Twenty minutes later the jailer told Bulldog to pack up and two Deputies escorted him to the airport. Before he left, he explained that he thought that I was going to accept the deal too."

"What a fuckin' snake!" Rod spat. "My father once told me that if you pick up a snake and it bites you, you knew it was a snake when you picked it up. Bulldog will never get a chance to bite me. To me, he's a fuckin' snake."

Sugar, who had been sitting patiently while Rod spoke to Ramrod, shouted. "We will be there for your hearing at ten o'clock, baby!"

"By the way," Rod continued. "We attended the funeral yesterday. The brothers were loved by many friends and family. There were a lot of tears."

"Thanks again for looking after Sugar."

"She a good woman."

"Did she tell you that I asked her to marry me?"

"No, she didn't." Rod smiled, glancing over at her.

Ramrod chuckled. "She told me that she wasn't accepting a fuckin' proposal from behind glass. She wants a proper proposal with a ring and everything that goes with it."

"I wouldn't marry your ass if I was her." Rod laughed.

* * *

Detective Hill called the Orlando International Airport, making reservations for a direct flight to Baltimore, Maryland. He was informed that the next available flight on American Airlines was at Gate 5 on Thursday morning, at nine o'clock.

It was Wednesday. He looked at his watch, it was ten o'clock at night. Hill rummaged through his suitcase, pulling out a pair of dark blue casual slacks and a loose knit white pullover shirt. Satisfied with his appearance, he left the motel room. Stepping outside, he hailed a taxi, requesting to be taken to the Pink Pussycat. If he had known it was a mere three blocks away, he would have walked. It was a clear, warm night. He stopped long enough at the entrance to the club to pay the two dollar cover charge. Entering into the club's deem interior, he took careful note of his surroundings, then seated himself at the horseshoe bar and ordered a long neck bottle of Budweiser.

"Is Nicole Redman here?" He asked the barmaid behind the bar.

"Who?" Glenda, the barmaid, asked.

"The owner." Detective Hill smiled. "You probably know her better by Peaches."

The barmaid shook her head and walked down the bar. She had whispered conversation with a waitress. He watched the two women glance in his direction. For the next fifteen minutes he sipped at his Budweiser, his eyes focused on the attractive young girl on stage, who was busy performing a slow striptease.

"Who are you? And, why are you asking about my sister?"

He heard the soft voice at his back and slowly tuned around to face a beautiful young woman in her very early twenties.

"Sister?" He said in surprise. "I didn't know Nicole had a sister!"

"What do you want?" Sugar demanded, putting her hands on her hips. "Is there somewhere that we can talk in private?"

"Nope!" Rod suddenly appeared at her side. If you have business with Sugar, then it's my business too."

Detective Hill showed his badge, then said. "I'm not here in my official capacity. I came as Nicole's friend."

"Follow me." Rod said, leading the way to the office and closing the door behind them. Sugar seated herself in a high back black leather chair behind the desk. Rod stood beside her chair and Hill stood facing them.

"What business do you have with Peaches?" Rod asked bluntly.

"I thought I'd tell her that there's a federal task force investigating several murders and cocaine trafficking, and her name came up. I know this because I was called to be a member of that task force. Assistant U.S. Attorney David Queen offered plea deals because he doesn't have a solid case against Rowe or Doyle. His surprise witness was standing across the street at a bus stop and witnessed the entire incident. He gives an accurate description of Rowe and Doyle, but he couldn't pick either from a photo line-up. He couldn't even read the words on the back of their leather jackets."

"Why are you telling me this?" Sugar asked.

"I've asked myself that a million times before coming here. If this was to get out, it would cost me my job. I investigated the death of Nicole's daughter. Nicole and I became close, more than just friends. I guess I still have a soft spot for her and wouldn't want to see any harm come her way."

"Are you sure they've got no evidence?" Sugar asked. "Johnny Rowe is my man."

"Absolutely nothing. Hundreds of people were interviewed yesterday. Agents were sent to prisons across the country offering get out of jail free cards to guys serving lengthy sentences. After exhausting their resources the task force was disbanded. I'll be flying back to Baltimore in the morning."

"Nicky has been missing for two days. It's unlike her." Sugar volunteered.

"Nicky." Hill grinned. "I assume that's Nicole. You shouldn't worry yourself too much, Nicole has a way of landing on her feet."

"I'm sorry. I call her Nicky, and I hope you're right."

"I am." Hill smiled reassuringly.

Rod cleared his throat. "I'll tell the barmaid that your drinks are on the house. If there's anything else I can do for you, let me know. When we hear from Peaches we'll tell her that you stopped in, what was said, and tell her to give you a call."

"Thank you. Also, would you please be discreet with the information?"

"No problem. You have my word on that." Rod promised.

* * *

Tony and Raul arrived at Fort Apache Marina at three in the afternoon. Their thirty-five foot Donzi was fueled and ready to go.

The powerful speedboat was powered by twin 427 Chevrolet high performance marine engines. Carrying its maximum payload, the Donzi had a top speed of 72 miles per hour, which was faster than any of the Coast Guard boats. Whenever they were running loaded with cocaine, they would speed across the open water in the darkness of night headed for the safe harbor of Boca Raton.

The sky was overcast and the local weather report called for northerly winds with six to eight foot waves, which meant they were in for a rough ride.

Four hours after leaving the marina they reached the island of Norman's Cay. Tony refueled the boat while Raul and two workers loaded the cocaine.

At seven o'clock they raced across the open sea for Boca Raton. For the next three hours they stood staring over the bow into the darkness. It was unlikely that they would see a bouy, a floating log, a small boat, or any kind of marker before crashing into it. Peering ahead provided them with a false sense of security. In the daylight hours sunglasses protected their eyes form the elements, but at night there was no such protection. The water stung their faces, their eyes squinting and tears stinging their eyes from the driving wind. Legend had it that at moments like this, they were at the mercy of the 'Fallen Angels'. The exact same sea had taken many lives, sometimes swallowing entire ships along with its crew. In the beginning, at least on their first few trips, there had been a sense of excitement and adventure. But those days were long gone! Tony and Raul were keenly aware that their careers and lives could end in the blink of an eye with one rogue wave.

At midnight they idled up to the pier behind Billy Bear's house. Swag had four five gallon cans of fuel sitting at the end of the pier. As Tony refueled the boat, Raul helped Swag unload the kilo's and carry them to a waiting van. Swag drove the van to his house, picked up the phone and called Chris at the motel.

Twenty minutes later, Chris, Peaches, Nuni and his men Bobby,

Ricky, and Frank hopped aboard a second boat and started the engine. Chris borrowed the boat from Don Aranow; who owned Fort Apache Performance Boats. The boat was thirty-five feet, with twin supercharged 427 Cobra engines. Don claimed that on a good day his boat would cut through the water at more than a hundred miles an hour.

Nuni brought two flashlights, but he was hopeful that the moonlight would provide enough light to walk the shoreline around the island. He had thoughtfully purchased blue jeans, a dark blue wind-breaker jacket, and dark blue toboggan hats for everyone. For Peaches, Nuni purchased a pair of tennis shoes and told her. "On this trip you're not wearing flip-flops."

The plan was simple. The boats would leave together. When they were half a mile from Norman's Cay, Tony and Raul would drift in the water for twenty minutes. Raul had estimated that it would be a ten minute walk around the shoreline to the compound. Chris would dry dock the boat, and everyone would hike to their destination. Once they were in position, they would lurk in the shadows. Upon hearing the Donzi approach and observing the guard walk to the dock, Nuni and his men would capture the men sleeping in the bunkhouse while Peaches and Chris entered John Leder's bungalow and captured him.

Peaches seated herself on the far right side of the boat on the rear bench. Nuni sat next to her with his arm stretched across the back of the seat. He wanted to pull her to him and hold her tight. But he would wait, hoping that someday she would feel the same for him as he did her. She crossed her legs, drawing Nuni's gaze down to her tiny feet. He broke into soft laughter. She wore a pair of multicolored flip-flops just to spite him.

Peaches caught him looking at her feet and smiled.

"One of these days, Alice." He smiled. "Pow! Right in the kisser."

Peaches laughed, pulling the toboggan hat down to cover her ears. She cupped her hands and blew hot air into them, rubbed her arms, and shivered. For a brief moment she wished she had worn the damn tennis shoes and socks! Her thoughts ran rampant. From her daughter, to fond memories of her mother and father, and on to Bulldog. It began to rain softly, making her drop her head, and helping to hide her tears. After a long moment of silence she was able to get her quiet tears under control.

She gazed towards the heavens not seeing a single star in the sky.

The boats were side by side, twenty feet apart, running sixty miles and hour when Tony pointed for Chris to swing wide, and come in from the back of the island. Tony and Raul slowed to an idle, going into a slow drift. Tony hoped the guard would walk down to the dock to meet them. After all, it was his normal routine. But what if he didn't? Pondering the thought, Tony prayed that he wouldn't have to shoot anyone. Nuni and his men were going to capture the men sleeping in the bunkhouse, while Peaches and Chris entered John Leder's bungalow and captured him. If anything went wrong, he knew that El Jefe would order them all killed. There would be no second chances.

* * *

Sugar and Rod had closed the Pink Pussycat at two o'clock. Sugar counted the cash and secured the money in a safe while Rod supervised the barmaids restocking of the bar and the bouncers nightly clean-up. By three a.m. they were letting the last of the workers out the rear door and locking themselves inside.

"Would you like a drink?" Sugar offered, stepping behind the bar to make herself a stiff one.

"Don't mind if I do. Just pass me a tall bottle of Budweiser." Rod grinned.

"I'm worried about my sister, and I've no idea what's happened to her ex-husband Charlie, or where Nuni is." Sugar announced, a tear forming in her eye. Rod reached across the counter of the bar and wiped the tear away with his hand.

"Don't worry, little one," he said. It was a feeble attempt of comforting her, but it was the best that he had to offer.

"Would you like to sleep on the couch tonight, and I'll sleep on the floor," Sugar offered.

"No, thank you. I'm really not accustomed to the comforts in life." Rod grinned.

She knew it was true. Rod was a man's man.

CHAPTER EIGHT
REFLECTIONS

The sea calmed as the Donzi neared the island, the moon peeking out from behind dark clouds. Tony and Raul felt a sense of relief while the other men dealt with a mixed range of emotions. Everyone knew that their lives depended on things going exactly as planned. Otherwise, some of them may not make it home to their loved ones.

From the moment their feet hit dry land, Peaches took the lead walking the shoreline at a rapid pace, staying close to the line of towering trees. After about a five minute walk, she caught sight of the dock, motioning the men to a sudden halt. She led the men into the shelter of the trees and knelt down on the damp earth. Peaches quickly removed the map of the island from her back pocket and began issuing orders.

"Nuni, position Frank, Bobby and Ricky where they can rush inside the bunkhouse and hopefully catch the guards sleeping. They can walk around the bungalow and come in from the backside. You watch for the guard to approach the dock. If Tony and Raul don't capture him, then shoot him if you have to. Chris, you and I are going into John Leder's bungalow."

Within minutes they were all in position to launch their attack. The light rain had slowly softened the ground, allowing them to move soundlessly across the beaten ground. They all saw a sudden flicker of a lighter, then the glow of a lit cigarette. Nuni was close enough to smell the smoke. A guard was sitting on the steps of the bungalow. As predicted, when he heard the roar of the Donzi's engines the guard stood up, tossed his cigarette on the ground and crushed it with the sole of his shoe and proceeded to walk down to the dock. Chris and Peaches stood in the shadows of the bungalow watching closely. Making a decision on his own, Nuni suddenly stepped out of the shadows behind the guard. He wrapped his left arm around the man's neck while shoving the heavy 45 automatic into his back. The guard froze. "Don't flinch!" Nuni quietly whispered. "I've got a real itchy trigger finger."

Chris and Peaches hurried silently up the stairs, pausing a brief second to remove the handguns from their waistbands. They stood inside the thin wooden door for a second, letting their eyes adjust to the darkness. They moved from the sparsely furnished front room to the rear of the little house, discovering John Leder sprawled across a double bed, the sheets pulled back to expose his body. He was wearing dark blue shorts and a gray tank top.

Peaches stepped forward to grab him by the ankle with both hands. She gave a hard tug, jerking him from the bed.

"What ... the ... fuck." Leder sputtered, coming awake. He hit the floor with a loud thud.

Chris shined a bright flashlight in his face, causing Leder to throw up a hand to protect his eyes from the blinding light.

"What's going on? Who are you?" he shouted.

Peaches smiled in the darkness. "I'm your worst fuckin' nightmare," she whispered.

The three men sleeping in the bunkhouse offered no resistance as they were awaken from their sleep at gun point. After tying their hands behind their backs, they were taken to the courtyard where they were joined by John Leder.

"Do you remember me?" Peaches asked Leder, stepping forward to yank the toboggan hat from her head.

"Peaches!" Leder gasped in shock.

At that moment Tony and Raul joined them, drawing a cold stare from El Jefe.

"I never expected to see you again."

Peaches suddenly turned her gun on Tony and Raul. "Tie them up too!" she ordered.

Nuni's three men immediately went into action. "Please ... we..." Tony was clubbed into silence while Raul stared at Peaches with sudden hatred filling his eyes, not bothering to resist as he was quickly tied up.

"What are we going to do with them?" Nuni asked.

"Wrap all three of them in chicken wire, then put them in the boat tied up at the dock. We will need some rope and six cinder blocks."

It was six o'clock, the sun just peeking over the horizon casting a spectacular glow. As dawn broke, the seagulls cried and a warm wind swept over the island taking away the last of the light rain drops.

The four captured men were Cubans, one of them spoke English. "We are workers. We do work for El Jefe. We mean you no harm. Ya have no reason to kill us."

"See that no harm comes to these men while I'm gone." Peaches instructed Chris. "Nuni and I will return within the hour."

"Are you sure you don't want me to take care of this?"

Peaches smiled down at Leder who was watching her closely. "No, it's personal!"

Tony, Raul, and Leder were wrapped in wire, then dragged roughly to the boat and thrown on the floor. Tony groaned as he slowly came to from the earlier beating he had taken. As Nuni started the engines, Peaches cast the ropes onto the dock. Nuni put the boat in reverse, backing away from the pier. He stopped, shoving the throttle forward. The boat jumped across the water racing out to sea. Three miles out, Peaches motioned for Nuni to shut the engines off.

"Help me stand Tony and Raul up on the back of the boat," she instructed. They started with Tony, getting very little fight as Peaches tied a cinder block to each of his feet. Raul came next, but he chose to put up a wiggling fight, so she coldly struck him over the head with the butt of her .45 automatic, stunning him enough to make him submissive.

"We...saved...you." Raul groaned, tears streaming from his eyes. "That you did." Peaches smiled, tying off the cinder blocks to his ankles. "And I'm going to save you too. I just wanted you both to know how I felt when I was on the back of the boat in a wire cage. Get them down and cut them loose, Nuni."

"You're one crazy bitch." Tony shook his head in shock.

When they were released from their wire cages, Peaches ordered Tony and his brother to stand John Leder up on the back of the boat. Following her orders to the letter they tied blocks to his feet. Leder suddenly found his voice.

"I will do anything…" Leder's pleading was cut short as Nuni back handed him across the mouth with a heavy hand.

"Are you going to push him into the sea?" Tony asked Peaches. "No, you and Raul are," she replied.

"But we told you that we've never killed anyone before." Tony begged, his eyes pleading.

"Sorry, but it's the only way I can be sure that I can trust you. None of us will ever speak of this again."

She reflected that Raul would never laugh again at the thought of her in the cage on the back of the boat.

The sea was calm, letting El Jefe see his reflection in the water. There was a loud plash, ripples, and a few bubbles. His own reflection was one of the last things John Leder would ever see.

* * *

No one spoke on the ride back to the island. Thoughts of what they had just done occupying them. Tony reasoned, it was not something he wanted to talk about. Raul simply tried to block the memory from his mind. Nuni never gave it a second thought. Peaches wondered how long it took for Leder to hit the bottom and how long he lived. She envisioned the look on his face, his hair waving in the current, and fish circling the wire cage. Could he see through the murky water? How long did he hold his breath? What were his last thoughts? Peaches stood up. Her eyes filled with tears as she gazed over the bow of the Donzi towards the horizon. She wiped her eyes with the back of her hand, and Raul wondered if she was crying, or was it the result of the forceful wind.

When their feet hit dry land, Peaches began issuing orders. "Chris, I need to speak with you in the bungalow. In private."

"Okay." He replied following her.

Once inside with the door closed, she spoke quietly. "I want you to take Bobby, Ricky, and Frank with you. Drop them off at the motel. Then go to your brother's house and divide the kilos equally between yourself, Tony and Raul, and me. Making it a three way split, as promised. Then return to the motel and pay Nuni's men off. Give them whatever you believe to be fair, and leave Nuni's money in a bag. Afterwards, you can stay at the motel or return to your apartment and wait for my call."

Chris looked out the door of the bungalow at the men tied up, who were still sitting on the ground in the courtyard. "Are you sure you want us to leave now?"

"Yes, I'm sure." She said, getting up and walking to the door. "Nuni, untie those men!" She stepped outside to speak with them.

Following orders, Chris and the men left in one of the boats.

"Thank you, Ms. Peach!" The worker spoke broken English communicated the thanks for the other workers. He wore a broad grin.

"Call me Peaches." She laughed at the shortening of her name. Her platinum blonde hair glistening in the sunlight. To the migrant workers, she looked like a goddess.

"Tell your men they are free to go, or they can stay and work for me. If they choose to stay, I will double their salary and provide better working conditions."

"We have no place to go, Ms. Peaches."

"Then you will work for me," she offered. On second thought, she asked. "What exactly do you do?"

"Whatever is asked of us. We fish, cook, clean the bungalows, wash clothes, and provide security."

Nuni chuckled. "The security could stand some improvement."

"What did he say?" Pepe, the captured guard asked Juan in Spanish.

Juan repeated what Nuni had said, explaining it in Spanish. Pepe grinned and nodded his head in agreement.

"Sometimes we help load boats and once a week we unload the airplane."

"Airplane?" Peaches questioned, raising her eyebrows.

"Yes." Juan pointed. "There's a landing strip on a small island two, maybe three miles to the west. The field is lined with fifty gallon oil drums that we set fires in if the plane has to land after dark. Every Wednesday the airplane comes, and we unload two thousand kilos. A boat came and we loaded two hundred kilos on it. Last night, Tony and Raul came and they took three hundred kilos to Miami."

"That accounts for five hundred kilos. What happened to the other fifteen hundred?" Nuni asked.

"They're inside the bungalow." Juan nodded.

Nuni and Peaches looked at each other, turned, and hurried inside the bungalow. In a room opposite where they had found John Leder sleeping, they discovered kilos of cocaine stacked four feet high against the rear wall. A broad smile appeared on Nuni's face as he began counting the stacks.

"I wonder where they came from?" Peaches said aloud. She stepped back outside and asked Juan. "Do you know where the airplane comes from?"

"Bogota, Columbia." Juan answered instantly.

Peaches pondered the thought. She had alot to think about. "There's no stove in the bungalow. How do you eat?" Nuni asked.

"We cook on an open fire in a skillet. We have no freezer. Sometimes someone will bring us fresh eggs, milk, and meat. We have plenty of food. Manual is the fisherman. Pepe dives for lobster."

"What can you cook us for breakfast?"

"American pancakes and coffee."

"Works for me." Nuni grinned.

"Just black coffee for me."

Peaches smiled. "Let's go for a walk." She suggested to Nuni, rolling up the bottom of her jeans. She slid her tiny feet out of the multicolored flip-flops. Nuni rolled his pants legs up, took off his shoes and socks and followed her. They waded into the water and felt the surge of the waves move first in than out. The sky was filled with white powder puffs. Huge palm trees blew softly, swaying back and forth. The water was crystal clear and when they stood perfectly still they could see fishes nibbling on their toes. The sand was as white as sugar and when they walked the beach barefoot it was warm to the touch. Norman's Cay was an unspoiled island, its beauty extremely captivating.

"We probably should have returned with everyone else." Peaches sighed, thinking of her sister and Bulldog.

"I'm glad we didn't." Nuni smiled, happy to share the time alone with her.

"You're a good man, Ulises Alvarado. You have always been there for me no matter what."

"That's how it's supposed to be!" Nuni professed his loyalty.

Following the shoreline, it took forty-five minutes to walk completely around the small island. Nuni pointed to two dolphins playing off the coastline. The smell of hot coffee mixed with fresh salty morning sea air greeted them as they returned to the bungalow.

"Breakfast is ready, Mr. Nuni." Juan called.

Nuni turned to Peaches with a grin. "Mr. Nuni. I like the sound of that."

* * *

"You've got a visitor, Rowe. I'll be back in five minutes." The jailer announced.

Ramrod had never slept so late, but he was physically and mentally exhausted. Alone with his thoughts there was just too much to think about. He washed his face, brushed his teeth, and ran his fingers through his hair. While dressing in the orange jailhouse jumpsuit he glanced at his tattoos. The jailer had asked about them when he was fingerprinted and photographed.

On his left arm above his elbow he had the number thirteen and a-half tattooed, which stood for twelve jurors, one judge, and a half ass chance. It was a constant reminder of his criminal conviction and his not fitting in with the norms of society. On his right forearm he wore a heart with a banner in loving memory of his mother. His tattoos were not skulls, crossbones, or the typical biker 'Fuck The World' messages. In his opinion, it was Hollywood and newspaper reporters that gave bikers a bad name, He reasoned that good news did not sell newspapers. The biker war was nothing compared to the atrocities that happened in other countries every day.

The jailer returned and escorted Ramrod to the visiting booth. Sugar and Rodney was there waiting for him. He sat down and picked up the phone. "Hi baby, you look beautiful."

"Why didn't you tell me about the surprise witness," she demanded immediately, anxious to hear his reply.

"I didn't want you to worry any more than you already were," he replied, wondering how she knew about the witness.

"Well, I have some good news for you," she said cheerfully. "The surprise witness saw everything, but couldn't pick you or Bulldog out of a photo lineup. He was standing at the bus stop across the street, and it was too far away for him to even read the back of your leather jackets. The federal task force has been disbanded."

"How sure are you of that?"

She's sure." Rod grinned, leaning over to talk into the phone over her shoulder. "Take my word for it, they've got nothing."

"My preliminary is at ten o'clock in the morning."

"We'll be there." Sugar promised.

"Does Harold know that the surprise witness can't identify anyone?" Ramrod asked.

"No one else knows," Rod replied.

"Call Harold. Tell him that I need to speak with him in person as soon as possible. I don't trust talking over the phone."

"I can do that brother," Rod smiled.

"Has anyone heard from Peaches or Charlie?"

"Not yet." Sugar shook her head.

"Time's up," the jailer announced.

"I love you, baby." Sugar said, blowing a kiss at Ramrod. "I love you too," he grinned.

* * *

"I want the bungalow cleaned. Take all of John Leder's personal belongings outside and burn them." Peaches instructed Juan. "By the way, how much were you paid a week?"

"We were paid by the month, Ms. Peaches. Two hundred dollars each."

"Well, from now on, you will each be paid a hundred dollars a week. Where can we buy lumber and supplies? There's some improvements to be made. Either myself or Nuni will be back next week. You're not to take orders from anyone else. Do you understand?"

"Si, Ms. Peaches." Juan smiled, nodding his head. Then explained. "The closest island is fifteen miles away. It's called Great Exuma. Georgetown, the capital of the Bahamas is there. The island has a dirt runway that can accommodate small planes and twin engine turbo props. There's no paved roads. But there's two motels, three bars, a grocery store, and places where tourists shop. Lumber and supplies are bought from the mainland of Miami."

Peaches nodded. "Keep a guard inside and outside of the bungalow at all times. If anything goes wrong, someone will be joining Leder real soon."

Juan quickly translated Peaches orders in rapid Spanish.

It was one o'clock in the afternoon when Peaches announced that it was time for her and Nuni to leave.

Minutes later Nuni fired the engines of the Donzi. Peaches cast off the ropes onto the dock. The craft slowly backed up. Nuni slowly shoved the throttle forward to full speed, sending the boat racing across the water. Peaches steadied herself, then slipped on her Ray Ban sunglasses. The wind whistled around them and her platinum hair blew wildly as they sped across the open water heading towards the dock at Fort Apache Marina.

CHAPTER NINE
LUCKY LADY

Swag made two rows of five kilos of cocaine on his kitchen table, carefully stacking them two high. He took measurements, then drove to a local shipping business where he purchased ten boxes and two rolls of packing tape. He returned home, packed the boxes and taped them closed. After half an hour of sweaty work he had ten boxes, each containing twenty kilos of cocaine. Five boxes were for Tony and Raul and five were for Peaches. He neatly stacked his brothers hundred kilos in his bedroom closet. Chris and the crew, consisting of Frank, Bobby, Ricky, Tony and Raul docked at the pier behind Billy Bear's house at one o'clock. The day was young, but the men were dead tired. Chris drove Nuni's rental van to the Holiday Inn, dropping off the men and promising to return in one hour. He went to his apartment, immediately going to his bedroom to pull open the accordion door. He unlocked the safe revealing two shelves of money.

He grabbed two stacks, ten thousand each, and wrapped the money in rubber bands. Then, he grabbed a blue gym bag from the floor beside the safe, tossed the money inside and zipped it closed. After securing the safe, he closed the closet door. Leaving his apartment, Chris locked the door behind him. Ten minutes later, he parked in his brother Swag's driveway.

"Did everything go alright?" Swag asked, greeting his brother at the front door.

"It was a great day!" Chris replied, smiling broadly.

"I thought it might make things easier if I packaged the merchandise. There's ten boxes, each containing twenty kilos. Your hundred is stacked in my bedroom closet."

"That makes things simple. I was wondering how I was going to keep everyone from knowing what was going on."

Chris walked into the bedroom, opened the closet door, grabbed four kilos and placed them inside the gym bag zipping it closed. Next, he walked back outside and opened the van's rear doors. There was a bed in the back with a storage space beneath it. As Swag carried boxes to the van, Chris neatly stored them. Then he drove to the Holiday Inn, parked next to Tony and Raul's Pontiac, and knocked on the motel room door. Moments later, Tony opened the door.

"Open the trunk of your car," Chris instructed. Raul joined them as Tony opened the trunk of the Pontiac. Chris opened a rear door of the van, quickly passing five boxes off to Raul.

"There's twenty kilos in each box," Chris explained with a grin. "Thanks." The brothers smiled, elated to finally reach the end of the promised road.

"Thank you." Chris smiled, grabbing the gym bag out from the back of the van and locking the door, as Tony and Raul prepared to exit the motel they handed the room key to Chris.

Chris headed for the room that Frank, Bobby, and Ricky shared. When he knocked on the door, Bobby answered. Chris entered to find Ricky and Frank sitting on the edge of the bed snorting lines of cocaine.

"I'm going to give you guys a choice." Chris said, getting right down to business. "You can have ten thousand in cash or a kilo of uncut coke."

"You mean to split between us." Frank asked.

"No. You each have the choice. That's not bad for a nights work, is it?"

"Hell no! I'll take the kilo." Frank grinned.

"Me too!" Bobby added.

"I guess that makes it unanimous." Ricky chuckled.

Chris opened the bag and passed out the kilos, then returned to the room Tony and Raul had occupied to wait for Peaches and Nuni's return.

Nuni and Peaches arrived at Fort Apache Marina at five-thirty. After securing the boat they walked to the bait shop and called a taxi cab. It was six o'clock when they knocked on the door where Chris waited.

"I need to speak with you, in private." Chris immediately informed Peaches. He stepped outside and into the parking lot, out of everyone's sight. Nuni walked inside the room, and waited.

"There's five boxes sealed with brown packing tape, each containing twenty kilos, beneath the bed of the van. You will have to open the rear doors to unload them."

"Thanks, Chris. I couldn't have done it without your help." She replied, sincerely.

"No problem." Chris smiled, pleased that he had her gratitude. She had shown him that she could be a fierce enemy or a great friend. "How was everything after we left?"

"It went very well," she smiled.

Rejoining Nuni in the hotel room, Peaches went directly to the phone and dialed the number for the Pink Pussycat.

Chris was on the opposite side of the room facing Nuni. "This is for you, bro. There's a kilo of cocaine and twenty thousand dollars in cash." Chris handed the gym bag to Nuni, adding. "I gave Frank, Bobby, and Ricky a choice between a kilo or ten thousand dollars. They each took a kilo, and were happy. That's not bad for one night's work!"

"Thanks bro!" Nuni grinned, giving Chris a half hug and a slap on the back.

"Hello?" Sugar answered the phone.

"How many times do I have to tell you to answer the phone in a professional manner? The name of our club is the Pink Pussycat." Peaches told her sister in faked seriousness.

"Nicky!" Charlotte Lynn shouted excitedly. "Where in the fuck are you? Are you okay? I've been going crazy. Everyone has been worried and looking for your ass."

"I will be there in a few hours, and I'll explain everything then."

"Charlie is still missing, and now Nuni is missing too."

"Nuni's with me, I don't want to talk about this right now. I called to let you know that we're okay."

"Hurry your ass here!" Sugar told her.

The second she was off the phone, Sugar ran from the office in search of Rod. From across the room he saw her coming with a huge smile on her face.

"What's up?" Rod grinned, pleased to see her smile.

"My sister just called. She's okay, and Nuni, is with her. They will be here in a few hours."

"Where has she been?"

"I have no idea. I asked, but she said that she didn't want to talk about it over the phone."

"Smart girl." Rod noted.

Nuni, Peaches, Frank, Ricky, and Bobby left the Holiday Inn before dark. It was eighty-five degrees, so Nuni rolled down the driver's side tinted window. Peaches rode shotgun, in the passenger seat beside Nuni. The other men road in the back of the van. Nuni, hung his arm half outside the window as they entered the turnpike. He set the cruise control while Peaches turned the radio up. Everyone snorted lines of cocaine and smoked a little marijuana in celebration of a job well done. Peaches had not mentioned the hundred kilos in the rear storage compartment to Nuni. The automobile was already loaded down with guns and the drugs owned by the other men. Not to mention the twenty thousand dollars in cash being held by Nuni. If they had a worry in the world, it was not at that moment. Nuni's sunglasses slid down his nose causing him to push them back up. He was anxious to get home, but distracted by Peaches singing softly to the Beach Boys. "Wouldn't it be nice..." She bobbed her head to the beat of the music.

When they arrived at Bobby's house, Peaches told Nuni about the five boxes and he unloaded the boxes and the guns into the trunk of his Lincoln Towncar. A few minutes later Nuni and Peaches drove away in the Lincoln, their business with the other men at a conclusion. Bobby would return the rental van.

Thirty minutes later Nuni backed his Lincoln under the carport of his four bedroom house. He lived on a cul de sac, making it all the more difficult for authorities to set-up surveillance. He hired a landscaping service to maintain his yard, explaining why the lawn was freshly mowed and the gardens well cared for. Nuni did not have a green thumb, but he enjoyed having a well kept home. In the backyard there was an enclosed Olympic swimming pool. The white brick ranch had all of the amenities. Air-conditioning, modern appliances, a sunken living room, and three bedrooms. Nuni's master bedroom had huge walk-in closets with his and her bathrooms. His bathroom had a glazed stone walk-in shower. Her bathroom had a long mirrored vanity with a white marbled sunken tub. Peaches went inside the house and opened the rear glass sliding door off the kitchen. She stepped outside, following a white crushed stone path in the backyard that led her through a rose garden to a gazebo. She sat down on the wooden swing, inhaling deeply, enjoying the sweet fragrance of the roses. For a brief moment, she was in a blessful state of mind.

Nuni unlocked the trunk of the Lincoln, unloading the boxes into the utility room at the rear of the carport. He stacked them neatly, one on top of another. Then, he closed and locked the door. He walked into the house, looked out of the kitchen window, and saw Peaches sitting inside the gazebo. Without hesitation, he opened the sliding glass door and walked outside to join her.

"The boxes are safely locked away in my utility room for now. Tomorrow, I will move them to my storage unit if that's alright with you?" Nuni offered.

"With all the shit that's going on, I think it would be a very good idea to move the kilos to a more secure place as soon as possible," she replied.

"Would you like the ten cent tour of my castle?"

"Of course." Peaches stood to follow him.

As they entered the house, Nuni said. "This is the kitchen and dining room. The pantry and laundry is through that door." Nuni pointed. It also led to the carport, the pantry was behind the utility room. "That's the living room." Nuni waved as they turned to walk down a hallway. They walked past a large bedroom equipped with a bathtub, shower, and a sink. There were two bedrooms at the end of the carpeted hallway. Nuni opened the last door on the right. "This is my sanctuary. It's where I lay my head at night." He gave a hand gesture towards the four poster, hand carved, mahogany king-sized bed.

"It's nice." Peaches said in earnest. She sat down on the edge of the bed, her hand caressing the softness of the mattress. It was cool to the touch. "Comfortable too." She said, then pointed to a nude painting of Marylin Monroe lying on her side on a bear skin rug. Marylin's eyes seemed to be staring at her and the painting was thoughtfully hung at the very foot of the bed.

"Did you paint it?"

"I think you know I didn't." Nuni smiled, staring at her in a way that was unmistakable. He was certain that she knew how much he wanted her.

"How much property do you have?"

"Almost an acre."

Peaches had taken note that the entire house was tastefully decorated with a great leather pit group in the sunken living room, a modern kitchen boasting Dutch ovens, and all stainless steel appliances.

"This is very nice. It's hard to believe you live in this big house all by yourself."

"I don't. I have a cat." Nuni chuckled. "She was here before me. I named her Ms. Prissy because she doesn't like to be held, or touched. The only time she will have anything to do with me is if I have something she wants, mainly food. She's white with a black spot around one eye. I also have a housekeeper, Ms. Florida. She cleans the house and washes and irons my clothes."

"Ms. Florida, huh?" Peaches smiled, imagining some beauty

queen in a bikini.

"Maxi is from Panama City, Florida. She's sixty-five, very thin and homely looking. I call her Ms. Florida because it makes her feel good."

Peaches smiled approvingly, then stood up to kiss him on the cheek. "We've got to get going. My sister is waiting for us."

"I'm making progress," Nuni beamed.

Peaches laughed as they made their way outside to the car. She knew exactly what he meant. He wanted her so bad, she could see the desire in his eyes whenever he looked at her. She opened the passenger door of the Lincoln and climbed inside.

Nuni walked all the way around the Lincoln, stopping at intervals to look under it. She wondered what he was looking for. Was he looking for a bomb, a bug, or maybe he was checking for a flat tire. He opened the driver's side door, slid inside and slipped the key into the ignition. He started the Lincoln and put the car in drive. They drove in silence for a full five minutes before Peaches could restrain herself no longer.

"What were you looking for under the car?" she demanded to know. Nuni smiled, thinking that she was a bossy little thing.

"Ms. Prissy likes to lay up against anything warm. I've almost run over her twice because she was lying under a rear tire."

Peaches shook her head and laughed.

Nuni added. "If you think that's funny, you should see how she reacts whenever I try to move her. The claws come out."

* * *

Fifteen minutes later Nuni parked at the rear of The Pink Pussycat. Entering unnoticed through the rear door, it allowed Peaches a chance to take note of how things had been going during her absence. The place was packed with laughing and conversing customers. She could see that the waitresses were constantly on the move, supplying drinks and smiles. Their conduct was professional and pleasant. On the stage an attractive red head was performing a slow strip, her costume that of a high school cheerleader. When one of the waitresses noticed her presence it set off a small welcoming crowd. The disturbance drew Sugar's attention from where she stood at the far end of the bar.

Sugar practically ran across the bar, throwing her arms around Peaches' neck and hugging her tight.

"What happened?" She demanded in a whisper. "Where have you been? Are you okay?" Charlotte Lynn fired one question after another without waiting for an answer.

"Give me a minute." Peaches told her.

The minute turned into a half an hour as she moved around the club giving her attention to the many customers who knew her from her previous performances at the club. Nuni stood at the bar watching her, while Rodney watched Sugar following in her sister's wake. In the presence of her sister Charlotte seemed to come to life, looking truly happy for the first time since he had met her.

Finally, Peaches took her sister by the hand and excused herself from the customers table. They went over to join Nuni.

"It's time I explain what's going on. Let's go to the office and talk," Peaches said.

Sugar followed her sister, thinking that she was dressed strangely in blue jeans, a dark blue wind-breaker, and multicolored flip-flops.

Rod followed as they walked through the club. Nuni opened the door to the office and held it open for Peaches and Sugar. Rod started to step through the door only to have Nuni place his hand flat to his chest. "Sorry, but this is private."

Rod gave a calm grin.

"He's with us." Sugar quickly interjected. "His name is Rod Anderson. He and Ramrod started the Argots together. 'Rod was watching the news in Anchorage, Alaska and saw that Ramrod was in jail. He immediately boarded the next flight. Ramrod asked him to look after me and he's been filling in for you since you went missing."

Nuni extended his right hand in a welcoming gesture, As Rod shook hands, he sized Big Nuni up. He was six feet tall, maybe two hundred and thirty pounds, with brown hair and brown eyes. His hair was cut short, well groomed, and at a first glance Rod could tell he was Hispanic. Although Nuni appeared to have never seen the inside of a gym, he had a surprisingly firm grip. Peaches sat down on the black leather couch, crossed her legs, and began telling her story of how she had been kidnapped. How she was taken to Norman's Cay, caged in chicken wire, and how she was saved by two men who were brothers. She told how she called Chris from a motel in Miami. How Chris had called Nuni, because she did not want to risk the F.B.1., D.E.A., or some other agency having a phone wired. Nor could she risk John Leder finding out that she was still alive.

"Where is this Leder now?" Rod demanded, his anger already showing his loyalty.

"He's no longer a threat." Nicole gave him a thank you smile.

"Let's just say he's the one looking for Davy Jones Locker." Nuni chuckled.

"You are one lucky lady," Rod grinned.

"Has anyone heard from Charlie?" Peaches asked.

"Not a word," Sugar said.

"I've been taking over things for Ramrod with the club while he's inside.

There's also a laundry list of people waiting for deliveries," Rod said.

"I have a hundred kilos that can be shipped now. Sometime next week, there will be another fifteen hundred kilos available. Sunday night, I'm flying to Maryland for a week. I'm excited about seeing Bulldog. Why wasn't Ramrod released too?" Peaches demanded.

There was a brief silence while Charlotte Lynn and Rod shared a look. Peaches caught the exchange, her heart tightening in sudden concern. "Tell me."

Rod explained. "The assistant district attorney offered them three options. Option one was to proceed to the preliminary. Two, was to plead guilty to one federal weapons charge for a two year prison sentence. Or three, sign a capias not to return to the State of Florida for five years and all of the charges would be dismissed. The way I see it, Bulldog took the deal and…"

"He took the fuckin' deal not to return to Florida for five years," She cried, cutting him off and tears filling her eyes.

Nuni rubbed her shoulders. "Are you okay," he asked.

"Fuck no, I'm not okay." She shrugged his hands off of her shoulders. She was too upset at Bulldog to want any man's touch. "Bulldog doesn't love me, the only person he cares about is himself. I don't want to ever see him again. Not ever!"

"Ramrod's preliminary hearing is scheduled for ten o'clock in the morning. Also, do you know a Detective Hill from the Anne Arundel County Sheriffs Department in Maryland?" Rod inquired, looking at Peaches for her reaction.

"Why do you ask?" Peaches asked, her face a blank mask.

"Because he was called to Orlando to be a member of a federal task force and he came to the club asking for you. He wanted you to know that your name came up in the investigation regarding more than one murder and trafficking in cocaine. He also shared with us the information about the surprise witness the government was relying on. The witness could not pick anyone out of a photo lineup. The task force has also been disbanded. He said that he investigated your daughters murder and the two of you had become very good friends. I promised that I would tell you to give him a call whenever I saw you."

Murder? Had Detective Hill really said that? To her recollection, he had always referred to her daughter's death as a hit and run, Wonder of wonders, maybe there was hope for Detective Hill after all.

CHAPTER TEN
NAUGHTY BUT NICE

It was three o'clock when Sugar and Rod closed and locked the doors of The Pink Pussycat. On the drive to Nuni's they drove to a fast food restaurant and grabbed a couple of hamburgers and cold soft drinks. Sugar took her time eating, chewing slowly on the ice from her orange soft drink. Chewing on the ice was something she had always loved. Nuni left a key to the side door beneath a planter and the carport light turned on. Inside the house, he left the dining room light on. As soon as they entered the residence, Sugar darted from room to room in search of her sister. All of the bedroom doors were open, except one. Rod followed behind her.

"She's either been kidnapped again or Nuni's getting lucky," he snickered.

Sugar went to a empty bedroom and closed the door. Rod went to the bathroom, undressed, and took a long hot shower. Afterwards, he wrapped a towel around his waist, picked up his clothes, and walked to the bedroom next to Sugar's. Closing the door behind him, he pulled the covers back on the Queen size bed and crawled beneath the covers, sighing at the feel of the cool sheets against his naked skin. He could not recall the last time he slept between clean sheets.

The next morning, Sugar was the first one to get up. She showered, dressed, then went into the kitchen to search through the cabinets for food. Finding them to be full, she looked inside the refrigerator, pleased to find it well stocked. She immediately started humming to herself as she started grabbing pots and pans from beneath the kitchen sink. Glancing briefly out of the long window over the kitchen sink she noted that the sun was high in the pale blue sky. Brewing a pot of coffee, she smiled to herself, thinking that Ramrod would be back with her real soon. She fried a whole plate of crispy bacon before cracking eggs into a bowl. She paused to preheat the oven in preparation of making a pan of homemade biscuits.

Peaches awoke bedside a sleeping Nuni to the smell of freshly brewed coffee. She left Nuni's bedroom wearing a ridiculously large T-shirt.

At the sight of her sister, Charlotte Lynn smiled, thinking of Ramrod singing at the cabin the morning after they first slept together. She began to sing, "Sugar in the morning. Sugar in the evening. Sugar in the afternoon." Peaches stood on her tip-toes, reached for a cup from a kitchen cabinet, and poured herself some of the hot coffee. She ignored her sister, sitting down in a chair at the kitchen table crossing one foot under her leg.

Rod walked into the kitchen looking rested and relaxed. He looked at Peaches and grinned. "Nice shirt."

Peaches calmly gave him the finger, making him laugh. "Would you care for a cup of coffee?" Sugar smiled.

"Black." He nodded, taking a seat across from Peaches at the table.

"Is that the way you like your women?" Peaches quizzed.

"The only way I fight with a woman is for the top or bottom. And I don't care if I win or lose," he replied with a smile, as he reached to turn on the television to catch the morning news.

* * *

"Good morning, Miami. Susan Lichtman of WTVJ Channel four with a live update from our local correspondent in Orlando. We have Richard Bower, reporting from the steps of the Federal Courthouse."

"Susan, it's absolute chaos. There's not an available parking meter within three blocks in any direction. Bikers from all across the County are filling in for today's hearing in support of the alleged outlaw biker, Johnny 'Ramrod' Rowe. We have the Argots, Dirty Dawgs, Sons of Iniquity, the Barbarians, and the Pack Rats. Throughout the night, bikers have been arriving. This is an unprecedented show of support. It's certainly going to be an eventful day."

"You heard it live from the Federal Courthouse in Orlando. We will continue to bring you up to date reports throughout the day. Today's weather is clear skies with expected temperature reaching the high 80's by mid afternoon. Susan Lichtman of WTVJ Channel four news reporting."

"Did you see that?" Peaches asked Rod from where they were seated watching the small television in the kitchen.

"I saw it." Rod said, but found it incredibly odd given the fact that the clubs are territorial and rivals. Rod wondered what had prompted the clubs to come to Orlando?

Nuni woke up to the smell of bacon and eggs. He crawled out of bed, showered, and joined everyone sitting around the kitchen table.

"Sleep well?" Sugar said with a teasing smile.

Nuni blushed.

Peaches rolled her eyes, shook her head, reaching over to grab a slice of toast. Buttering the toast, she decided she was not going to feed off into her little sister's playfulness.

Rod was moving around like a cat on a hot tin roof. After watching the morning news, he could not stand still. He was anxious to join in on the action.

* * *

While Harold was taking a shower someone called three times. The fourth time he thought surely it must be a matter of great importance. He stepped out of the shower, wrapping a towel around his waist, and rushed to answer the phone.

"Hello?" Harold answered, glancing at his watch. It was 9 o'clock. "Harold?" Came the soft reply. "The washer is broken and I can't wash any clothes."

"For Christ' sake Emily, call the Maytag repairman!"

Harold's wife Emily never took the initiative to do anything without first consulting him. She would never prepare dinner before calling and asking what time he would be home. He wished she would make some decisions on her own. At least sometimes she could think for herself.

"I wasn't sure what to do."

"Call the Maytag repairman," He repeated. "I have to get dressed for court. I'll call you tonight."

"I love you."

"I love you too."

* * *

After breakfast Peaches showered, then slipped into a yellow summer dress with white high heels. Sugar dressed in a tight black mini-skirt with a ruffled white sleeveless blouse, and black high heels. While the girls gossiped and applied makeup, Nuni and Rod stepped out to the enclosed swimming pool.

"Did you have a good time last night?" Rod grinned. "Indeed I did." Nuni chuckled.

"You've got a real nice place. I really appreciate your letting us stay with you."

"The way I see it, Peaches has made us family." Nuni said thoughtfully.

Within minutes they were back inside, calling for the women to get a move on it. While everyone seated themselves in the car, Nuni did his ritual, walking around the Lincoln, checking under the tires for Miss Prissy. Thirty minutes later, he parked in an underground parking garage downtown and Nuni announced that he would rather not be seen in the courtroom, especially since his Lincoln had been described leaving the house in Altamonte Springs before the raid. Not to mention his having five boxes containing a hundred kilos of cocaine stacked in his utility room.

"If you don't mind, I'll wait in the car." Nuni suggested. Rod, Sugar, and Peaches walked two blocks to the Federal Courthouse. They passed by crowds of wolf whistling bikers, up the courthouse steps, and on into the courtroom. It was 9:45 a.m. Per Ramrod's request, Harold had the bailiff save seats in the front row for them. Harry Swogel and Harold Glazer entered the courtroom five minutes later. Harold announced to them that the Assistant U. S. Attorney had made a final offer. If Ramrod would plead guilty to possession of illegal firearms, he would recommend two years probation.

"Did you tell Ramrod?" Sugar asked.

"I did."

"And?" Sugar questioned, staring into Harold eyes.

"He told me to tell David Dart Queen to shove his deal up his ass."

"Did you tell him that?" Peaches laughed softly, mindful that they were in a courtroom surrounded by a crowd of spectators. "I did." Harold grinned.

"Oh fuck! Here we go." Peaches reported as two guards escorted Ramrod into the courtroom. Every seat was filled with media and bikers. The hallway was packed with bikers and outside the courthouse motorcycles lined the street.

Harold Glazer, Harry Swogel, Attorney David Queen, and Special Agent H. Thomas Moore took their places at the counselor tables.

"All rise!" The Bailiff announced. "Court is now in session, the Honorable Magistrate Judge Rudolph McCallister presiding."

"You may be seated." Judge McCallister said, adjusting his black robe as he sat down.

"Your honor, we are here before you this morning for a preliminary hearing. But before we begin, the government would like to enter a motion for the hearing to be closed to the public and the media."

"Objection, your honor." Harry Swogel snapped. "This comes as a complete surprise to the defense. We were not made aware of this motion before now."

"Your honor, the government was given no notice that the courtroom would be filled with outlaw bikers."

The bikers remained silent, not a word was spoken about David Queen's comment.

"I can assure the court that this was also a surprise to us as well as our clients."

"Gentlemen, this is a free country. The constitution protects the rights of citizens to assemble and to peaceably protest anything they disagree with. However, in the interest of maintaining order, this courtroom is closed to the public, excluding the media. No cameras will be permitted."

"Bullshit!" A biker yelled as the pack of bikers headed out of the courtroom.

Rod and the girls elbowed their way into the crowded hallway. They were being crushed, so Peaches screamed out to the bikers. "We're Argots, the ones you are here to support."

An Argot biker shouted. "The girl in the yellow with the platinum blonde hair. That's Peaches."

"That's her sister with her!" Another biker yelled.

The crowd cheered, stepped back, making room for the girls to sit on the bench.

Rod grinned and stood beside them.

Marshal Willard had served with the U.S. Marshall's Service for nearly twenty years. He was responsible for the security at the Federal Courthouse. The second the bikers began arriving in Orlando, he called for assistance from other Federal Agencies. The Sheriff of Orange County called for assistance from neighboring counties, who sent off duty police officers. The mayor was taking no chances, he called the governor and requested that the National Guard be placed on high alert. As the bikers entered the courthouse, one by one, they were walked through a metal detector. Every possible security measure had been taken.

"Your honor, the government has offered the defendant numerous plea offers. He has chosen not to accept any of those offered. It is with much regret, we do not wish to proceed with any charges at this time."

"Do I understand you correctly. Are you presenting a motion to dismiss all charges against the defendant?" Judge McCallister asked bluntly.

"Yes, your honor." David Queen replied. Judge McCallister scowled. "The charges are dismissed, with prejudice."

"With prejudice means the government can never refile the charges."

Harold explained to his smiling client.

Ramrod gave Harold a sudden impulse hug. Reporters rushed from the courtroom, in a hurry to get their version of the verdict on the news first.

"All charges were dismissed!" Someone shouted.

The bikers in the corridor gave a loud cheer.

Peaches stood on a bench in the hallway shouting. "Brothers, come celebrate with us at The Landing in Daytona beach tonight! There will be an open bar from six o'clock until closing." The Pink Pussycat was a high class club, the doors would never be open to outlaw bikers. The Landing would be happy to get the business, and whatever the cost, it was worth every penny to show her gratitude for their offered support.

Nuni was sitting in the Lincoln smoking a joint and listening to the radio when he heard the cheers coming from the streets.

As they left the courthouse, Ramrod was bombarded by reporters chasing after them. "Do you intend to sue for damages? Do you feel vindicated by the charges being dismissed?"

"No comment." Ramrod smiled, hugging Sugar close to his side.

The afternoon news showed two miles of motorcycles descending upon Daytona beach with stragglers bringing up the rear. State troopers were out in force, especially on Interstate I-4. The mayor of Daytona was notified the bikers were on they way and they were in a partying mood.

After watching the evening news, Detective Sergeant Hill grabbed a cold beer. Twisting off the top, he dropped into an easy-chair to prop his feet up. He had a strange admiration for the outlaw bikers, and he was happy to see that Nicole was doing okay. He wondered if she was ever really missing.

Marsha watched the news, not one bit surprised by anything Nicole might get herself into.

A stunned Manny finished watching the news, wondering what in the Sam-hell was going on. Why was Nicole on television with a bunch of bikers?

Bulldog grinned as he watched the news. He was elated that the bikers had rallied to Ramrod's defense; happy to see the woman he loved safe and unharmed; happy to see the charges against Ramrod dismissed. He picked up the phone at the cabin and dialed the number for The Pink Pussycat. The head barmaid answered and informed him that Ramrod, Peaches, Rod, Nuni, and Sugar were in Daytona celebrating.

At the end of the night, the bar tab at The Landing was fifteen thousand dollars. Peaches was happy to pay it, truly loving the brotherhood. Ramrod was friends with all of the club presidents, having been responsible for supplying them with crystal meth and cocaine for years.

On the drive back to Orlando, Peaches sat next to Nuni and Rod rode shotgun. Ramrod and Sugar kissed and teased each other in the backseat. Nuni felt the warmth of Peaches soft body pressing against his then her hand rubbing his leg. He looked at her and she smiled. He thought to himself, this little bitch knows she's giving me a hard on.

"We need to talk when we get back to your place," Peaches whispered in his ear.

"Keep doing what you're doing to my leg, and we're going to be doing a lot more than talking," he promised.

It was four o'clock in the morning when they pulled under the carport at Nuni's house. Ramrod and Sugar walked through the house to the sliding glass doors leading out to the indoor pool. Suddenly, laughing with drunkeness Ramrod snatched Sugar up in his arms and leaped into the deep end of the pool.

"Ahhh…" Sugar screamed as they hit the water. Still laughing,

Ramrod climbed out of the pool. "Asshole!" Sugar sputtered, coming up for air. Ramrod laughed harder, walking into the house in search of a cold beer. Nuni and Peaches strolled down the hallway into his bedroom and closed the door behind them.

Ramrod returned to the pool area to find Sugar dripping water at the side of the pool. He tossed back the last of the beer in his hand, then slowly approached her.

"Baby please..."

Ramrod cut her words off by crushing her to him and kissing her violently. She groaned in response, feeling a hand reach beneath her mini skirt. He pulled her soaking wet bikini underwear off and tossed them onto the concrete walk. Her firm breasts and hard nipples were exposed through her white blouse.

"You're a creep," She giggled, coming up for air.

"But you love me, don't you?" He nibbled at her lower lip.

"Yes! Are you going to marry me?"

"I dunno. I don't handle rejection all that well," he smiled, busy hiking her skirt up around her waist. "But I might ask again someday," he teased. Ramrod unzipped his jeans, pinned Sugar against the wall of the pool house, pulled out his manhood and shoved it deep inside her tight pussy. He kissed her neck and she trembled at his touch, wrapping her legs around his waist. She loved the way he squeezed her breasts and enjoyed the multiple orgasms that only he could give her.

* * *

"Wake up, Nuni." Peaches whispered against his ear.

"What the fuck?" Nuni growled, looking at the alarm clock next to the bed. It read seven a.m. "I don't do mornings."

"I have a flight to catch, and you have to drive me to the airport. But first we need to talk."

"About what," he asked, wiping the sleep from his eyes. He sat up in bed, combing his fingers through his hair.

"While I'm gone, I need for you to take care of some things." Peaches sat up beside him.

"Like what, baby?"

"From a secure phone, call Tony and Raul. Go with them to the island as soon as possible. Tell Juan that you will be sending Tony and Raul to pick up the fifteen hundred kilos. Bring the kilos to Orlando and put them inside of your storage unit. When the plane arrives from Bogota, Columbia on Wednesday hijack the load. Find out the name of who John Leder was doing business with and tell the pilot to deliver a message. The message is simple: 'Peaches wants a meeting.' Then move the hijacked cocaine to Orlando immediately."

"Are you fuckin' insane?" Nuni asked In disbelief.

"Just do it! I know what I'm doing." She finished, climbing naked out of the bed.

"If I'm going to do all of that, then you're going to have to get back in this bed and take care of daddy." Nuni demanded.

Peaches shook her head, but pulled the sheets back and slid back into bed. At eleven o'clock, she caught a direct flight to Baltimore, Maryland.

* * *

Saturday afternoon Nuni called Tony and Raul and made plans to return to Norman's Cay Sunday afternoon. By noon Monday, Nuni wanted the boat loaded with the fifteen hundred kilos and en-route to Miami. From there, he would pick the load up in a rental van and take the cocaine to his storage locker in Orlando.

When Nuni inquired further about the Wednesday delivery, Juan explained how things worked.

"On Wednesdays, we run the generator. We need the power for the radio, which allows us to communicate with the pilot. When the plane is sixty miles from the island the pilot radios in with a special call sign. He says, 'Naughty but nice to Norman's Cay.' We reply, 'Naughty but nice is cleared for landing.' Then we rush to the island, unload the plane, and give the pilot a suitcase filled with money, and everyone leaves."

"Well, my friend, that's not quite how Peaches wants things done this week." Nuni gave a hard smile.

CHAPTER ELEVEN
MONEY TALKS

From the airport, Peaches caught a cab to Regency Towers. She had only been gone for a week, but it seemed much longer. As the taxi stopped at the front entrance, she couldn't recall the last time she had entered the building through the lobby. She walked inside, pressed the up button for the elevator, and the round button illuminated. The door chimed, then instantly opened. She stepped inside, pressing the button for her floor. The door closed, and the elevator moved effortlessly upwards.

When the door opened, she stepped out. Within a minute, she was turning the key in the door of her apartment. Everything was just as she had left it, except for a foul stench coming from the kitchen. With very little effort, she found the source of the odor. It was coming from her garbage. The bag was filled with egg shells, discarded cans of tuna fish, uneaten food, and two empty milk cartons. She walked into the living room, opened the curtains, then the sliding glass door. As a breeze circulated through the apartment, she grabbed the foul smelling trash bag and tied it closed, carrying it with her to the elevator taking it down to the basement garage. The second the doors opened she saw her beloved yellow Volkswagen parked next to her silver Mercedes-Benz. To her left, there was a stained section of concrete, a reminder of her shooting Ryan 'Dollar' Porter. If it bothered her, no one would ever know because after her daughter's death she had learned to show no signs of emotion. She turned to use the dumpster just outside the building, opened the lid, and tossed the bag of garbage inside. Returning to her apartment, she walked out onto the balcony, placing her hands on top of the black wrought iron railing. As she looked out over the City, she drew in a deep breath of fresh air, her thoughts wandering to Charlie. Where was he? She walked to her bedroom, picked up the phone, and dialed the number to his house. There was no answer.

At five o'clock, she uncovered the Mercedes and drove to Charlie's house in Milllerville. His prized 1965 Corvette Stingray was not parked in the driveway. She parked, walked to the front door and rang the doorbell, repeatedly. There was no answer.

Nicole saw a business card stuck in the door, along with a sealed envelope. She grabbed the card and read it. It was from the Anne Arundel County Sheriffs Department, a Detective Hill. Peaches opened the envelope and read the letter inside. "Charlie, please call me. I'm going crazy! All my love, Dee Dee." Below Dee Dee's signature was her phone number. Peaches stuck the envelope and letter in her back pocket, then walked completely around the house. All of the doors were locked, the garage empty, and there were no broken windows. She concluded that there was no obvious signs of foul play. She sat in the driveway for ten minutes contemplating what she should do next, deciding to return to her apartment and call Dee Dee. Maybe she had heard something by now.

On the drive back to her apartment, she stopped at a car wash in Glen Burnie and had the Mercedes cleaned inside and out. Two guys hand dried the car with towels while a third vacuumed the inside and cleaned the windows. She handed one of them her receipt and a generous tip, then drove away. In the pit of her stomach, she felt that something was terribly wrong concerning Charlie. He would never up and disappear without saying a word to anyone. She feared that something bad had happened to him.

She parked the Mercedes in the underground parking lot, looked over at her little yellow bug, smiled, and said, "It's your turn tomorrow."

Returning to her apartment, she walked into her bedroom to use the phone. She called Charlotte Lynn at the Pink Pussycat. She told her sister that she was at the apartment after having returned from Charlie's house and receiving no answer to her repeated knocks. Further, she had made reservations for a return flight to Orlando for Friday afternoon.

"What time?"

"I'll be flying T.W.A. and landing in Orlando at four o'clock."

"Ramrod and I will be there to pick you up," Sugar promised. "I'll see you then."

Next, Peaches dialed Manny's number. "Hello." he answered. "Hello yourself." She teased, laughing.

"Nicole, how are you? Where are you?"

"I'm fine. I'm at my apartment. I need your bank account number, so I can return your money. Are you free for lunch tomorrow? Marsha and I will be seeing you Wednesday, as usual."

"Does Marsha know that you're back?"

"Not yet, but I intend to stop by her house tomorrow. Right now, I need your bank account number," she insisted.

Manny gave her his bank account number, wondering to himself how many women would have actually been so determined to return his money. After they said their goodbyes, Manny was looking forward to just the two of then having lunch, he had a lot of questions for her.

Peaches reached into her back pocket, opening Dee Dee's letter in search of a phone number. Finding one, she dialed it. Dee answered on the third ring.

"Hello, Dee Dee. This is Nicole, Charlie's ex-wife."

"Nicole?" Dee Dee repeated, surprised by her calling. "How did you get my phone number?"

"I'm sorry. But I opened the envelope you left on Charlie's front door. I just left his house two hours ago. There was your letter and a business card from a detective from the Anne Arundel County Sheriffs Department."

"I saw the card. I was there yesterday."

"You and I need to talk in person. Friday, I will be returning to Florida. This is going to be a hectic week, but is there any way that you could come here Thursday?"

"When and where do you want to meet?"

"How about at Charlie's house at noon?"

"I'll be there." Dee Dee promised.

Returning the receiver to its hook, Peaches went into the bathroom to run a hot bubble bath. She sat on the edge of the bathtub, swirling the water while adjusting the temperature slightly, then stripped off her clothes. Climbing slowly into the bathtub she sighed her pleasure, relaxing to soak in the hot suds. It felt good just being able to take a deep breath. Fifteen minutes later she toweled herself dry, picked up the dirty clothes from the floor and stuffed them inside the plastic dirty clothes hamper. Continuing to towel her hair dry she made her way into the bedroom, slid beneath the cool white linen sheets and stretched out naked, enjoying the relaxing feeling of being in her own bed.

It was Sunday morning when she was awaken by the ringing of the telephone. Dazed, she rolled over to pick up the receiver. "Hello?" She yawned. Daylight showered the room, coming through the sheer yellow curtains covering the bedroom window.

"It's about time you answered the damn phone. I don't know if I should be pissed off for your not showing up to work, for not calling, or for making me worry myself sick. I didn't know if you were alive or dead." Blaze Starr's agitated voice came over the line.

"Hi Blaze." Peaches sat up in bed. "I'm sorry but things have been crazy. I just returned from Florida last night."

"I know things have been crazy. I saw you on the evening news. When will you be coming back to work?"

"I'm sorry, Blaze. This isn't how I planned on telling you, but I'm moving to Florida. I'll be leaving Friday."

There was a long pause on the other end. "I'm sorry to see you go, but I hope you're happy. Make sure you stay in contact, and if you ever need me just pick up the phone and call."

"I will. I promise. I'm going to miss you."

"Me too, honey." Blaze's subdued voice came over the line. "I'll talk to you soon."

"Okay, bye." Peaches slowly hung up the phone, she laid in bed for a long time thinking about the friends she would be leaving behind and the ones she hoped to take with her. She hated how things had worked out with Bulldog, but there was Nuni waiting back in Orlando. For her, their relationship was not about love. He was loyal to her and that was all that mattered. He was someone that was devoted to making her happy and she was certain that he loved her. Peaches looked at the alarm clock on the night-stand. It was 10 a.m. She stretched and yawned, rolling to the side of the bed to place her tiny body on the carpeted floor. She stretched her arms over her head and yawned for a second time. "Shit!" She cursed to herself.

She was torn between waking up or crawling back under the covers and going back to sleep. She got up and walked into the kitchen where she started her day by rinsing out the coffee pot. She filled it with water, poured coffee grounds into the container on top, placed the coffee pot on the electric stove and flicked the burner on, pausing long enough for the coffee to began percolating. While the coffee was brewing she went into the bathroom to brush her teeth, wash her face, and comb her hair. While getting dressed she wondered if Marsha would be taking the children to church this morning.

Returning to the kitchen she put two slices of bread into the toaster. After a quick breakfast of toast and coffee, she left the apartment taking the elevator down to the underground garage. She walked to her little Bug and unlocked the door. The weather had finally broke outside and the day promised to be fairly cool, the snow on the ground finally falling away with the changing of the Seasons. She spent ten minutes just waiting for the engine to warm up, babying the car until the engine purred softly. Twenty minutes later, she parked in Marsha's driveway. Walking through the front door, she smelled the unmistakable smell of bacon frying.

Marsha was in the kitchen reaching for something in a cabinet when Peaches snuck up behind her, grabbed her waist and yelled. "Gotcha!"

"Ahhhh ..." Marsha nearly jumped out of her skin, hating it when someone tried to scare her half to death. Nicole smiled and snatched her into a tight embrace.

"My God, you scared the shit out of me, but I'm glad to see you. Are you okay?"

"I'm okay." Peaches assured her softly.

They spent a long moment hugging one another, valuing their closeness all the more.

"We need to have a family meeting." Nicole stepped back. "We do, huh?" Marsha grinned. "You look nice," she added.

Nicole was dressed conservatively, wearing a blue flowered dress with blue flats. If Marsha planned on taking the children to Sunday church, she would go with them.

"Are you taking the kids to church this morning?"

"Not today. Before you scared the shit out of me, I was looking for a cake mix. Today is Carla's birthday."

"How old is she?"

"Twelve."

"Damn girl, I didn't realize so much time had gone by. Where did the time go? I remember when Megan was just six. Jimmy and Danny were both seven. Carla was ten, and Travis was fourteen."

"In just a few months, Travis will be getting his driver's license."

"Speaking of kids, where are they?"

"Sleeping, and you better not disturb them."

"I just told you that we're having a family meeting."

"After lunch."

"That doesn't work for me. I'm having lunch with Manny." Nicole countered.

"Oh. You are, are you?" Marsha smiled. "Should I be jealous?"

"I would." Nicole replied with a laugh.

She left the kitchen and walked down the hallway banging on bedroom doors. "Aunt Nicole's here. Wake up! We're having a family meeting in twenty minutes."

Nicole walked back into the kitchen to find Marsha standing there with her hands on her hips.

"One of these days I'm going to kick your ass, girl." She snapped.

They looked at each other for a long second, then burst into laughter.

Closer to fifty minutes later the entire family was gathered in the living room, curious as to what was going on. The extra time hand been taken up with the children swarming all over Nicole in a loving welcome.

"Happy birthday, Carla." Nicole smiled at the pretty auburn haired girl. "Thank you." Carla smiled, happy that her auntie Nicole could be there for her birthday.

"Well, I'm going to get right to the point. By a show of hands, who would like to live in the sunshine state of Florida?"

Everyone was taken by surprise. Heads turned, but they simply looked at one another. Marsha's mouth was wide open in awe. Totally speechless! Nicole continued. "In Orlando, just twenty miles away from Disneyworld. It's less than an hours drive to the ocean. Sunshine, fruit trees. Oranges, grapefruit, and tangerines. You can pick fresh fruit right off the trees whenever you want. Come on, let me see those hands!"

"I want to live in Disneyworld," little Megan announced, throwing up her tiny hand.

"Count me in!" Travis chuckled, adding. "With the ocean comes girls in string bikinis."

"You're so gross!" Carla sneered at her brother, but raised her hand. She wanted to be wherever her Aunt Nicole would be. She idolized her Aunt and loved being around her.

Marsha laughed. "You're growing up too fast," she told her son. The twins, Jimmy and Danny, were the last to raise their hands. "Well, that settles it." Nicole declared victory.

"No, it doesn't." Marsha quickly retorted. "Go back to bed children, you're all dreaming."

"Don't you want to live in Florida?" Nicole questioned.

"I would love to, but it's not quite that simple. We have a home.

The kids have school, and friends. I'm making a decent living and able to support them. I can't just give up that security. And, what about "Manny?"

"He's moving to Florida too!" Nicole laughed, then added. "He just doesn't know it yet."

"If Manny agrees to go, then maybe I'll consider it." Marsha conceded. "Pack your bags, baby." Nicole beamed, getting to her feet from where she was seated on a sofa.

Nicole looked at her watch. It was 11 o'clock. She walked to the kitchen, picked up the phone, and dialed the number for Manny's apartment.

"Meet me at the front entrance in ten minutes."

"Where are we going?"

"Wherever you want to have lunch."

Ten minutes later, the little Bug pulled up to the curb of the building. When she saw Manny standing in the foyer, she beeped. He walked outside to join her, opening the passenger door of the little car and taking a seat.

"This is one time that I'm thankful for having short legs."

Nicole kissed him on the check, then drove away from the apartment building.

"Where's the Mercedes?"

"I drove it yesterday. Today is the Bug's turn."

"I see." It was obvious, at least, to him, that she thought of her cars as Marsha did her children.

"Where are we going for lunch?"

"Wherever you want." Nicole replied smiling.

"It's been a while since I've been to Shi-lo's."

"Sounds great."

Shi-lo's was a small restaurant on the waterfront that specialized in seafood. Mainly lobster, crab legs, and oysters. It also served mouth watering steaks and hot sandwiches.

Nicole parked in the crowded parking lot and together they

walked down the wooden planked sidewalk to the restaurant's front entrance. The building was supported by pilings extended over the water. Manny held the door open allowing Nicole to walk through ahead of him.

"You look beautiful!" Manny complemented her.

"Thank you," she blushed, pleased that he noticed. "It's just a dress."

"They walked to a table that offered a view out of a huge bay window, overlooking the ocean and the docks. Manny pulled a chair out for her. Huge ships were docked and boats of all shapes and sizes cruised the harbor waters. Manny seated himself across from her wearing a pleased smile.

"What business do we have to discuss?"

Peaches returned his smile. "Would you like to live in Florida? Me, you, Marsha and the kids. The kids voted unanimously to move, they are excited about it. Marsha will go if you do."

Manny grinned. "It's not what I thought we were going to discuss. First, I would like to know why you needed to borrow half a million dollars. And, why you were on the evening news?"

"May I take your order?" The waitress interrupted.

"Yes, I would like a bowl or clam chowder and a Coca Cola." Nicole smiled at the middle aged lady.

The second the waitress walked away, Manny turned his full attention onto Nicole, waiting for her to answer his earlier questions. He was not going to let her sweep them under the rug. Not this time.

"Why did you need the money?" he pressed. "I was kidnapped," she answered truthfully.

"Kidnapped," he said in stunned disbelief. "From where?"

"I was kidnapped from my nightclub."

"Your nightclub?" Manny repeated in total confusion.

"Yes. I opened a club in Orlando called the Pink Pussycat. It belongs to me and my baby sister, Charlotte Lynn. Everyone calls her Sugar."

"Who kidnapped you?"

"That's another story. The important thing is I'm fine, and it's not going to happen a second time."

"How can you be sure of that?"

"My friends took care of it."

"Your friends? I don't think I need to know anything else." Manny sighed, feeling mixed emotions.

"Manny, nobody in this world means more to me than you, my sister, and Marsha. You know that. Haven't you ever thought about moving to Florida? The weather is gorgeous. Orlando has more golf courses than Betty Crocker has cookies. You could buy a house big enough for you, Marsha, and her kids. You adore them and they love you. By the way, today is Carla's birthday. She's twelve. In two months Travis will be sixteen and old enough to get his driver's license. You need to be around people who love you, instead of being alone in your apartment."

"Will I be seeing you and Marsha this Wednesday?"

"Of course."

"Good." He shook his head, "I need a little time to think this over." After lunch, Nicole dropped Manny off in front of his building. She kissed him softly on the lips, then drove off feeling confident that everything was going to work out great. Hopefully, by moving to Florida she would be leaving some painful memories behind. The death of her daughter, Charlotte. The deaths of Sheila 'Missy' Watts, Jeff Miles, Harold Bennett, Tony Bedsoe, Dornonic Coroza, Ryan Porter, and Roger Pickett. Less not forget, her dear friend Joyce "Stormy' Winland. And now, Charlie was missing. There had been so much death in such a short period of time. It was time to move on, she thought.

* * *

Nuni called the motel where Tony and Raul had been staying,

hoping that they were still hanging around. He was in luck. Tony had found an apartment for him and his brother Raul, but they were still buying new furniture and preparing to move. Raul wanted a big screen TV and a stereo system. Tony wanted a Jacuzzi. The two men agreed to meet Nuni at the dock at Fort Apache Marina around two o'clock that afternoon. The weather forecast was sunny with expected highs in the 80's and clear blue skies.

CHAPTER TWELVE
THE BIG BANG

Nuni's gold two-tone Lincoln Towncar was a year old, with less than eight thousand miles on the odometer. He purchased the car brand new right off the showroom floor in 1971, and it still had that new car smell.

Arriving in Miami at one o'clock, Nuni stopped at a grocery store. Grabbing a shopping cart, he proceeded to purchase two hundred dollars worth of food, careful not to buy items that would require refrigeration. He purchased a few luxuries that he anticipated being eaten before they spoiled, such as steaks, cheese, milk, cereal, and bread. He thoughtfully purchased tortilla shells, canned goods, coffee, sugar, noodles. packaged gravy, ketchup, mustard, flour, spices, four one pound cans of Crisco grease, and a twenty pound bag of potatoes. He reasoned that if he was stranded on an island, he would want fried chicken, so he stopped at a KFC and bought a bucket of fried chicken with mashed potatoes, gravy and cole slaw. Tony and Raul were waiting at the dock and quickly carried the groceries to the boat. Nuni asked if they knew of a place where they could safely unload the kilos of cocaine. "Why not use the same dock that El Jefe used? I'm sure he won't mind."

Tony chuckled. "When we return to the mainland I'll show you where to meet us in Boco Raton."

"Sounds good to me." Nuni replied, chuckling at the thought of what Tony had said about John Leder not minding if they used a dock that was once his.

* * *

Many miles away Anthony Caruso cringed at the thought of his little princess loving anyone other than himself. Fortunately for Charlie, a death sentence had not been issued. Caruso had ordered him to be kidnapped from his home and taken to a nearby Holiday Inn. His orders were very specific. After a week Charlie was to be released with instructions to never see Dee Dee Caruso again.

* * *

Peaches walked into her bedroom closet, undressed, and hung the blue flowered dress from a hanger. She grabbed a pair of cut-off jeans, slipped them on, and admired herself in the full length mirror hanging from the back of the closet door. The cut-off jeans exposed the cheeks of her ass and that would give the boys something to fantasize about, she thought. She picked out a white halter top and slid her tiny feet into a pair of multicolored flip flops.

With the setting of the sun, she walked outside and stood on the balcony to watch the lights of the city come to life. It reminded her of her childhood when she and her sister spent hours chasing fireflies, catching them in vented mason jars. She gazed at the night sky, searching for the Big Dipper. Before now, she never had trouble finding it. It was the Little Dipper she had a hard time finding. Astrology was her worst subject in school, but it always fascinated her. Suddenly, she saw a falling star blazing across the heavens, and she quickly made a wish.

* * *

Monday morning, Peaches suddenly came awake as if startled out of a nightmare. She popped up in the bed like a Jack in the box. She could not recall having a nightmare or hearing the phone ring. The alarm clock had not been set the night before and there was no knocking at the door of her apartment.

She looked at the clock on the nightstand. It was 7 o'clock in the morning. Shaking her head with a little smile at her jumpiness, she decided to get out of bed since she was awake. She thought about calling Harold Glazer, who was normally in his office by 8 o' clock, She climbed out of bed, showered, and dressed casually wearing tight fitting blue jeans, a light summer blouse, and flipflops. She walked into the kitchen, preparing a pot of coffee and two slices of toast.

"Good morning. You have reached Harold Glazer's office." The receptionist answered.

"Is Harold in?"

"May I ask whose calling?"

"Nicole Redman."

"Please hold."

"Good morning." Harold answered, obviously happy to hear from her. "You did a great job in Orlando," she commended him.

"Orlando was interesting, but I'm quite sure you didn't call just to congratulate me."

"I need to see you in person."

"Can you be here before ten?"

"Of course. I'll see you then." She replied, then hung up the phone.

At ten o' clock, Peaches seated herself in the waiting area at Harold Glazer's office. Before the receptionist had time to speak, Harold stepped from his office and motioned for her to come in. As she stepped inside his office, he closed the door for privacy.

"How have you been," he asked. "I thought about coming to see your club when I was In Orlando, but I didn't feel that it was an appropriate time to make a social call. I'm quite sure that at least one of those agencies were keeping a watchful eye on me."

"That's okay. I wasn't there anyway." She replied, frowning at the thought of where she was at the time.

"What can I do for you?"

"Wire five hundred thousand dollars to this account." She said, giving Harold the information on a slip of paper.

"Manny?" Harold chuckled. "How's he doing?"

"You know Manny?" She asked, her face blushing.

"We are very good friends. Last year, we played golf every

Saturday."

"You know everybody!" Peaches declared.

Harold smiled. It was true. He knew everybody that was anybody. "I also have the information that you need to access your account if I'm not available. I've spread the Trust Fund account between three banks."

"That's great!" Peaches smiled. "Friday, I will be moving to Florida."

"I'll miss you!" Harold grinned his affection, then added, "The money will be transferred to Manny's account before noon."

"Thanks, Harold. I will miss you too!" She smiled, blowing him a kiss. Peaches spent the rest of the day shopping, hanging out at the beauty parlor, then a high end spa. She had her hair trimmed, redyed platinum blonde, and blow dried. Then, she treated herself to a manicure and pedicure.

She followed that with time at the spa, receiving a full body massage.

* * *

At Fort Apache Marina, Tony and Raul refueled the boat and filled four five gallon cans with gas for the return trip. If they left before five, they could reach Norman's Cay before dark. It was a beautiful day, and they were well rested and in good spirits.

Raul untied the Donzi, tossed the ropes onto the dock, and shoved off. Within minutes they were out of the inlet and into the open sea challenging waves at full throttle. At times, the boat went airborne flying ten to twelve feet above the waves. The boat immediately dipped down to settle for a brief second on the choppy sea. It was the ride of a lifetime, exhilarating. Tony compared the feeling in the pit of his stomach to dropping unexpectedly in an elevator. Raul thought it was more like riding a roller coaster when it was falling from its highest point.

When they docked, Juan and the other men were there to greet them. Raul handed Juan two buckets of KFC along with half a dozen new blankets. "Thank you!" Raul grinned. The blankets were a welcomed gift. At night, it was often chilling to the bone.

"You're welcome." Raul returned his smile, thinking it was much better working for Peaches that his former employer.

"Let's get the boat loaded!" Tony barked, anxious to leave before dark. Juan had thoughtfully boxed the kilos, twenty to a box stacking the boxes inside the bungalow. Then they carried the boxes in their arms down to the dock. Raul slowly tossed the boxes to Tony, one by one, having him stack them neatly in the boat's cabin. After the Donzi was loaded, Raul refueled the tanks, Tony shoved off from the dock quickly steering for open water. On every trip they prayed that it would not be their last. Neither of them cared to be lost at sea in pitch blackness, wearing nothing but a life vest in shark infested waters.

It was 1 o'clock in the morning when the Donzi reached its final destination, crawling slowly towards the dock. Nuni was waiting with a U-haul van that he rented in Orlando, It took an hour to unload the cargo. Nuni covered the boxes with a brown plastic tarp, then drove to the Holiday Inn on Ocean Drive and rented a room for the night. He thought it would be less conspicuous to drive back to Orlando during the day when there was more traffic.

Early Tuesday morning Nuni checked out of the motel and drove straight to his storage unit, where he unloaded the drugs.

Back in Baltimore, Nicole spent the day with Marsha and her children, trying to convince her of how beautiful and fun it would be to live in Florida; especially Orlando. Of course she tried to sell the main attraction of Disneyworld, swearing that there would he so much to do. Nicole even mentioned the Greyhound Dog Track just outside of Altamonte Springs.

"Wait until you see those greyhounds chasing a fake furry rabbit. It's so hilarious." Nicole laughed at the thought of the fun they would have. "Then there's Jai-Lai. It's played on a hardwood indoor court.

Men wearing tight shorts and tank tops propel a ball against a wall using a hand held curved basket. It's really fast paced. People wager on who they think will win the game. Not to mention the weather in Florida is gorgeous. You'll never get stuck in the snow."

"No, I'll get stuck in the sand. Stuck is stuck!" Marsha laughed.

"Are you thinking about it?" Nicole asked, wearing a pleading little smile.

"I'm giving it some thought." Marsha replied, nonchalantly. "How much thought?" Nicole asked, laughing.

"Stop it!" Marsha said, making a fist and holding it in the air in a threatening gesture.

Nicole laughed heartily.

* * *

Early Wednesday morning Nuni left for Miami. He was supposed to meet Tony and Raul at the Marina by eight o'clock. He drove the rented U-Haul van, stopping to purchase twenty boxes and several rolls of brown packing tape. When he arrived at the docks, Raul carried the folded boxes to the Donzi, Tony drove his car and Nuni followed in the U-Haul to the dock in Boco Raton where they would unload the hijacked cocaine. The van would be parked there until they returned. Nuni locked all of the doors and left the keys on top of the right front tire.

* * *

Nicole and Marsha knocked on the door to Manny's condo.

At the same time, more than a thousand miles away Nuni, Tony and Raul pulled up to the dock at Norman's Cay.

Manny greeted the girls with a kiss and a warm embrace. They stepped inside, taking off their shoes and light jackets, then walked across the plush white carpet to where Manny had chilled glasses of bubbly champagne waiting for them on a side board.

"Have a seat. Make yourselves comfortable." He insisted.

"This is nice." Nicole declared, rubbing her hand over the soft brown leather cushions of his newly purchased pit-group.

Manny grinned, pleased that she approved of his taste in furniture.

"Carla told me to thank you for the flowers and two hundred dollar gift certificate. She insisted that I drive her to Macy's right away. She couldn't wait to buy some new clothes." Marsha reported, smiling,

"I'm glad she enjoyed it." Manny grinned.

"Have you given any thought to moving to Florida." Nicole, could barely contain herself.

"As a matter of fact, I have. I think it would he a very good investment if I were to purchase a house in Florida." He held up his hand before Nicole could get too excited. "But I'm old, set in my ways, and I like my privacy. For myself, I would prefer to live in a condo near a golf course and restaurants. I'm thinking Marsha and the children could live in the house, rent free."

"So you'll go." Nicole asked.

"Of course." Manny replied.

"Hot damn!" Nicole jumped to her feet, throwing her arms over her head and doing a little dance. She Immediately turned to a laughing Marsha. "Now you've gotta go. Manny's buying a house for you to live in!" Nicole told her with a happy smile.

"What would I do with my house?" Marsha asked, not really knowing what else she could say.

"Sell it!" Nicole suggested. "With the equity you won't need to worry about a thing. You will have plenty of money. Besides, you said that you would go if Manny went!"

Marsha laughed. "I guess you got me there."

Manny excused himself, heading for his bedroom, signaling that he was suddenly hungry for something other than the spoken word. He returned from the bedroom wearing a white robe and black slippers. Thick gray hair on his chest was accented by a gold chain with a Saint Christopher medallion. On his left wrist he wore a gold Rolex watch that Nicole gave him as a Christmas gift. It was the year he had taken them along with Marsha's children to Honolulu. Manny often recalled to mind the two women leaving his suite and returning minutes wearing grass skirts. They wore leis around their necks and flowers in their hair. Beneath the grass skirts the two women had been completely naked. They had been such a blessing since coming into his life, and he often wondered at how easily lust could turn into love.

With a quick gesture of his hand, he motioned for the girls to join him in his bedroom. Entering the room the women smiled at the sight of the satin sheets pulled back on the round red velvet bed and the sound of soft music playing softly in the background. Marsha quickly stripped Nicole naked, ready to show how much she had missed her. Nicole more slowly returned the favor. They lay on top of the bed, kissing, and fondling each other while Manny seated himself in a chair bedside the bed to watch, his breathing heavy with the sight of their beautiful naked bodies. The girls took turns driving each other wild until they climaxed. Nicole crawled over to Manny, going down on her knees to open his robe, she hurriedly took his thick manhood deep into her mouth and sucked him until he exploded.

They dressed, returning to the living room, and talked more about the move to Florida. Many and Marsha agreed to fly to Orlando the following weekend. By then Nicole was confident she could find a condo for Manny and a house for Marsha and her children, something they would both be happy with. She would make it a priority.

* * *

"Naughty but Nice to Norman's cay." The pilot called over the short wave radio.

"Norman's Cay to Naughty but Nice, you are cleared for landing." Juan replied.

Nuni glanced al his watch. It was 3 o'clock in the afternoon.

"Okay, lets get to the island." He ordered.

Juan grabbed a fully automatic assault rifle. Nuni tucked his stainless steel Colt .45 into his waistband. Juan, Manual, Cheeva, Pepe, Tony and Raul, and Nuni boarded the Donzi and sped off, the boat sitting low in the water. Five minutes later they moored the Donzi a short walk from their destination. They walked to the landing strip, arriving just in time to see the airplane circling the island high in the sky. A few minutes later it landed in a cloud of dust and a cooling breeze.

Nuni, Raul, and Tony hid in the cover of the trees while the regular men went out to meet the plane. He was afraid that the sight of unknown men would spook the pilot. Juan would signal when they were finished unloading. Thirty minutes later Juan gave the all clear signal with a brief wave of his hand. Nuni and the two brothers quickly sprinted unnoticed up to the blind side of the airplane, slowly creeping around to confront the pilot who was angrily questioning Juan.

"I need the money…" he was demanding, but the words trailed off at the sight of the three armed men.

"Who do you work for?" Nuni asked as he pointed the assault rifle at the pilot's head.

The pilot shook his head, suddenly afraid of what would happen if he did not return to Columbia a with the expected money.

Juan slammed the butt of the rifle into the pilot's stomach. He dropped to his knees clutching his stomach.

"I need the name of your boss."

"Pa..b...lo Escobar." The pilot croaked out.

"I can't understand you." Nuni said, smiling down at the man looking up at him.

"Pablo Escobar!" The man gasped.

"Well, I want you to go back to Columbia and tell your Jefe that John Leder is dead. I'm taking this load, and if he wants to talk he should contact someone named Peaches. She owns a nightclub in

Orlando, the Pink Pussycat. She wants to meet with him to discuss their doing business."

The pilot slowly climbed to his feet. "Pablo Escobar is going to be very upset if I return without his money."

"Just give him the message. Peaches, at the Pink Pussycat. If he wants his money, then he will have to contact her."

Within minutes, the airplane raced down the dirt runway going airborne in a cloud of dust. The pilot stopped at Great Exuma to refuel, then continued on to Bogota, Columbia.

Everyone returned to Norman's Cay. Nuni, Tony, and Raul returned to the small island, loaded the cargo of cocaine into the cabin of the Donzi and raced across the ocean to Boca Raton where they unloaded it into the rental van. Nuni drove to the same Holiday Inn that he had used before on Ocean drive and rented a room, while Tony and Raul returned the Donzi to its dock at Fort Apache Marina.

Thursday morning, Nuni checked out of the motel, drove to his storage unit in Orlando and unloaded the new batch of two thousand kilos. The unit now contained a staggering amount of thirty-five hundred kilos of pure uncut cocaine. The street value in the tens of millions.

* * *

Sweating profusely, the pilot arrived in Bogota without the drug lord's money. He was immediately taken to a sprawling hundred acre ranch where the powerful Pablo Escobar ruled like a feudal lord. Pablo Escobar stood five-eleven. He weighed two hundred and ten pounds with a dark growth of beard, brown eyes, and dark curly hair. Pablo walked from his modest ranch style home to the center of the courtyard. A circle of his henchmen stood in the sunlight totting automatic weapons.

"They did not give me the money." The pilot announced at the sight of Escobar. "I was instructed to tell you that John Leder is dead and someone named Peaches wants to meet you."

"Peaches, who in the fuck is Peaches?" Escobar shouted in anger.

"She owns a nightclub in Orlando. It's called the Pink Pussycat."

"You just let them take my kilos?" Pablo screamed.

"I have no choice. They had guns!" the pilot pleaded.

From the small of his back Escobar suddenly produced a .45 caliber automatic. Without a moments hesitation he shot the pilot in the head, blowing a hole out of the back of his skull in a spray of gray matter. The pilot was dead before he hit the ground. Two men ran forward to grab the pilot's legs and drag him away.

Pablo Escobar was a man of few words with a low tolerance for men who did not follow his instructions to the letter.

CHAPTER THIRTEEN
ROME FIRES BURNING

Pablo Escobar spoke to the remaining men standing in the courtyard. "Go to the nightclub in Orlando and bring this bitch Peaches to me."

His men never questioned his orders. Those who dared to ended up living very short lives. While those who pleased him were always well rewarded.

Pablo owned a fleet of airplanes, and pilots were a dime a dozen. However, finding experienced pilots that could land in a field during a rainstorm were not that easy to come by. With a cargo valued at more than a million dollars, pilots had to prove themselves over a long period of time. In the beginning, Escobar purchased stolen DC-6's. The airplane had a stall speed of fifty-one knots and could land on top of water. Of course, it had to be unloaded quickly because it would sink in fifteen minutes. The problem was stolen DC-6's were not readily available and the twin engine Cessna 402 could carry a payload of two thousand kilos and land safely on a dirt airstrip.

Two of Pablo's men flew in a seaplane to Norman's Cay and spoke with a very agreeable Juan, despite the automatic rifle he kept pointed in their direction. Nuni had warned Juan that Pablo Escobar's men might show up and following his instructions to the letter, he sent them to The Pink Pussycat. The two henchmen rented a vehicle on the mainland and drove to Orlando.

* * *

Thursday afternoon Dee Dee met Peaches at Charlie's house at 2 o'clock. Peaches was the first to speak as they met at Charlie's front door.

"I called for a locksmith to meet us here. I want to make sure Charlie isn't injured, tied up, or dead. Someone could have robbed him and taken his Corvette."

Dee Dee suddenly looked really concerned. "I was tempted to break a window." Dee Dee admitted.

"When was the last time you saw or spoke to Charlie?"

"It's been about a week since we talked. My father forbade me from seeing him. He said that Charlie was a drug dealer, and he wasn't going to tolerate my dating him."

"Do you think your father is responsible for Charlie's disappearance?"

"I asked him and he said no. But when I was six years old, a neighbor hit me while I was riding my bicycle. The neighbor and his car came up missing. Do you think Charlie was kidnapped?"

"No one has asked for a ransom, so I would rule that out."

When Russell the locksmith arrived, Peaches paid him two hundred dollars to unlock the front door and leave. Russell had known her from when she was a dancer at the Blue Onion and he was confident that her intention were not to rob someone's house.

Both women went from one room to the next, searching for any clue that might lead them to Charlie's whereabouts. They found nothing out of place and nothing to aid them in their search. Nicole locked the door on their way out of the house.

"I will give you a call if I hear anything." Peaches promised. "Likewise." Dee Dee replied.

Dee Dee climbed into her car. At the corner she made a right turn, speeding off in the direction of the turnpike. Peaches in her Mercedes-Benz sped off in the opposite direction.

Peaches stopped at a pay phone. She took the business card from the rear pocket of her jeans she dialed the number.

"Detective Hill." He answered.

"I heard that you were looking for me."

"Nicole? Where are you?"

"I'm in town. Do you have time to meet for a cup of coffee?"

"At the White Coffee Pot in fifteen minutes."

"I'll see you there." She promised.

Peaches arrived at the restaurant a little more than fifteen minutes later. She parked in front, walked inside, taking a seat in a booth with a view of the parking lot. She ordered a cup of coffee just as Detective Hill parked, entering the restaurant a couple minutes later.

"Hi!" He grinned, his pleasure at seeing her obvious. He took the seat opposite her, one thought weighing heavily on his mind.

"Thank you for stopping by my club with the information!" She smiled her thanks.

He waved her thanks away. "I was glad I could be of help. But there's something I must know."

"Anything." She agreed.

"I've been dying to know why you left my apartment that night?"

Peaches gave a sad little smile. "I had a nightmare. When I woke up you weren't there! And I needed you to be there."

"You left a note that simply read fuck you."

"It was more comfort than you left me!" She snapped.

At that moment the waitress returned with Peaches' coffee. "Would you like something, Sir?"

"Coffee." He forced a smile.

"Anything else for you, Miss?"

"No, thank you."

"Is that your silver Mercedes-Benz convertible parked at the door?"

"Yes, it is."

"I saw the license plate. Peaches is your stage name and now you own a club in Orlando called the Pink Pussycat."

"My sister, Charlotte Lynn and I own it. I believe you've met her. Charlotte's stage name is Sugar. Tomorrow I will be moving to Orlando."

"Did you find out who was driving the car that killed your daughter?"

"He was a hitman." Nicole smiled brightly, then explained.

"He died in a car explosion two years ago. His name was Domonic Coroza."

Detective Hill nodded, his eyes taking in her beauty with a look of longing. "I love your hair. You look beautiful."

Peaches blushed. "Thank you!" She smiled, then said. "Well, it's crunch time. I've got to go. If you're ever in Orlando, stop by the club. Your drinks are on the house."

"I'll do that." Detective Hill smiled. He walked Peaches to her car, then watched her until she was out of his sight. He stood there wondering how things might have been if he had not left her alone that night.

* * *

"Charlie, I have a question for you. Do you want to live or die?"

"I want to live!" Charlie replied truthfully, his eyes pleading.

Two medium built, dark haired Italian looking men, held him trapped inside a motel room. Charlie was covered in sweat, deathly fear causing him to fidget where he sat on a straight backed chair.

"There are conditions to you being granted your freedom. First, you can never tell anyone that Dee Dee's father was responsible for your being kidnapped. Second, you can never and I mean never, see Dee Dee again. Do you understand and agree to these conditions?"

"Yes!" Charlie was quick to say.

"Then you are free to go. Your clothes, money, and possessions are laying on the bed. Your car is parked in the front parking lot. Take a shower and go home. If it becomes necessary that we meet again, it will be for the last time. Do we understand one another?"

Charlie nodded his head dumbly.

The two men in dark suits left the motel room, closing the door quietly behind them.

Charlie quickly dressed, not bothering to take the suggested shower. Putting on his watch, he looked at the time; it was 1 o'clock in the afternoon. He exited the room into a short carpeted hallway, lined by a number of other motel rooms. Turning right he went down to the entrance into the lobby and headed across the polished tiled floor, his eyes searching around in fear encase his abductors changed their minds about letting him go. Going out into the parking lot, he went directly to where his Corvette was parked. He hurriedly climbed into the car and started the engine. He drove directly home, not daring to relax until he was safely behind closed doors. He locked the door behind him, breathing a sigh of relief. He immediately showered, shaved, and changed his clothes. Then he went to the kitchen and grabbed a cold bottle of Coca-Cola from the refrigerator. Next, he made a bologna sandwich and topped it with potato chips. After wolfing down half of the sandwich, he picked up the phone and dialed Nicole's apartment.

"Hello?" She answered.

"I need to see you now!" Charlie said in urgency.

"Charlie?" Nicole gasped in surprise. "Where are you? Where have you been? Everyone has been looking for you! We've been worried sick!"

"Don't call anyone, please. Just come to my house as soon as possible."

"I'll be there right away!"

A little over an hour later when Charlie heard the doorbell, he looked through the peephole to find Nicole standing on the other side. He opened the door to let her in, quickly locking it behind her.

"What happened to you?" She demanded, noticing that he looked haggard and drawn.

"I was kidnapped."

"So was I." She replied. "Who kidnapped you?"

"You were kidnapped too?" He asked.

"First, tell me what happened to you." She persisted.

"They made me eat cat food and gave me dog treats for dessert."

"Who did it, Charlie?"

"Dee Dee's father sent two thugs to kidnap me. They held me in a room at the Holiday Inn. They made me take my clothes off, forcing me to sleep on the floor in a corner. This morning they asked me if I wanted to live or die. To live I had to agree never to tell anyone that Dee Dee's father kidnapped me. I can never see Dee Dee again. They said that if they have to return that it would be for the last time."

"What did you tell them?"

"What do you think? I'm here ain't I?"

"I was kidnapped from my club. Your former employer, John Leder ordered his men to bring me to Norman's Cay. Leder said that he gave you the east coast, not Florida. He blamed me for the Heathens and the Argots going to war over drug turf and he claimed I was responsible for the F.B.I. and the D.E.A. involvement. His men wrapped me in chicken wire and took me three miles out to sea and stood me up on the back of a boat. They even had two cinder blocks tied to my ankles."

"How did you get loose?"

"I offered his men five hundred thousand to let me go."

"What happened?"

"I'm here ain't I?" She smiled, hitting him with his own words.

"Holy fuck! Now, John Leder's going to kill all of us." Charlie panicked. "No, he's not." Peaches spoke coldly. "Things have been insane, Charlie. The F.B.I. and D.E.A. formed a task force. The cabin in Pennsylvania was raided, along with the house in Altamonte Springs. Bulldog and Ramrod were charged with murder, attempted murder, conspiracy to commit murder, and federal firearm violations. Harold Glazer represented them. Bulldog accepted a deal not to return to Florida for five years. I don't ever want to see him again! Some of the club members are saying that he's no brother of theirs. The charges against Ramrod were dismissed, and the federal task force has been disbanded. Now, I'm moving to Florida tomorrow."

"What am I supposed to do?"

"What you've been doing. It's business as usual."

"Have you ever eaten cat food?"

"No, I haven't." The mere thought of it nearly made her puke. "It was horrible."

"You lost some weight. What are you going to tell Dee Dee?"

"Fuck that! I'm not calling her!"

"I promised her that I would if I heard anything."

"Then tell her that I went to Disneyworld with another girl. Tell her that the long distance relationship and my only seeing her on the weekends wasn't working out for me."

"Are you sure that's what you want me to tell her?"

"I'm lucky to be alive. The next time her father will have me killed."

When Peaches returned to her apartment she called Dee Dee to relay the message.

* * *

"I'm sorry for thinking you had Charlie killed." Dee Dee stood before her father in his office. "You were right, he's just like all the other drug dealers. He was at Disneyworld with another girl. He said that our long distance relationship just wasn't working out for him."

"You've spoken to him?"

"No, his ex-wife called me."

Dee Dee burst into tears. Anthony Caruso held his daughter in his arms, brushed the tears away with his hand, and safely assured her. "Everything is going to be okay, Princess."

* * *

TWA Flight 254 from Baltimore to Orlando landed Friday at 4 o'clock and Nuni was anxiously awaiting for Peaches' arrival. It was a gorgeous day with temperatures in the high 80's. She exited the airplane to find Nuni smiling and waving his hands to get her attention. She acknowledged his presence with a big wave in return.

Nuni hugged her affectionately, giving her a quick kiss. "Do you have any luggage?"

"Four suitcases. I'm moving to Orlando."

Nuni grinned from ear to ear, knowing she would move in with him. "I've got plenty of room at my place." He offered, adding. "Ramrod and your sister are staying there. It's cool! We've kept the home fires burning."

After Nuni, picked up her luggage and loaded the suitcases into the trunk of his Lincoln, she requested he take her to the nearest Harley-Davidson dealer.

"Sure, there's one on 17-92 near the Steak and Shake. We can stop there afterwards," he suggested.

On the drive he told her all about his trip to Norman's Cay, and the thirty-five hundred kilos that were now in his storage unit.

"We've got to get busy moving it," she announced. "I thought my sister and Ramrod were picking me up?"

"I'm a bully!" Nuni grinned.

At the Harley dealership Peaches picked out a 1971 black Harley-Davidson Wide-Glide. It was chromed to the max, fully loaded, with fringed black leather saddle bags. A salesperson approached them.

"How would you like to finance that beauty?" the salesman asked, smiling.

"I'll pay cash," she replied. "Make the title, registration, and tags out to Rodney Anderson."

"His address?"

"What's your address, Nuni?"

Nuni gave the salesman his address. "When would you like delivery?"

"Now." She answered, already busy digging into her purse. Peaches paid for the Harley with crisp One Hundred dollar bills. The salesman placed a temporary tag on the bike, handed her the temporary registration and a set of keys for the bike, informing her that the title would arrive in the mail in about ten days.

"Can you ride a Harley?" She asked Nuni, as they stepped outside of the dealership.

"It's been awhile." He admitted.

"Give me the keys to the Lincoln and I'll follow you to the house."

It was 5 o'clock when Nuni pulled under the carport and parked the Harley. He had dropped Ramrod and Sugar off at the club before going to pick Peaches up at the airport. Rod had stayed behind. Hearing the unmistakable roar of the Harley engine, Rod walked outside to see who it was.

Nuni was climbing off of the motorcycle as Peaches stepped out of the Lincoln. She smiled and yelled to Rod. "How do you like your new motorcycle?"

Rod stood there speechless. No one had ever given him a gift like this before. Certainly nothing like this. He ran a hand through his curly brown hair, walking around the bike, admiring its beauty and lines.

"Are you for real?"

Nicole just smiled, slipping her arms around Nuni's waist.

CHAPTER FOURTEEN
FLYING HIGH

Rod straddled the Harley, starting the engine with a grin. "For the first time in my life, I really don't know what to say."

"There's no need to say anything. Take it for a spin." Peaches suggested. Rod put the motorcycle in first gear slowly driving out of the driveway and down the street. He stopped at the corner, looked both ways, turned right rapidly accelerating while shifting gears. The sound of the Harley's pipes faded into the distance. It felt great to feel his hair blowing wildly in the wind. How long had it been since he felt like this? It had been so long ago he could not remember.

Peaches walked to the backyard and sat down on the swing inside the gazebo. She could smell the sweetness of the freshly cut grass, the fragrance of the roses, and something warm and fuzzy rubbing against her leg. She looked down to find a white cat with a black spot around its eye looking up at her.

"Hi, kitty." Peaches smiled, reaching down placing a hand under its warm belly and picking the cat up. With the cat resting comfortably on her lap she gently stroked it, talking softly to the cat as if it was a baby. "Coochie..coochie...coo. Yes, you're a good kitty, aren't you?"

The cat purred that deep sound of contentment that only cats could make.

Rod stopped at the Rymar Shell gas station on highway 441. He filled the gas tank, checked the fluids, and stepped back to admire his new Harley. Fifteen minutes later, he returned to Nuni's, parking the motorcycle beneath the carport.

Nuni looked out the kitchen window and saw Peaches sitting by herself in the gazebo and thought it would be nice to share a quiet moment with her. He opened the sliding door, stepped outside, and saw Miss Prissy laying quietly in Peaches lap. She was gently stroking the cat, making it move its head back and forth as it purred. Nuni reached down to pet the cat's head. Miss Prissy responded by arching her back. Her claws came out and she swiped across the back of Nuni's right hand. He cursed, jerking his hand back, bleeding from the vicious scratch. "You treacherous little bitch!" he yelled.

"Are you alright?" Peaches asked, giggling.

"For two years I have fed that ungrateful cat and tried to befriend her, to no avail. You're a total stranger and she takes to you like a kid does cotton candy. Go figure."

"Animals have a sixth sense."

"And cats have nine lives. Miss Prissy just used up another one of hers."

Nuni declared.

Peaches giggled, sat Miss Prissy gently down on the ground, then stood up.

"What's on your agenda?" Nuni wanted to know. "Are you going to the club with us? Or would you like to stay at the house this evening?"

"I'm not staying here." Peaches said flatly.

"Then I suggest you get ready. We're leaving in ten minutes."

"There's no need to rush." Rod said, stepping into the backyard.

"Ramrod and Sugar are perfectly capable of taking care of the club until we get there." He turned his attention completely on Peaches. "I don't know how I can ever repay you or thank you enough, but I promise that I will never part with the Harley."

Peaches smiled. There was something about Rod that she found extremely attractive. She was not sure if it was his character, charisma, or mannerisms. Maybe he was just plain hot by any woman's standards. Whatever it was, she had to watch herself around him.

Twenty minutes later, Rod parked at the curb in front of the Pink Pussycat. He warned the bouncers that if anyone put so much as a scratch on his new Harley they would all be looking for new jobs in the morning. The bouncers gathered around the 1200 cc black Wide Glide and gazed upon it in envy. Under the neon the black paint looked metallic and the chrome sparkled, reflecting the colors from the neon lights.

Nuni parked the Lincoln at the back of the club and he and Peaches entered through the rear door.

At 8 o'clock. two Columbian men were stopped at the front door and turned away because their clothes were in appropriate. There was no written dress code, but being unshaven and wearing cut-off jeans and sandals was a stretch.

The taller of two Columbians grinned broadly. "We are here to see Ms. Peaches. Pablo Escobar sent us."

"Wait here, I'll give her your message."

Peaches was seated at the bar, nursing a concoction that her sister mixed in a tall glass. The burly bouncer came over to whisper in her ear. Without saying a word she stood up and walked to the front door of the club moving a fast pace, her heart beating just a little faster in her excitement. Ramrod, Nuni, and Rod dashed from opposite sides of the room to follow her.

"I'm Peaches." She introduced herself to the two Columbians.

"Pablo Escobar sent us to bring you to him at his ranch in Bogota, Columbia. We have an airplane wailing for us in Miami. My name is Paco and my friend here is Lupe."

"Where are you staying?"

"In our car. We arrived yesterday afternoon. We rented a car and drove here to Orlando. We did not think to bring any extra clothes."

"Tonight, you will be my guests. Rod, rent a room at the Holiday Inn downtown for these men. Buy them some appropriate clothes. Tomorrow I will go with you to Columbia."

"Are you insane?" Nuni frowned. "You're not going anywhere without me!"

"Ulises, I give the orders, not you." Peaches snapped, "Rod, will you please see that my instructions are followed?"

"No problem." Rod grinned.

"Nuni, can I see you in my office?" Peaches barked angrily.

Nuni followed her back inside the club to the office. He closed the door behind them. "You and that fucking cat have a lot in common!"

He spat angrily.

Peaches took a seat in the chair behind the desk. "Nuni I trust you more than you know." She explained. "I don't want to disrespect or hurt your feelings. But, I'm the boss, I'm the one who says jump and you're the one who says how high."

"Yeah, well you've got life all fucked up if you think for one second that's going to work for me."

"Don't you think I know that? That's why we can't have a personal relationship. We are friends. Business partners with fringe benefits."

Nuni suddenly laughed. "You are some kind of woman. I guess I'll have to live with that." He went around to give her a hug. By 8 o' clock Rod returned with Paco and Lupe. He seated them at the bar so they could have a front row seat to watch the girls perform. They were now dressed in casual slacks and shirts with brown leather cowboy boots.

"Run them a tab, Glenda." Rod ordered the barmaid. "You guys order whatever you want. I'll be back to check on you."

Rod went to Peaches' office walking in without knocking.

Peaches looked up surprised by his sudden entrance. "Is everything okay?"

"Everything's fine. Are you really going to Columbia with them tomorrow?"

"Yes."

'If you want me to go with you, I will." He offered.

"Thanks, but no. I have thirty-five hundred kilos of Escobar's cocaine. He's not going to kill the goose that lays the golden eggs."

Rod chuckled. "He might not take kindly to your killing John Leder."

"A man in his position has no loyalties except to himself. It's all about the money. He would kill me if he didn't get his money."

"You've got balls, girl."

"If he wanted to kill me he would have ordered it by now." She reasoned.

They exited the office together. She walked to the bar, moved Paco over one stool and sat down between two men.

"Are you having a good time." She asked them. "Yes, Ms. Peaches. The girls are very beautiful."

"Don't get too drunk, we will be leaving early in the morning. Where is the plane?"

"At a private airport, just outside of the city limits of Miami. It belongs to a business associate of Pablo Escobar. It's a seaplane. Scorpio is waiting for us there."

"Scorpio?" She repeated.

"That's the pilot's nickname." Lupe explained,

It was 2 o'clock in the morning when Paco and Lupe returned to their room. Peaches promised she would be there around ten o'clock in the morning.

At 9:30 there was a knock on the motel room door. "Are you guys ready to go?" Peaches smiled.

"Of course." Paco returned her smile.

* * *

Agent Moore, Sweeny, and Pete Elliot met for breakfast at the house of Pancakes in Fern Park, Florida. They seated themselves at a corner table so they could talk in private.

"May I take your orders."

"Three coffees." Moore ordered, while looking at the menu. There was a small pitcher of cream in the center of the table and a wicker basket filled with sugar packets. As the waitress poured coffee they ordered breakfast waiting until the waitress departed before speaking.

"Pete, after we disbanded the task force we discovered there was a leak of information," Moore reported. "What? Who?"

"Detective Sergeant Hill from the Anne Arundel County Sheriffs Department in Millersville, Maryland. He called the Pink Pussycat; and asked for Nicole Redman. We still had the club's phone tapped.

When we heard the phone conversation we set up surveillance. Hill was followed to the club and observed entering the back office with Rodney Anderson. He also called information from his motel room and asked for the number to Nicole Redman's apartment at Regency towers in Baltimore, Maryland."

"Why haven't you busted his ass?"

"The wire tap wasn't authorized. We have no evidence."

"So, what happens now?"

"We are going to feed our rat some cheese." Moore grinned.

"We also have an informant working inside the club." Agent Sweeny added just as the waitress arrived with their food.

* * *

Peaches dressed in a pair of faded jeans, a white tube top, and her multi- colored flip flops. In her travel bag she carried a change of clothes, tennis shoes, and personal hygiene. Perfume, lipstick, deodorant, a razor, and a white windbreaker.

"We have to search you and your travel bag for weapons before we get on the seaplane," Paco explained with a frown. If it was his choice he would not bother, but the pilot gave specific instructions.

"That's fine, but I didn't bring a gun." She smiled, then asked. "Did you have a hard time finding me?"

"No, but we went to Norman's Cay first. At the point of a gun a man told us where we could find you."

"You have a very nice club." Lupe added.

"We thought we would have to take you by force. We never expected you to be so nice. Your hospitality was most generous. Thank you," Paco said.

"You are both welcome anytime, and if you ever need a job, come see me."

"I want to help dress the girls." Lupe chuckled.

"I don't think that position is available." Peaches laughed. The baby blue sky was filled with scattered white powder puff clouds and a flock of birds flying South. Paco turned the radio to a country station and set the cruise control.

"What kind of birds are those?" Lupe asked, arching his neck to look out of the window.

"The kind that can fly!" Paco laughed. "It won't be much longer and we will be flying too."

Thirty miles beyond the city limits they exited the turnpike, still in Dade County. They drove past an old dilapidated faded red barn, then down a one lane asphalt road. Paco turned right onto a dirt road and drove for another quarter of a mile before coming to a stop in front of a huge brick home. Behind it was a cleared field used as a landing strip. The twin engine seaplane was fueled and the pilot was anxiously awaiting their arrival. They left the rental car and walked to the seaplane. Peaches stopped to put her hands in the air and Paco gently patted her down for a concealed weapon. Next, he searched her travel bag. The pilot started the engines. Lupe offered Peaches a helping hand as she stepped inside the plane.

"I didn't know seaplanes could land on a dirt runway." She spoke her thoughts out loud.

"Some only have platoons," the pilot responded. "This is an eight passenger twin engine Gruman Goose. It has platoons and wheels and can land pretty much anywhere. The name's Michael Coffey. Most people simply call me 'scorpio'. Welcome aboard."

As they taxied down the runway, the pilot called back over the intercom. "I'm sure glad you're here. I damn sure didn't want to end up with the same fate as the last pilot."

"What happened to the last pilot?" Peaches questioned,

"When he returned without the money, El Jefe shot him right between the eyes." Paco spoke grimly.

"He hit the ground like a sack of potatoes." Lupe added.

CHAPTER FIFTEEN
TRASH TALKING

"Give me one reason why I shouldn't kill you." Escobar demanded of Nicole.

Pablo and Peaches sat across from one another at a round glass topped table beside an Olympic swimming pool behind the white stucco ranch style home. They had a clear view of the plush grounds overlooking Pablo's vast estate. Armed guards stood back watching and waiting for El Jefe's every command.

"You killed my dear friend, Johnny." Escobar was saying. "I have done business with him for many years. On top of that you stole my drugs." He could not help but admire the woman's beauty.

Peaches stared back at him without blinking. "I was kidnapped from my club by his order!" She retorted. "I was taken to Norman's Cay, and he ordered me killed. Your friend ordered his men to cage me in chicken wire, then throw me into the ocean."

"How did you escape?"

"I offered his men half a million dollars if they spared my life. They accepted."

"What happened to Johnny?"

"We traded places and I came here to do business."

"I want my money."

"I counted on that. If you wanted me dead you would have sent a hit team after me." Peaches turned slightly in her chair to motion at the armed men surrounding them.

"I'm not sure what to do here. I have never done business with a woman."

"Maybe that's the problem," she smiled. "This can be the first time."

Pablo laughed. "I just might find myself liking you."

"I think you'll like me better after you hear what I have to offer."

"I'll like you better when you pay me my money. Did you bring it with you?"

"No, I didn't. First, we have to negotiate a price."

"Negotiate?" Pablo turned his head sharply to look at her. "The price is fifteen thousand dollars a kilo."

"You can do better than that." She smiled at him coldly, knowing Leder had sold kilos to Charlie for sixteen thousand.

"What do you suggest is a fair price?"

"Ten thousand a kilo."

"I should shoot you myself." Pablo growled. "Johnny paid twelve."

"Then, I'll pay twelve." Peaches replied, quickly extending her hand to shake on the deal.

Pablo laughed heartily. "Twelve it is!" He returned her hand shake. "Now, when will you pay me the money?"

"In forty-five days you will receive all of the money that's due to you. It can be in cash, wire transfer, or however you want it. But, I want to continue doing business for a very long time. It was either come to you with my offer or close down the business on the Miami end."

"You are smart, but are you sure you can handle this?"

"I am."

"Then, we can do business. Come, I want to show you something. Can you ride a horse?"

"It's been awhile." She smiled.

Pablo looked to his left in the direction of the barn and yelled to one of his men. "Saddle the white mare for Peaches and the black for me."

The white mare Chastity was gentle and very easy to ride. The black horse was named Crow and he was a full blooded Arabian stallion. Crow jumped around working himself into a frenzied lather, anxious to run. They rode to the top of a great sloping mountain top overlooking a distant village. "That's where I grew up. My family was very poor. We had no electricity or running water. On Sunday, if we were fortunate, my mother cooked a scrawny chicken for dinner."

Pablo grinned in remembrance of his humble upbringing.

"Most people have no sense of appreciation. Do you have a sense of appreciation?"

They dismounted to stretch their legs.

"I was raised in the country in a modest trailer in the sticks in a place called Adel, Georgia. Mama cooked on a wood burning stove and she canned vegetables and fruits. My father taught me how to hunt, fish, and to clean what I killed by the age of twelve." She paused to pat the mare on the neck. "But we had electricity and running water. I would like to believe that I have appreciation."

Pablo grinned, delighted that she understood the point he was making. "Tonight you will be my guest for dinner. I will have a room in my bungalow prepared for you. Tomorrow the pilot will return you to Miami. I will make arrangements for someone to drive you to your home in Orlando.

Have you had the pleasure of Columbian cuisine?"

"No, I haven't," she replied with a warm smile.

"Then you're in for a treat. What's your birth name?"

"Promise you won't laugh."

Pablo nodded.

"Nicole Ester Scott."

"Why would I laugh? It's a beautiful name."

Quickly changing the subject, she announced. "I didn't bring any nice clothes. I brought another pair of jeans, a blouse, and tennis shoes."

"There is no formal attire required to eat outside on a porch in the moonlight. Come, there's one more thing I want to show you."

They mounted the horses and Peaches followed him for a quarter mile down off the mountain. They finally dismounted beside a narrow path running through dense evergreen woods. The smell of chemicals and kerosene filled the air. Walking behind him they came to a huge canvas tarp about twenty by forty feet wide. The tarp hung above a crude make shift lab where cocaine was being manufactured. Fifty gallon drums of acetone, round canisters of ether, and five gallon cans of kerosene were spread about the immediate area.

"This is where the coca leaves are made into powder cocaine. It's nothing fancy."

"It looks and smells nasty." Peaches exclaimed.

"It does, doesn't it." Pablo laughed his agreement. He had never given it much thought after the first hundred times of smelling it. To Pablo Escobar, it all smelled like money.

After giving her a complete tour of the mini drug factory and its many workers, he suggested they return to the ranch. Thirty minutes later they dismounted. There were three buildings spaced around the main living quarters, all with white stucco siding.

"I now have hot water, electricity, and indoor plumbing." He reported with a smile. "And, there's a shower in the guest's bedroom if you would like to freshen up before dinner."

"Thank you." Peaches answered, gently stroking the white mare's head. "You're a good girl, Chastity." She hugged the horse around its powerful neck.

Pablo motioned for a worker as they stood before the barn.

"Feed the horses and put them away." He ordered. They walked without talking to the ranch house, then Pablo spoke a few words in Spanish to a woman. "Alicia will show you to your room. She speaks no English."

Peaches followed the woman into the house, down a hallway with a dark Spanish tile floor to a bedroom at the rear of the house. The room was modest, but well kept. There was a single bed covered in fresh linens, a mirrored vanity with a matching chair, and a bathroom with a badly stained white porcelain sink. The shower and toilet were equally stained from the hard water. Between the trip by plane, the horseback ride, and the visit to the awful smelling lab, she welcomed the opportunity to shower.

After showering, Peaches dressed into the change of clothes that she had brought with her, then sat down at the vanity brushing her hair and applying eye-liner and lip gloss.

Alicia returned to the room, motioning for Peaches to follow her. Pablo was already seated at a table on the porch. He gestured for Peaches to seat herself across from him. It was not a date, and he was far from being a gentleman, but he had also taken the time to shower and made himself presentable.

"For an appetizer we are having ajicace."

"I have no idea what that is." Peaches said with a smile.

"Chicken soup." He laughed. "There's arape, which is made from cornmeal. I suggest you butter it generously. It's tasty when it's buttered. For the main course we are having empendas. This is a stuffed pastry filled with chicken and cheese. For a side dish we have Con Cozo."

Peaches' eyes said it all, wondering what in the hell Con Cozo was? Before she could ask, Pablo smiled and said. "White rice cooked in coconut milk."

Peaches smiled approvingly.

"I must warn you." He continued. "Most Americans get sick if they drink the water. Instead, can I offer you coffee or whiskey."

"Whiskey will be fine."

The meal was exquisite. Peaches thought that the meal turned out to be surprisingly tasteful. After dinner they moved to the opposite side of the porch and rested in rocking chairs while Alica cleared the table.

"What a gorgeous sunset." Peaches said, admiring the view and the array of colors, bright orange, red yellow, and blue. Bogota in its own right was beautiful, featuring lots of rolling hills, woods, and plush grasslands.

"How did you get into this line of business?" Pablo suddenly asked, while lighting a cigar. He took a moment to offer her one.

"No thanks." She said to the offering. "It's a long story."

"We've got all night." He replied puffing on the Cuban cigar.

Nicole shrugged her shoulders in resignation. "My daughter

Charlotte was six years old when she was murdered. She was playing hopscotch in the street in front of our house when she was struck by a car and killed. The police ruled it a hit and run accident. In my opinion, it was murder. The car was found abandoned in a grocery store parking lot a mile away. It was stolen earlier that morning and used in an assault on a man who lived in an adjacent neighborhood. I took an oath to find the man driving the car and hold him accountable."

"Did you find him?"

"Yes. He was a hitman for the Baltimore Mafia. But in order to find my daughters killer I danced at bars and frequented late night clubs. I met my boyfriend at the bar where I danced. My boyfriend Bulldog was the Sergeant of Arms for the Argots, a motorcycle club in Pennsylvania. My ex- husband Charlie served time with a friend who had a cocaine connection. He introduced Charlie to his connection, then Charlie was expected to sell fifty kilos a month. I acted as the middleman and sold his kilos to the Argots. When Charlie needed to sell more I suggested the club open a chapter in Orlando. It just made sense, the Argots were already selling the Heathens crystal meth. The Heathens started the war claiming Florida their territory. Before that, I had never heard John Leder's name."

"What happened to the hitman?"

"One morning when he went to start his car, it exploded."

"Did you pay Johnny's men the money you promised?"

"I did. I honored my agreement. But I wasn't going to live my life hiding. I returned to the island in the middle of the night with five armed men. First, we captured the man guarding Leder's bungalow, then the men asleep in the bunkhouse. I went inside the bungalow, grabbed Leder's feet and yanked him from the bed. He was shocked to see me alive and pissed at the men who betrayed him. I ordered him caged in chicken wire."

"It's a fantastic story!" Pablo shook his head in amazement. He blew out a thick puff of smoke. "How do you know that he's not still alive? Maybe the men took another bribe?"

"I thought about that, so I watched him slide off the back of the boat. He screamed like a little girl, cried like a baby, and pleaded for his life until the last second - to no avail. I never despised anyone as much as I did him. By the way, the war is over. I met with the club presidents of the Sons of Iniquity, Dirty Dawgs, and other outlaw biker clubs Friday night. We got them together at a bar called The Landing in Daytona Beach. We celebrated the charges against the Argots president, Johnny Rowe, being dismissed. I picked up the bar tab. The Heathens no longer have a cocaine connection, so they will have to reevaluate their position. Bulldog accepted a plea bargain. His brothers have disowned him and he's no longer in my life. The bikers know and respect me. I have become a full pledged Argot."

"You are a savvy business woman. I believe we will be doing business for a very long time to come."

"I am in the process of moving my home from Maryland to Florida. I own a club in Orlando with my sister, Charlotte Lynn. Her stage name is Sugar."

"You are full of surprises."

Peaches smiled. "My sister calls me Nicky. The Argots club President is my sister's man. I have Johnny Rowe firmly on my side."

"Is she as savvy as you?"

"She's smarter than me. And much more domesticated. She can cook, preserve, and sew."

"To me, you seem to be highly intelligent." Pablo reflected, still puffing away on his cigar.

"I have another idea."

"Let's hear it."

"You could make a water tight container, possibly from plastic, and have it molded into the shape of a bomb. The head could be made to screw on and off. One container could carry eighty kilos of cocaine. Two stacks of five, placed side by side, four high. If you were to put some type of a homing device inside the cap, powerboats equipped with a tracking device and divers could retrieve them. The depth on the south side of Norman's Cay ranges from fifty to eighty feet." Peaches explained.

"You want me to drop my cocaine into the ocean?" Pablo laughed heartily. "It would take twenty-five containers to hold two thousand kilos. What if one breaks, leaks, or is lost due to a defective homing device. Who will pay for the loss? Will you pay for it?"

"I never thought about that." Peaches admitted. She took a swig of whiskey, then passed it back. "I didn't say it was a good idea."

Pablo laughed before taking a drink from the bottle himself and handing it back to her. "I'm getting pretty drunk." He declared. "But I don't think I'll ever get drunk enough to dump my cocaine in the ocean."

* * *

Nuni paced the floor. He was worried sick about Peaches. He wished she would call, walk through the front door, or somehow let him know that she was safe and sound. He walked around the club aimlessly with no sense of what he should do.

"Boss, is everything alright?" A bouncer named Bowdy asked out of concern.

It was obvious to everyone that something was weighing heavily on Nuni's mind. Bowdy had been given the authority over the other bouncers and he felt it was his job to make sure the boss was happy.

"I never should have allowed Peaches to go to Columbia by herself."

Nuni snapped, then instantly wished he could retract his words.

"What's she doing there?"

Nuni shook his head, suddenly taking on a guarded look. "Bowdy, don't you ever repeat what I just said to anyone." Nuni said in a deadly serious tone.

"I see nothing, hear nothing, and say nothing." Bowdy promised.

Nuni stepped outside, looking up at the stars. He took in a deep breath, then exhaled loudly. Wherever Peaches was, he wished that he could be there at her side.

The bartender Glenda stepped outside to grab a breath of fresh air. She only had a few minutes left on her break. "It's a beautiful night, isn't it?" She said at the sight of Nuni.

"It doesn't get much nicer than this." Nuni reflected.

Never in his wildest dreams would he have imagined himself managing a nightclub. He had been a hustler every since he could remember. He had started by hustling as a pool player, being compared to some of the all time greats. He was a gambler, playing poker when the opportunity presented itself and placing wagers on everything from a dog race to a football game. To Nuni, selling cocaine was nothing more than another business opportunity. He just happened to know people who were interested in purchasing large amounts of cocaine.

Glenda lit a cigarette, blowing a cloud of blue smoke towards the still night sky. Nuni thought it was a disgusting habit and wondered why people thought it cool to smoke cigarettes.

* * *

Charlie still had not left his house. He ate, watched television, showered, and slept until noon each day. His mind was torn between his terrifying experience and his broken heart.

It felt as if someone had reached deep inside his chest and literally ripped his heart out. With his every breath he longed to be with Dee Dee and his hatred for her father grew. Anthony Caruso was the only thing in the way of what he wanted most.

If only Anthony Caruso was out of the way. He wished the man would suddenly drop dead from a heart attack, or maybe drive his car off a cliff. Then there was the possibility of his being shot dead by a rival mob boss. Charlie called upon whatever God there was in heaven to strike the man down dead.

Many miles away Dee Dee had not stepped outside of her house since Charlie had rejected her so badly. She mopped around, wearing a white robe and furry pink bunny slippers. She spent every waking moment reminiscing about the time she had spent with Charlie. The night they met; their walk on the beach, the first time they made love, and the limousine ride to the opera.

It was all right there in her mind. How could she have misjudged him so badly? How could something that felt so right, be so wrong?

* * *

It was a beautiful night. The woods were filled with unfamiliar sounds. Hoots, howls, ca-ca's, whimpers, tweets, and shrill whistles. In the backwoods of Georgia, the churping of crickets were the norm. So Peaches felt right at home on Pablo's vast estate. They sat in rocking chairs on the porch passing a fifth of Jack Daniel's whiskey back and forth.

"Do you know where the Big Dipper is?"

"No." Pablo gave a half drunken smile. "I quit school in the eighth grade and I never studied astrology, but I have always gazed at the heavens and wondered what was out there?"

After studying the night sky for a few minutes, Peaches pointed. "I'm pretty sure that's the Big Dipper. It's been a long time since I've been able to find the Little Dipper." She said, then thoughtfully added. "I quit school in my tenth grade year."

"Weren't you the slightest bit afraid to come here by yourself?" Pablo wondered.

"I insisted on coming by myself."

"You are a brave woman!"

"No, I'm not. When I was stood up in the cage on the back of the boat, I learned the meaning of fear. I was scared shitless! For a moment I didn't know what to say or do."

"You said something."

"Yeah, I offered the two Cuban brothers five hundred thousand dollars if they spared my life. When they looked at each other and grinned, I thought I was a goner, so I shouted, "Fuck all you muther fuckers!""

Pablo burst out laughing. "You shouted that?" He spoke through his laughter, while passing her the bottle of whiskey.

"If not those exact words, then it was something very close to it." Peaches explained, taking a swig of the whiskey before giving the whiskey back.

Between puffs on his cigar and swigs of whiskey, Pablo laughed heartily.

When the bottle was empty, they called it a night.

In the comforts of the guest room, Peaches reflected on the risky trip she had decided to make to Bogota, Columbia. It had been a fruitful day, she mused. She fell into a peaceful sleep, wondering what Nuni and Sugar were doing back in the States.

CHAPTER SIXTEEN
MAKE IT HAPPEN

As Peaches was leaving Bogota and flying over the lush green forest she came to the realization that she had committed herself to selling two thousand kilos of cocaine in forty-five days. The most the Argots had ever sold in one month was slightly more than three hundred. The thought was overwhelming.

* * *

Saturday morning at 10 o'clock Ramrod was standing on the concrete driveway in front of Nuni's house with his motorcycle. Rod had already washed and dried his new bike. Now, he was waxing it and polishing the chrome. Sugar stepped outside in frayed cut-off jeans wearing a white blouse with no bra. On her pretty feet she wore red open toed sandals. The sight of her immediately caught Ramrod's eye. Her hair was in pigtails. Her nipples pressed hard against her buttoned blouse and the temptation was just to much for him to resist.

"Show time!" Ramrod shouted, turning the water hose towards her.

He held his thumb over the nozzle squirting her from head to toe. Her white blouse molded itself to her well rounded breasts, exposing them in all their glory.

Sugar yelped, cupping her hands to cover her breast shouting a string of obscenities. She ran across the lawn, opened the front door of the house and disappeared inside. Ramrod and Rod laughed.

Sunday, Rod looked through the classified section of the Orlando Sentinel in search of a house for rent or to buy. There was a two year old four bedroom ranch with one and a-half baths and central air for sale near the rental house in Altamonte Springs. It was also on a lake and the asking price was a hundred and ninety-two thousand dollars.

"Would you like to live in Altamonte Springs." Ramrod asked

Sugar as she washed dishes at the kitchen sink.

"No, there are too many bad memories. Look for a place on this side of the city."

Ten minutes later, Ramrod and Rod fired up their bikes. Sugar crawled onto the sissy seat behind Ramrod's 1951 Panhead. His Harley was painted emerald green metalflake to match his 1970 Chevrolet Caprice Classic, which was still at the cabin in Pennsylvania. Sugar wrapped her arms around Ramrod's waist and they drove off. Like it or not, someone had to check out the rental house on Pot Lake. Also, while they were in the area they planned to check out the house for sale on Prairie Lake Drive. They rode side by side. One speeding up to take the lead, then the other. It was a game they had played from long before, like cat and mouse.

When they parked in the driveway of the rental house, it brought back nothing but bad memories for Ramrod and Sugar. The trio walked down to the lake.

"I'll live here if no one else wants to," Rod offered. It was a beautiful home and it held no bad memories for him.

"Where's the clubhouse?" He asked.

"It's less than half a mile from here. When we leave I'll show you. Since we're here let's go inside." Ramrod suggested.

There was not much furniture, but to their surprise the house was not all that badly damaged. It took them all of twenty minutes to clean up and cart out the trash and destroyed furniture.

Leaving the property the Harley's roared down the street. They had decided it best not to wear any colors. Rod no longer had club leathers, his jacket having burned along with his home and family.

Ten minutes later they came to a burned out husk of a building. Ramrod pointed and they pulled into a graveled lot and parked. Rod stared at the building, noticing that the heat from the fire had been so intense that it caused the roof to collapse. The fire had been so hot it had melted the paint on the cinder blocks. The ground was black where the motorcycles had been stacked and set on fire.

"Seeing this brings out the worst in me." Rod spat, shaking his head in disgust.

"No one was prepared for retaliation. When we returned from the cabin, we thought our show of force would be sufficient."

Sugar's eyes filled with tears as she remembered the brothers who were killed and beheaded. Some of them had lived in the house on Pot Lake. She could never live there again.

Arriving at the advertised house located at 3715 Prairie Lake Drive, they were met by a male real estate agent. The four bedroom home's best selling feature was that the district had the best public schools in Florida. Lyman High was within walking distance.

"We don't have children." Ramrod smiled.

"We aren't married either." Sugar gave him a look.

The home was beautiful, but it was too big for just the two of them. Plus, Sugar was insistent on them living on the opposite side of the city.

* * *

Peaches looked at her watch as she stepped out of the taxi cab. It was 4:05 p.m. She grabbed her overnight bag, thanked the driver for his services, and walked to the side door of Nuni's house. Before she could knock, the door was opened by a smiling Nuni.

"Let me take that!" Nuni took hold of her bag. He hugged her, then kissed the top of her head. "I've been worried sick about you."

"That's sweet, but I'm a big girl." She reminded him as they entered the kitchen.

"Did everything go okay?" He asked.

"Things went very well. Bogota is beautiful! It's a huge evergreen jungle."

"I heard they're still having civil wars and rebels running around in the mountains."

"Maybe so, but I never saw any of that. It was quiet. Very peaceful.

I never heard a gunshot."

"Was Pablo Escobar upset about your killing John Leder?"

"Of course he was. They were friends. But he was more upset with his cocaine being hijacked and his not receiving any money. When the pilot returned he killed him for not having his money."

"Did he threaten to kill you?"

"A couple of times." She took a seat at the kitchen table. "He offered to sell me kilos for fifteen thousand each. I counter offered to pay ten. That's when he said that he should have shot me," she laughed.

"You're only paying ten thousand for a kilo." Nuni asked in disbelief. "No, that's what I offered to pay. He said that Leder was paying twelve, so I agreed to pay the same."

"Wow!" Nuni said, shocked by the price.

"That's between us. It's not for anyone else to know. By the way, where is everyone?"

"They went to inspect the damage to the rental house after the raid and to look at another home that's for sale. I expected them back by now."

At that moment they heard the sound of Harleys downshifting as they neared the house. The sound was unmistakable, reminding Peaches of the Toys for Tots run from years ago and the roar of hundreds of Harley's.

The second Sugar walked through the side door she saw her sister sitting at the kitchen table. She ran over to give her a tight hug around the neck. Ramrod and Rod entered the kitchen.

"I missed you."

"Did you find a place?" Peaches questioned her, returning her sisters hug.

"No, it was too big for just the two of us."

Rod smiled. "It's good to see you back." He and Ramrod took turns giving Peaches welcome home hugs, then joined her at the table.

Ramrod looked at Sugar with a grin. "It's time to rattle those pots and pans, baby."

"Would you like coffee, tea, or me?" She teased.

"I've already had you this morning, so fix me something that's going to take care of these hunger pains."

"Do you want breakfast or lunch?"

"Breakfast, with toast and pancakes."

"After breakfast, we need to have a serious talk." Peaches announced. "So, don't be taking off on me. I'm going to take a quick shower."

"Are you hungry?" Sugar yelled as her sister hurried from the kitchen and down the hallway. "Guess not." Sugar pouted when she received no answer.

Peaches closed the door to Nuni's bedroom, stripped naked, and walked into the spacious bathroom, stepping into the huge shower stall. Water jets sprayed from all directions, the hot water revitalizing her. She took her time in the shower until she felt totally refreshed. Exiting the bathroom she found Nuni waiting for her in the bedroom. She took her time dressing, sitting down at the vanity applying eyeliner and lip gloss. Lastly, she took her time brushing her hair so that she could gather her thoughts.

"Nuni." She began. "I can't do this by myself. I need a partner and I trust you. But I need a silent partner. I call the shots and I make the decisions. Your job would be to make sure the deliveries are made on time, to solve problems when I'm not available, and to collect the money owed to us."

Nuni was pleased to help her run things. "I can do that," he beamed.

After breakfast Peaches shocked everyone by announcing that she had forty-five days to sell two thousand kilos of cocaine. Actually, in forty- five days she had to pay for four thousand kilos. The two thousand Nuni hijacked and the two thousand to be delivered.

"Are you fucking insane?" Nuni snapped, hearing the details for the first time.

"You do know the most we've sold is three hundred kilos in a month." Ramrod offered in concern.

"We've got to do better. Think big or stay at home! John Leder did it, so there's no reason we can't. It's going to require personal sacrifices, hard work, and long hours. But the payoff will be huge. Four thousand kilos sold at twelve thousand five hundred each is fifty million dollars. If we sell our kilos for twenty thousand each, we net eighty million dollars. Every month afterwards we net forty million."

"Do you have a plan?" Rod asked bluntly.

"I do." Peaches smiled. "We need to get all of the club presidents together for a meeting at the cabin. The Sons of Iniquity, the Dirty Dawgs… all of them. We are going coast to coast. Nuni will be in charge of distribution. I intend to front each club president a hundred kilos."

"I'm not so sure that's a good idea." Nuni protested.

"Don't worry." Peaches smiled. "Everything will be conditional. The club presidents must unanimously agree that if a club shorts us, the loss will be distributed equally among them, and the club presidents will decide how to deal with the problem."

"What about the Heathens?"

"They no longer have a supplier, so they pose no future threat. I want the meeting setup for this Thursday. Get on the phone and make it happen. Nuni, rent a house near the cabin. Furnish it and have a thousand kilos there by Thursday."

"By Thursday? This is Monday, and today is almost over."

"Make it happen." Peaches ordered.

Peaches called Marsha, then Manny, and made arrangements for them to fly to Orlando the following weekend. They would arrive Friday afternoon, spend the weekend, and be back in Maryland before noon on Monday. Manny called and reserved two first class round trip tickets. Marsha would pay a friend to watch the children until her return.

* * *

"If I'm going to make this happen I need some help." Nuni told Ramrod. "I'll call the cabin and have one of my brothers find a house to rent. If you rent a U-Haul tonight you can shop for furniture. Load the boxes filled with kilos, then load the furniture in front of the boxes. When you arrive in Harrisburg, call the cabin and one of the brothers will escort you to the rental house and help you unload. Drop the U-Haul off and you can drive my car. Right off hand I'd say you've got the easy job. I'll post two brothers at the house for security. Afterwards, you can fly home Friday."

While Nuni was out shopping for furniture, Ramrod was making calls.

At 6 o'clock, Rod and Peaches opened the Pink Pussycat.

"It's good to see you back." Bowdy greeted Peaches.

"It's good to be back." Peaches smiled, then asked Glenda. "How has been business been?"

"It's better when you're here. Will you be performing tonight?"

"Why not?" The thought of strutting her stuff excited her.

The first girl to take the stage was tall, thin, and homely looking. She wore a gaudy pink outfit with a white fur wrapped around her neck that she swirled in her right hand.

"What's the name of the girl on stage and who hired her?" Peaches demanded, looking disgusted.

"Her stage name is, Fancy. I think Nuni hired her." Glenda quickly explained.

"That's the reason business is down." Peaches declared, already headed for her dressing room.

Peaches dressed in her fireman's outfit. Black boots, yellow raincoat, red hat, and she carried a fire extinguisher filled with water. When she took the stage the crowd went wild. In the midst of hoots, hollers, whistles, and wolf calls, she squatted. Opening her legs she rubbed some bearded guys face in her twat, then quickly danced away before he could grab her. Peaches looked over at Glenda giving her a huge wink. "That's how you entertain a crowd and sell drinks." She said exiting the stage.

Peaches walked to her dressing room, changed clothes, then returned to sit on a stool at the bar.

CHAPTER SEVENTEEN
THE PROPOSAL

Tuesday morning at 7 o'clock Ramrod opened the door to Rod's bedroom and yelled. "Breakfast is on the table!" Rod stumbled to his feet. "Give me five minutes."

Rod dressed, washed his face, running his fingers through his hair. As he brushed his teeth the smell of bacon and eggs filled the air. Finishing, he joined Ramrod and Sugar in the kitchen. When he was seated at the kitchen table, Ramrod made an announcement. "I have a proposal. Sugar and I have decided we would like to live in Florida and maybe raise a couple rug rats."

"That sounds great!" Rod immediately congratulated them.

"Well, I was thinking that you could take my place at the cabin in Pennsylvania."

Sugar walked to the hall closet to grab a black leather jacket off of a hanger. She returned to pass the jacket to Rod.

Rod looked at the jacket in surprise. The Argots colors were on the back with both upper and lower rockers. His wings were on the front along with his name. Below his name was the patch for club 'President'.

"Are you sure this is what you want?"

"Absolutely. We started the Argot chapter together. It's time for you to take your rightful place. You also need to be there to make sure everything is in order for Thursday's meeting. So, I suggest you get an early start today." Rod ate breakfast, packed his saddle bags, and left for the cabin in Pennsylvania. It was before 8 o'clock.

Peaches woke up with her left arm laying across Nuni's bare chest. Glancing over she smiled at the sight of his dick standing at attention. Without a moment's hesitation she mounted him, letting his rock hard shaft slid deep inside her warm tight pussy. Nuni quickly came awake with a groan of pleasure.

"Ride me cowgirl." Nuni urged through gritted teeth.

Peaches obeyed, riding his manhood for fifteen long minutes. Her body breaking out in a deep sweat. Her pleasure building with each deep thrust into her womb. Suddenly Nuni rolled her over onto her back, holding her legs in the air, and pounded her hard, reaching deep into the back of her pussy. In one final stroke they climaxed together. He fell on the bed beside her with a hearty laugh, causing Peaches to smile.

"I like the fringe benefits!"

She joined in his laughter. Together they went to the shower, taking turns washing each others backs.

"After breakfast, I've got to get on the road." Nuni announced. "Have you got everything together?"

"I believe so. The truck's loaded. One of Ramrod's brothers is renting a house for us."

Ten minutes later, Nuni and Peaches sat down at the kitchen table for breakfast.

"Where's Rod?" Peaches asked.

"He's the new club president and he's on his way to the cabin to make sure things are ready for Thursday's meeting."

"He should have waited and left with Nuni." She snapped. "I didn't know when Nuni was leaving?" Ramrod replied.

"See, this is what I mean. There's a lack of communication between us!" Nuni concluded.

Ignoring his comment, Peaches continued. "Nuni, take an extra ten thousand dollars with you. At the meeting give each club president one thousand dollars. That should be more than enough to cover their expenses."

"How much are you going to charge for a kilo?" Ramrod inquired. "On the first two thousand kilos, we're charging twenty-five thousand dollars per kilo. The cocaine is uncut and being fronted. That will pay for the four thousand kilos. Then the price will be reduced to twenty thousand per kilo, provided there's no losses. There will be no profit until after we sell the first two thousand kilos. Everyone needs to understand that.

"I'll be flying to Harrisburg Thursday. I intend on driving Nuni's Lincoln to the airport and leave it in long term parking. My flight departs from Orlando at seven in the morning. Someone needs to be at the airport to pick me up. Nuni will fly back with me Friday morning. Our departure flight leaves at ten and arrives in Orlando at three in the afternoon. If everything goes as scheduled we will be at the airport to meet Manny and Marsha when their flight arrives at three-thirty. Ramrod, you and Charlotte Lynn will stay behind and take care of the club."

"Gee, who didn't know that?" Sugar quizzed.

Rod had rode his bike through the night arriving at the cabin around 7 o'clock in the morning. The brothers knew he was coming and they had voted him in as their new club president. Bulldog's pearl white Panhead was parked at the front door. Rod parked his Harley and walked into the cabin. He was welcomed by Rooster, Craven, Jammer, Capote and Tiny. They were all wired after a heavy night of drinking and snorting crystal meth.

"Where's Bulldog?" Rod demanded.

"He's sleeping." Rooster replied, nodding towards Bulldog's bedroom door.

Rod went over and kicked the door hard with the sole of his black biker boots. The door banged back against the wall with a loud smack.

"What the fuck?" Bulldog growled, sitting up on the edge of the bed. "Get your shit together and get the fuck out of here!" Rod barked at him, then turned on his heels to go wait in the outer room.

Bulldog sat on the edge of the bed to pull on his jeans. He slid on his boots, pulled a shirt over his head, then walked out of the bedroom to confront Rod, who was standing in the middle of the living room. Word had already spread that their new club president was out for blood and that Bulldog's head was on the chopping block. All of the members were well aware with the Florida events surrounding Ramrod and Bulldog, and now it was judgment day.

"What's up?" Bulldog demanded.

"I didn't stutter. Get your gear and get the fuck out of here! As the new club president, the first thing on my agenda is to get rid of the trash. I'm taking your colors!"

"Fuck you! That's what you're going to have to do, take them!" Bulldog spat.

"My pleasure. After you." Rod grinned, his eyes cold as ice, as he opened the front door of the cabin.

Bulldog stepped off the porch, squaring off. The club brothers surrounded them in a large circle. The ground was hard and dry, the air filled with a stiff breeze. The two men circled. Bulldog threw a hard right punch, causing Rod to spin in behind him with a single lightning move kicking Bulldog brutally in the back of his knee sending him pitching off balance. Rod stretched out his right foot catching Bulldog across the jaw, sending him to the ground in a dead fall. Lunging forward after the falling man, Rod struck out with a powerful swing of his left elbow. It landed squarely on the jaw. Bulldog hit the ground like a sack of potatoes, knocked out cold in less than a minute. The other bikers stood around stunned at the skill and brutal strength of their new president.

Without a word, Rod re-entered the cabin making his way to Bulldog's former bedroom. He grabbed Bulldog's leather club jacket and pulled out a pocket knife, cutting off his colors, both rockers, and the Sergeant of Arms patch. Bulldog was just getting to his feet when Rod threw his patchless leather jacket in his face.

"You've got five minutes to get the fuck out of here, or I'll burn your Harley and bury your sorry ass wherever you fall." Blood was running from Bulldog's mouth down the right side of his cheek.

"What, no vote? This isn't how things are done." Bulldog spat, looking at the many brothers surrounding them. When there was no answer, he spat blood on his leather jacket. Walking to his Harley, he started the engine, and fish-tailed down the driveway leaving a trail of dust and gravel behind. The exhaust roared as he shifted through the gears; then faded in the distance.

"Bulldog ran out on his brothers in Florida," Rod shouted. "He deserted Ramrod, Peaches, and his fallen brothers. If any brother here isn't willing to put his life on the line for his brothers, get on your bike and get the fuck out of here now!"

No one spoke.

Rod then asked. "Is the rental house ready?"

"It's a half mile down the road. There's three bedrooms and one full bath. The utilities are already turned on." Kapote reported.

It was 2 o' clock in the afternoon when Nuni stopped at a gas station in

Harrisburg and called the cabin for directions to the rental house.

"Turn right on Highway twenty-seven and I'll send a brother to meet you there." Rod explained.

Rod and four brothers met Nuni at the rental house and helped unload the truck.

One hour later, Nuni began unpacking while Rod and Craven returned the U-Haul truck.

* * *

"Follow me." Ramrod told Sugar, taking her by the hand. "We need to talk."

As they walked down the path leading to the gazebo, he stopped to pick a white rose from a bush. Rod stopped only long enough to stick it in her hair, making her smile in delight. Then he motioned for her to sit down on the swing inside the gazebo.

"I don't know if you are prepared for what I'm about to say."

Sugar suddenly felt her hands trembling. She expected him to say that he was returning to the cabin because he could not live the life she wanted. Instead, she watched him get down on one knee.

"Will you marry me?" He asked, taking her left hand to place a one carat diamond engagement ring on her finger.

"Oh, yes!" She cried, throwing her arms around his neck to kiss him happily. "I love you, Johnny Rowe!" She declared, stopping to admire her ring. To her, it was stunning.

"And I love you with all of my heart."

"I want a proper wedding," she said. "Mama would have wanted that. I want a wedding gown and Bridesmaids. I want you to wear a tuxedo or a suit and tie. I want a reception afterwards with plenty of photos. Lots of photos."

Ramrod laughed at her excitement. "Whatever you want, Sugar." He smiled.

She kissed him a second time, then ran inside the house in search of Peaches. "Nicky…Nicky!"

Peaches ran from the bedroom concerned and thinking that her little sister needed help.

"Look!" Charlotte Lynn beamed, proudly displaying the ring on her finger.

"Congratulations." Peaches hugged he sister. "When's the wedding?"

"I don't know." She laughed, then looked over at Ramrod as he entered the house.

"You pick the day and I'll be there," he promised.

"Where are you going on your honeymoon." Peaches asked. Again Sugar looked at Ramrod for the answer.

"I guess we have a lot to think about," he laughed.

"I hate to break up the party, but I only have a few hours to find a house for Marsha and her five kids. Not to mention a condo for Manny."

"How old are her kids?"

"Travis is the oldest at sixteen. Carla is twelve. The twins, Danny and Jimmy are nine, and the youngest Megan is eight."

"The house that we looked at in Altamonte Springs would be perfect for them. It's four bedrooms on a lake with three acres. It has the best school district in Florida."

"How much is it?"

"The owner is asking one hundred and ninety-two thousand, but you may be able to negotiate."

"I still need to find a condo for Manny and an apartment for myself."

By six o'clock that evening Peaches had rented a two bedroom apartment for herself in Winter Park. The rent was three hundred a month, and it had all of the amenities she wanted. Such as an outdoor swimming pool, laundry, and air conditioning. For Manny, she located a two bedroom condo on a golf course at the Grand Hyatt in Orlando. It was on the 7th floor with a private balcony, which provided a beautiful view of the city. The listing price was recently reduced by thirty thousand dollars. Going from one hundred and eighty thousand dollars to one hundred and fifty. She felt confident that Manny would love the location.

* * *

Peaches drove Nuni's Lincoln to the Orlando International Airport and parked it in the long term parking. Her flight to Harrisburg was on time.

Hours later she disembarked from the plane to find Rod standing at the gate waiting for her. He was driving Ramrod's Chevrolet Caprice. While they drove towards the rental house he bought her up to date with how things had gone with the drug delivery. A little over an hour later they stopped at the rental house to check in with Nuni. Peaches hugged him.

"See, you didn't think it was possible. But, you did it."

"I still can't believe we're doing all of this work for nothing. We're not making a dime for selling two thousand kilos. It's nuts!"

"Nuni, you remind me of my ex-husband Charlie. You're not looking at the big picture. The first two thousand kilos pays for all four thousand. On the second two thousand, we will make forty million dollars. Every month from that point on we'll make fifteen million dollars. Is that worth busting your ass?"

Nuni blushed, realizing how foolish he must have sounded.

Peaches reached inside her purse and pulled out ten manila envelopes and handed them to Nuni with instructions. "Put a thousand dollars in each envelope and give them to Rod. I need you to stay here, but I will return in a few hours."

"Whatever you say." Nuni sighed.

* * *

Club presidents from all over the country gathered inside the cabin. The Sons of Iniquity from California, the dirty Dawgs from Arizona, and the Pack Rats from Washington state were among the many outlaw biker clubs. They were seated around the living room taking turns sniffing lines of crystal meth.

Rod began the meeting by passing out the envelopes filled with one thousand dollars in cash. Peaches stood in the center of the room and began speaking. "I seriously doubt that any of you have ever done business with a woman," she announced with a cold little smile, noting the nods from the group of hardened men. She continued in a firm voice. "My brother Argots will confirm that I'm all about business. For showing up today, I am giving each of you one thousand dollars to cover your expenses. If any of you have a problem doing business with a woman, take your money and leave now. For those who stay, I intend to make your club very wealthy." Peaches paused, to give any of the club presidents a chance to leave if they wanted to. None left.

"My plan is to front each club president one hundred kilos of uncut cocaine for twenty-five thousand dollars a kilo, But, it must be unanimously agreed upon that if any club defaults, or fails to honor the commitment here today, the other clubs will unite and stand against the rogue club. Also, club presidents will share in the losses and vote on punishments. After two thousand kilos are sold and the money is collected, the price will be reduced to twenty thousand dollars per kilo."

"I have two questions." The Dirty Dawgs' president stood up. "Where do I sign up? And, when do I get the merchandise?"

"Does anyone wish to not participate?" Peaches questioned. "Do we look crazy?" The Sons of Iniquity president demanded.

His view seemed to be the opinion of all those present. The deal was too great for them to pass up, knowing that what she was offering would make their clubs wealthy and strong.

"If everyone has agreed to the terms, you can take a hundred kilos with you today. In the future I can only guarantee shipments of ten kilos, next day delivery. But we can send numerous shipments to different locations."

"How do we pay you?" Rocky, the Dirty Dawgs' president asked.

"In cash, and as quickly as you can get it to me. My partner is named Nuni. He will personally be in touch with each of you. He handles the shipments, and money. As a matter of fact, Rod could you send someone to take his place at the house and bring him here to meet everyone?"

"Sure, no problem."

Rod took Craven to the rental house and returned with Nuni. As introductions were made, each of the presidents took the measure of the man they would be dealing with.

"I'm your guy! Whatever you need I'll find a way to deliver it. All payments will be made in cash and delivered to me personally. I want no misunderstanding about this."

"One more thing guys," Peaches added. "We need to move two thousand kilos a month, and that's starting now. Sell it to street hustlers, taxi cab drivers, little old ladies, or nursing homes. Just move it."

The Argots broke out samples of the cocaine, crystal meth, and tapped a cold keg of beer. It was time to party.

"Where's Bulldog?" Peaches wondered out loud.

"He's gone! When Rod arrived yesterday, the first thing he did was beat Bulldog's ass, strip him of his colors, and toss him out of the club." A club member explained.

"Bulldog gave up his colors?"

"Nope. He told Rod that if he wanted his colors that he would have to take them, and Rod was happy to oblige. He beat his ass in front of the entire club."

The Dirty Dawgs and the Sons of Iniquity presidents overheard the conversation and spoke up.

"If Bulldog hadn't called us, no one would have rallied in support of Ramrod in Orlando. Every one of us were looking for Peaches!"

"He told us that he was going crazy in jail, not being able to do anything about you being missing, and unable to protect his club president." The Dirty Dawgs president added.

"Holy fuck!" Rod cursed himself for being a fool.

Peaches hurried from the room to the bedroom her and Bulldog had always shared. Everyone had it all wrong. How could she not trust her heart where Bulldog was concerned. Where had he gone? What could he possibly be thinking. She wondered if he would ever forgive her for her betrayal.

CHAPTER EIGHTEEN
DIRTY MONEY

After leaving the cabin Thursday morning, Bulldog went to the bank, withdrawing his money and closing the account. His first thought was to return to the cabin with a gun and kill Rodney Anderson, understanding that he would most likely die in the process. He had been shamed in front of his brothers and lost the fight without throwing a single punch. The humiliation was overwhelming. He did not want to return. None of his brothers protested his being ousted without a vote. It was time for him to get on his Harley and get in the wind. His old friend Freddy Moon owned a bar in Groton, Connecticut. It was called Fiddler's Three. Two years earlier, Freddy offered him a job as night manager and had promised the position would always be available should he ever change his mind. Bulldog mused that the position of night manager was just another title for security or bouncer. It was not truly a management position.

He did reason that at the moment it was his best option. If he stayed local, he knew it was just a matter of time before he returned to the cabin. So, he packed his bags with cash and headed north.

Bulldog rode throughout the day, his thoughts turning towards Peaches and how much he truly loved her. When the news had come down through the grapevine that she was safe and sound, his entire heart had given a sigh of relief. Now, he was riding away from the woman he loved.

Freddy Moon was sitting on a barstool near the front door of his bar when he heard the sound of the Harley approaching. He watched Bulldog park and walk out of the dark night and through the door. Freddy quickly came to his feet, a smile of greeting lighting his face. They shared a firm handshake and a slap on the back.

"You sure are a sight for sore eyes." Freddy continued to grin. Freddy was five foot six, and a hunred and sixty pounds of whip cord muscle. He was also a full blooded Cherokee Indian. Long coal black hair hung down his back and brown piercing eyes looked out of hawk like features. He was in his mid thirties, never married, and partied every day of his life.

Bulldog bellied up to the bar. "How long have you owned this place?"

"Eight years this May." Freddy motioned to the barmaid. "Give my friend whatever he wants to drink."

The barmaid gave Bulldog a warm smile taking in his handsome good looks with pleasure. Freddy laughed. The females had always been kind to his big friend.

Bulldog gave her a nice smile in return. "I'll have a long-neck bottle of Bud and a shot of Wild Turkey on the side." He said, then turned his attention back to Freddy. "Is the position of night manager still open?"

"You know it is." Freddy replied, slapping his old friend on his back. "But there's no wearing colors in the bar. It gets rowdy enough with the drunken sailors."

Groton, Connecticut was home to a submarine base and Fiddler's Three was a favored hangout.

"I don't wear colors anymore." Bulldog said flatly. "What happened?"

"C'mon Freddy. You watch the news, so you already know what happened in Florida."

"I didn't catch every report." Freddy said in confusion.

"To make a long story short, we had three choices. One, go to trial on all of the charges. Two, plead guilty to federal firearm violations for a two year sentence. Or three, sign an agreement to leave the State of Florida and not return for five years. I was madly in love. The love of my life had been kidnapped, and I was going nuts and feeling helpless. The thought of going to jail wasn't very appealing. I could do nothing to help anyone from jail, so I took the deal. When I was released, I called in favors. Outlaw bikers from across the country rode into Orlando in support of Ramrod's hearing, and to search for the woman I loved. Her name is, Peaches. She lives in Maryland, so accepting the deal was no big sacrifice. Not everyone saw it that way."

"I saw bikers on the news shouting her name as she left the courthouse. What happened to her?"

"I don't know. She doesn't want anything to do with me."

"Man, that's fucked up."

"Yeah, tell me about it." Bulldog frowned. He downed the shot of Jack Daniel's, then chased it with a beer.

"Where are you staying?"

"I don't know yet."

"There's an efficiency apartment behind the bar. It's nothing fancy, but it's available and the rent is reasonable enough. It's free. It has a bed, shower, and a kitchenette with a stove, refrigerator, and sink."

Bulldog grinned broadly, "I was sold when you said it was free."

* * *

"I can only ship ten kilos at a time." Nuni explained to the club presidents. "But you can pickup or I'll deliver larger quantities."

Five club presidents took one hundred kilos with them. Nuni took addresses for deliveries. Shipments would be made through the United States Postal Service. If a club needed more product, they needed to provide an address for each package.

Rod called Ramrod and broke the news about Bulldog, After hearing the story about how he had taken Bulldog's patch, Ramrod said that he thought Rod could have handled that a little better.

Rod was beside himself, wishing that he could turn back the hands of time, have a do over. Sadly enough, he knew that was not possible. He offered a twenty-five hundred dollar reward for Bulldog's whereabouts.

Peaches had to gain control of her emotions. She wanted to break down and cry but she could not show her vulnerability, especially in the presence of the club presidents. She quickly wiped a tear from her eye, laid out double lines of cocaine, and snorted a line into each nostril. She grabbed a large clear plastic cup, filled it with beer from the tapped keg, raised the cup high in the air, and shouted. "Let's party!"

"Help yourselves." Rod yelled to the brothers.

Her innermost thoughts were of her beloved Bulldog. She should have known better, she told herself. She should have listened to her heart, used her own judgment, and not have been so easily influenced by those so quick to jump to conclusions.

The Sons on Iniquity, the Dirty Dogs, and the other clubs were now banded together in brotherhood. There would be no more biker wars over territory. If any member betrayed the brotherhood, the penalty would be severe.

The party continued well into the early hours of the morning. Rod had taken on the responsibility of distributing and keeping track of the cocaine at the rental house. Four club presidents had taken a hundred kilos, and those were en-route to their stash houses. Nuni had addresses to ship six packages. It left Rod responsible for five hundred and forty kilos to be released or shipped upon orders from Nuni. All transfers were to be logged into a book, but the stash was also available to be sold by any Argot brother.

* * *

Friday night, Glenda Miles, the head barmaid, picked up Sugar from Nuni's house and gave her a ride to work. "Where is everyone?" Glenda asked.

"Ramrod's at the club making some repairs. Everyone else is in Pennsylvania, but they will be back tomorrow afternoon." Sugar smiled, then stuck her hand out, wiggling her ring finger. "Ramrod and I are engaged."

"Wow." Glenda said, impressed.

"It's just one karat, but I'm going to have a beautiful outdoor wedding with bridesmaids."

"I'm happy for you." Glenda smiled.

* * *

Charlie and Dee Dee were nursing broken hearts, each of them sick with longing for the other.

No one had heard from Chris Delgato since the trip to the island. Peaches surmised that he was preoccupied with selling his hundred kilos of cocaine.

Marsha and Manny were packing suitcases, preparing for their flight in the morning. Manny called Avis Rent-A-Car and reserved a new Cadillac Coupe Deville. Then he called the Holiday Inn in downtown Orlando and reserved adjacent rooms for him and Marsha.

At closing, Ramrod announced that he wanted to stay at the club and finish installing a second shower in the girls' dressing room. It had to be done during the club's down hours because he could not work in it when the girls were present.

Glenda offered Sugar a ride home. The two had become fast friends since Sugar's arrival at the club, and during the night they talked, somehow drinking a little bit more than they should have. Arriving at Nuni's they found the house to be dark and silent. Not wanting to go inside by herself, Sugar invited Glenda in for a nightcap.

Glenda parked her red Chevy Nova in the driveway, the car looking exceptionally nice for being five years old. Sugar stumbled through the house, turning lights on as she went, including the front porch and backyard lights. She turned on just about every light in the house before heading for the kitchen. She filled two tall glasses with ice, adding Jack Daniel's and Coca-Cola. With a drunken giggle she passed a glass to Glenda.

Out of the corner of her eye, Sugar caught something moving on the patio. Immediately she realized that it was the cat, Miss Prissy. She opened the door.

"I bet you're hungry!" She said to the cat. She had never thought to feed the cat. She went through the cupboard until she found a can of cat food. She dumped it on a saucer, then filled a bowl with milk.

"There you go, Ms. Prissy." She said, smiling with a tipsy grin. Glenda reached down to pet the cat.

"You don't want to do that." Sugar said, making Glenda snatch her hand hack. "Peaches is the only person she has warmed up to."

Glenda noticed the swimming pool through the open door. Seeing her interest, Sugar flipped a light switch on the wall beside the door, and aqua colored lights lit up the water. With a shared laugh, they hurried outside as quickly as possible to plop down on lounge chairs. They leaned back to sip their drinks and talk.

"Why is everyone in Pennsylvania?" Glenda asked. "My sister has other business ventures," Sugar replied. "Does she own another club?"

"No." Sugar laughed. "It's nothing like that, but, I can't talk about it."

"That's fine. Have you spent much time in the pool?"

"No, I haven't."

Glenda walked to the edge of the pool and slowly put her hand in the water. "It's bathtub warm," she reported.

"It's heated all year," Sugar smiled.

Glenda looked around the yard, noting that a privacy fence ran around the perimeter.

"I've always wanted to go skinny dipping at night. How about it, are you game?"

"I'll do it if you will," Sugar giggled.

The girls stripped, and holding hands, on the count of three jumped into the pool. They splashed into the water with a loud scream, the water felt incredibly wonderful as they swam slowly side by side to the deep end of the pool. Treading water, they turned to face one another, admiring each others bodies. Sugar's breasts were larger, but Glenda's were perfectly proportioned, her pink nipples standing high and pointed.

Sugar was eight years younger, but Glenda's body had sculptured abdominal muscles. They swam further into the shallow side of the pool, and stood close in four feet of water. Glenda tenderly brushed the hair from Sugar's face with her fingers, pulled her close and kissed her hard on the mouth. At first it was a shock to Sugar, but she was just drunk enough to return the passionate kiss. Soon they were caressing each other's bodies, their hearts beating faster, and their skin becoming sensitive to the touch. Glenda maneuvered Sugar's ass onto the edge of the swimming pool, leaned her backwards, slowly positioning her legs over her shoulders. using two fingers, she separated the lips of her moist pussy and slowly, almost meticulously, licked the gash of her pussy until her tongue touched her clit. Glenda slid her hand beneath Sugar's ass, teasing her pussy until she was squirming around in uncontrollable throes of passion. Within minutes, Sugar climaxed,

"This is my first time with a woman," Sugar admitted.

"Mine too!" Glenda laughed. "Bowdy asked me earlier where everyone was."

"What did you tell him?"

"That I didn't know. There's something about him that gives me the creeps."

"I wouldn't want anyone, especially my sister, to know that we did this."

"Neither would I!" Glenda said flatly.

"But now it's my turn to do you," Sugar suddenly smiled.

Glenda sat on the edge of the pool with her feet in the water and leaned back.

* * *

Nuni and Peaches arrived at the Harrisburg International Airport at ten o'clock Saturday morning. Twenty minutes later, they boarded TWA flight 765 for Orlando, Florida. After seating themselves,

Peaches brought up something she had been planning for some time. She spoke in a near whisper.

"Now that you're in charge of distribution you're not going to have time to manage the club."

"I can take care of both," Nuni insisted.

"No, you can't. I don't think you fully understand what your new position requires of you. It's not just the distribution. You're going to have to count and bag forty-two million dollars. You're going to need help. You will need people you can trust and money counting machines. And, with money there is no trust. You will need cameras monitoring the room where the money is counted, stacked, and kept. Every time you have two million dollars bagged, move it to the storage unit. Only two people will know the location of the storage unit. That's you and me. We also need to make sure the kilos aren't being cut or shorted between the time they leave here and delivery. So, workers handling money or delivering packages will be required to take a polygraph every ninety days. We have a lot of product on hand. To meet our goal we must move two thousand kilos."

"Damn that's a lot of cocaine," Nuni reflected in a whisper.

"Nuni, if you are going into this venture with a negative attitude, perhaps you should reconsider taking on this much responsibility?"

"No, I gotcha. It's just a lot to digest." Nuni replied.

"I'm thinking that an army duffel bag will hold two million dollars. The canvas is durable and the army green is less conspicuous. I would love to see the expression on Pablo's face when he receives twelve duffel bags filled with cash."

Thirty minutes later at the International Airport, Manny and Marsha boarded American Airlines flight 264, bound for Orlando.

"How are you feeling about this move?" Marsha asked of Manny.

"At my age, living in a warmer climate will be a blessing. How do you feel about it?"

"I'm terrified! It's going to be an adjustment."

"If you need anything, call me."

Marsha nodded her head. "I need a drink. I'm scared to death of flying." Manny smiled, gently placing his hand over hers.

Nuni and Peaches flight arrived in Orlando first. While Peaches walked to long-term parking to pick up Nuni's Lincoln, Nuni collected their bags. All of Peaches plans fell together with perfect timing. The second Nuni stepped from the terminal, she pulled up to the curb, popping the trunk, so he could toss in the luggage. They waited around for another thirty minutes for Manny and Marsha's plane to arrive. The flight arrived on schedule.

Peaches greeted them with a warm embrace, introducing Nuni only as her club manager.

Manny went to Avis to pick up the rental car he had reserved, while the rest of them rode the escalator down to the baggage area to claim their luggage.

When Manny pulled up in a yellow Cadillac Coupe Deville, Nuni was there to load the bags into the trunk.

"I'll ride with Nuni," Peaches said. "You guys follow us to the house."

"I rented rooms for Marsha and myself at the Holiday Inn downtown. I'd like to check in first, if that's alright."

"That's fine, follow us." Peaches agreed.

Marsha sat next to Manny, the beige leather interior feeling soft and plush, that new car smell filling her senses. In the other car, Nuni stretched his arm across the top of the front seat, making Peaches feel very uncomfortable. Manny had never seen her with another man, and add to that her thoughts of Bulldog made her really feel guilty.

Manny parked at the front entrance of the Holiday Inn, hurrying inside to the front desk to check in. Nuni followed them inside with the luggage, a bellhop stepping forward to see that their bags got safely to their rooms.

"If you would like to unpack and freshen up, Nuni and I will go downstairs and have a cocktail. You can meet us in the lounge," Peaches suggested.

"For dinner, I'll cook something on the grill at my house. Bring along your bathing suits." Nuni offered.

"We will meet you in the lounge in twenty minutes." Marsha promised, then looked at Manny for his approval.

In the lounge, Peaches ordered a Tequila sunrise. Nuni ordered a long necked bottle of Budweiser.

"I need you to do something for me. It's important." Peaches told him.

"Anything." Nuni agreed.

"I'm still reeling over the news about Bulldog," she explained. "It will be better if we stay friends and partners for now. I need the time to work things out in my own head."

Nuni understood, having sensed that the information about Bulldog had stunned her. He was wiling to give her all of the space she needed. "I've got your back," he smiled. "Why don't you give Sugar a call and have her take some steaks and ribs out of the freezer?"

Peaches laughed. "Are you serious? Do you honestly think that frozen meat is going to thaw in a half an hour?"

Nuni shrugged his shoulders. "When we get back to the house, I'll go to the store and buy some fresh meat."

"Good idea." Peaches smiled, more than grateful for his buying fresh meat. Nuni was a good and loyal friend, but not the man she loved or could ever love. It had always been Bulldog and it always would be.

CHAPTER NINETEEN
ALL IN THE GAME

Everyone sat around the pool at Nuni's having drinks. Ramrod fired up the grill, while Nuni and Sugar made a quick trip to the grocery store to buy t-bone steaks and beef spare ribs.

"Tell me about the house you picked out for me," Marsha quizzed Peaches.

"It's a four bedroom ranch on a lake, and it's in the best school district in Florida. That's all I'm going to tell you. In the morning you can check it out for yourself."

"Did you find me a condo," Manny inquired.

"Yes, I did. It has a golf course and a spectacular view overlooking the city."

"Then, I'll love it." Manny assured her.

At five o'clock Ramrod and Sugar left to open the club. After an enjoyable dinner and several more drinks, Manny and Marsha decided to follow Nuni and Peaches to the club. Manny pointed for Marsha to look up when he spotted the pink neon sign above the Pink Pussycat.

Peaches led the way past the crowd gathered at the front door, bypassing the identification check and cover charge. She gave them a quick tour of her office and the dressing room that she shared with her sister. After the tour, she ordered Bowdy to seat Manny and Marsha in a booth near the stage. It was a first class operation. Even nicer than the Two O'clock Club.

"I've never seen you perform," Marsha reminded Nicole.

"You will tonight," Peaches promised. "Ramrod and my sister will be managing the club. They're getting married."

"I wouldn't mind being a barmaid here, I bet the girls make great tips." Marsha smiled.

"Marsha Bennett!" Peaches declared. "At night you need to be home with my nieces and nephews."

"I could be a manager," Manny grinned. "I don't have any kids."

Marsha stuck her tongue out at the two of them.

At ten o' clock Manny asked for directions to the Holiday Inn. Then he said with a smile. "But we won't be leaving before you and Sugar perform." Marsha smiled, pleased with Manny's response.

Ten minutes later Sugar took the stage, dressed in an Indian costume. Her feathered headband touched the floor. It was monstrous! The feathers were colorfully arranged in bright red, white, blue, and yellow. Leather multi-colored tassels covered her nipples. She wore knee-high, tan leather, pearled boots that were fringed at the top. A patch of leather covered her front and back side, hung by a string tied around her waist. Sugar had moves that could wake the dead, not forgetting that she was drop dead gorgeous.

"I could never do that!" Marsha said with a smile of wonder.

"I seem to recall you and Nicole wearing a costume in Hawaii. Grass skirts if I recall correctly." Manny grinned broadly. "And as I recall, you wore them exceptionally well."

Sugar exited the stage to be replaced by Peaches, who was wearing her fireman's outfit, consisting of a yellow trench coat, red hard hat, black boots, and tight black shorts. She began dancing and stripping provocatively, moving around the stage with a sensual grace, exposing, first black g-string panties, then her tassel covered nipples.

Marsha was immediately transported back in time to the moment when she had first taught Peaches her first dance moves. Since that time she could see that her dear friend had come a long way. The audience was going wild, clapping, and giving excited cat calls. Suddenly, Peaches grabbed her red fire-extinguisher, pointed the hose in the direction of Manny and Marsha, and pulled the trigger. Manny ducked, dodging the stream of cold water, but Marsha was not as quick, The stream of water doused her from head to toe.

"You'll pay for that!" Marsha sputtered.

The crowd burst into loud laughter.

At 11 o'clock Manny and Marsha wished everyone a good night, and returned to their room.

* * *

The second the barmaids and dancers arrived for work, Freddy Moon introduced Bulldog as the new night club manager. There were two other bouncers, Jake and Eddie. Jake had worked at the bar for four years, his huge size being enough to intimidate most men. Eddie was short, stocky and held a third degree black belt in Karate. Eddie had only been working as a bouncer at Fiddler's Three for about a year.

The dancers performed inside of black steel cages, which hung suspended from the ceiling. Every fifteen minutes, they were given a break. When one dancer stepped down, another took her place. There were four cages situated around the bar.

The girls whispered amongst each other, wondering where Bulldog was from? Each of them secretly wondering if he had a significant other. His powerful build and model good looks drew them to him like moths to a flame.

From the moment Bulldog was introduced to Ginger, their eyes locked, sparking an instant attraction. Freddy immediately cringed at the thought of it becoming a problem. Employees were not permitted to date each other. Freddy Moon had seen too many fights caused by domestic quarrels. There was always girls being jealous of other girls. You had men being unnecessarily overprotective, or upset because of their girl flirting with another man. Then there was the drunken sailors using verbal abuse or touching a girl. It was a good rule to not allow relationships on the job, and the girls needed their freedom to flirt and hustle the drunken sailors for tips. He decided to pull Bulldog aside and explain how he ran things.

"My rules are pretty simple," Freddy began. "Number one: Don't steal from me. Number two: be dependable. When it's your shift, be there! Lastly, don't date another employee. If you do and I find out, you'll find yourself looking for another job. I don't care if you have a drink or two. Your drinks are free, but don't get drunk while you're working. Any questions?"

"Nope." Bulldog replied.

On his first night, Bulldog broke up two fights, sending two drunken sailors peacefully back to the navel base, earning the respect of his fellow bouncers. Bulldog was not a trained fighter as Rod had been, being more of a street brawler with no formal training. What he did have was years of experience managing rowdy bikers who loved nothing more than a good fight. So when he broke up the two sailors, he did so with a smile and a good, natural laugh.

The dancers teased and taunted him when he passed by their cages. He felt like a piece of fresh meat being thrown to hungry lions, but he appreciated the attention. Bulldog was trying to let the Argots, the fight, and Peaches fade from his broken heart.

Ginger was five seven with blue eyes and fiery red hair. She was blessed with a perfect set of 38 double D's and her smile was captivating. Bulldog was already having fantasy sex with her. Her g-string and tassel covered breast leaving very little to imagination. He could visualize his face being buried in her little red, furry patch. He wanted to fuck her doggie style and watch her tits bounce as he pounded her. He fantasized about laying on his back, running his fingers through her long red hair, allowing her to suck him off. The way she looked at him when he passed by, let him know that he would have her. It was just a matter of time.

* * *

Sunday morning, everyone met at Nuni's house for breakfast. Sugar prepared a large country breakfast. There was biscuits, gravy, pancakes with maple syrup, grits, bacon, ham, and fried eggs sunny side up. There were even oranges and grapefruit, peeled and cut into slices in small bowls.

"I could get used to this!" Manny said between bites of food.

"I haven't yet." Ramrod laughed, then forked in a mouth full of food. "Mama taught her how to cook," Peaches said proudly. "I was more of a daddy's girl."

"Thank you for a fantastic breakfast." Marsha complemented Sugar. Shortly after breakfast, Manny, Marsha, and Peaches left for Altamonte

Springs to view the four bedroom home on Prarie Lake Drive. Nuni was already busy filling orders and managing the cocaine business. It was a gorgeous day. By 10 o'clock the sky was baby blue with temperatures in the mid eighties. The sun was hot on the skin and glaring on the eyes.

"I like your friends," Manny admitted. From the start, he had doubted whether he would approve of her friends. They were mostly bikers, but not at all what he had expected, the media and movies portraying them badly. It was the image that they projected that he disliked! He admired Ramrod and Rod for being the men that they were. Not to mention they rode motorcycles too. Manny liked how well cared for the motorcycles were, the powerful sound they made, and for a second he toyed with the thought of buying one for himself. The brothers had given him a lot to think about. In Florida there was plenty of good weather all year round. When he mentioned he might buy a Harley for himself, the girls had something to say about it.

"Don't you think you're a little old for that," Marsha asked.

"He's not too old," Nicole snapped in his defense. "But I don't think it's a good idea. I like you in one piece, just the way you are."

"Old, huh?" Manny grinned, glancing over at Marsha. "You know what I meant." Marsha laughed.

Nicole turned on the radio, tuning in a country station and started singing.

"Why are you in such a good mood," Marsha asked, "Because I'm in the company of the ones I love," she smiled. Manny grinned. He loved the girls. They were his family.

"Wow!" Manny exclaimed, impressed with the outside appearance of the house as he pulled into the driveway. The newly paved asphalt driveway was large enough to easily accommodate two vehicles. The house was a rich brown brick, accentuated by black shutters. Four feet high bushes ran the length of the house. The flower beds were freshly mulched, the sweet smell of cedar chips filling the air.

Marsha pointed. "Look at the garden."

In the middle of the front yard there was a garden of red, yellow, pink, and white roses. In the center sat a concrete bird bath with a water fountain and a large stainless steel flag pole. In honor of her late husband, she would proudly fly the flag of the United States of America. She thought, Harold would like that.

The house was beautiful, before she even stepped inside, Marsha felt like she had already come home. The amenities made the home all that much nicer. An enormous shower had been added to the half bath in the master bedroom.

From the outside patio she saw the sandy beach with a floating platform in the lake for her kids to enjoy. She could already imagine the twins diving or jumping from the platform. She decided that this was going to be a good move after all.

It would give her family a new beginning. They had suffered over the loss of her husband long enough. It was time to let him go and move on.

"Do you like it," Manny asked.

"I love it."

"Then it's yours," he stated flatly.

"Just like that." Nicole laughed, excited to see Marsha so happy. A fish jumped in the lake as if to welcome them.

Marsha threw her arms around Manny's neck and hugged him close. Tears formed in her eyes and she tried hard not to cry. She was unable to help herself, the tears fell anyway. Manny removed a handkerchief to blot at her tears.

They drove back to Orlando. It was time for Manny to inspect the condo at the Grand Hyatt. The manager of the condos came to escort them upstairs. "There are a lot of amenities." The well dressed manager began his sales pitch. "There's indoor and outdoor swimming pools, a fully equipped workout room. But, the best feature is the eighteen hole golf course. It was designed by the world renown, Robert Trent. There's also an exclusive clubhouse for members only." He opened the door leading into the highrise condo.

As they followed the manager inside, Manny frowned at the sight of the gold carpet. "I hate gold carpet." He said in distaste.

The manager cleared his throat, with a quick smile. "Did I mention that there's a sports shop, a bar, and a five star restaurant on the premises?"

"What color of carpet would you like?" Marsha asked Manny, glancing over at Peaches in amusement.

"Plush white, no shag."

"We'll take care of it." Nicole promised him with a kiss on the cheek.

The threesome walked out onto the balcony, the view was breathtakingly beautiful and Manny looked forward to seeing it at night.

"This meets all of my requirements, and then some." He told the manager.

"I wasn't sure how you would feel about the extra bedroom." Nicole smiled, happy that he was pleased.

"Now, I have a bedroom and a playroom." Manny teased the girls, making the manager blush.

Marsha and Nicole laughed. They looked forward to seeing what surprises he had up his sleeve.

Sunday night, Nicole broke down and slept with Nuni, but her heart wasn't in it. Simply put, she did not have the same feelings for him that she shared with Marsha and Manny, and certainly not the pleasure she felt in Bulldog's arms. She was certain that Nuni had deep rooted feelings for her. It was confusing, too complicated for her to think about.

Monday morning, Marsha and Manny flew back to Maryland. While boarding the airplane, in hindsight, Marsha wished she had thought to bring along a camera and taken photos to share with her children. When Travis voted to move to Florida, he failed to take into consideration his feelings for his girlfriend, Dorothy Ellis. Just a year ago he proclaimed his love by gifting her with a promise ring.

Manny insisted on taking care of the moving expenses for himself, Marsha, and Nicole. One of his friends owned a moving company.

Nicole's stage name was Peaches, and many of her friends called her Peaches, but not Marsha and Manny. To them, she would always be Nicole. In one week, Nicole planned to return to Maryland and pack up the entire apartment. She would then drive her Mercedes-Benz to Orlando. The mere thought of Marsha driving cross country with five rowdy children was way too much for Manny. He offered to pay for both Nicole's Volkswagen and Marsha's Mustang convertible to be shipped. After the girls agreed, he purchased first class tickets for Marsha and her children to fly to Orlando with him. In just two weeks the moves would be complete.

* * *

At ten o'clock Monday morning Agent Moore called Pete Elliot from his office in downtown Orlando.

"Hello, Tom. What can I do for you?"

"I received a call from my informant last night. Our girl Peaches has been out of town attending a meeting in Pennsylvania."

"I'd like to be a fly on that wall. Peaches isn't your average criminal. She's highly intelligent, calculating, and not to be underestimated."

"She's going to make a mistake. They all do. It's just a matter of time. I think it's time to feed our rat some cheese."

Moore chuckled at his own humor. He clicked off from Elliot, then dialed another number.

"Anne Arundel County Sheriffs Department," the switchboard

operator answered.

"This is special agent H. Thomas Moore from the Orlando office of the F.B.I. Is Detective Hill in, please?"

"One minute, Sir." The operator replied, connecting the call. "Sergeant Hill." Hill answered,

"Agent Moore here, how are you? Do you have any follow up information on Charlie or Nicole Redman?"

"No, I don't. I left my card on the front door of Charlie Redman's house, but I haven't heard from him."

"We have information that his ex-wife Nicole attended a meeting in Pennsylvania this week I don't want to go into any specifics, but should you hear anything I would appreciate a call."

"If I hear anything I'll call you right away. How's the weather?"

"Great. Perhaps you should consider relocating?"

"I've been giving that some serious thought. By the way, if you dial the area code three zero one, and then two ... five ... five ... five ... four, zero one, the call will go directly through to my office."

"I'll put that number in my Rolodex for future reference. You take care of yourself."

"You too."

* * *

One week later outlaw bikers from other states joined the alliance. The Rotten Bastards had chapters in Michigan and Ohio. The Bad Boys controlled most of the New England states. The Pack Rats covered Washington State. Home based in Seattle, they were now expanding to Canada.

At the end of the first week, four hundred kilos were sold. Nuni was looking for new ways to ship large amounts of cocaine around the country. His plan was to keep five hundred kilos at the rental house in Harrisburg, and five hundred at Charlie's storage unit in Maryland. His second thought was that shipping would be much faster and simpler if he had five hundred kilos in California and Washington State.

Nuni set up a bedroom in his house with surveillance equipment, the cameras covering every square inch of the room. He purchased an enormous heavy wood folding table, and four electric bill counters, two of them would be just in case of an emergency. He purchased boxes of money wrappers for all denominations. Everything from a one dollar bill to a hundred dollar bill was covered in the boxes of money wrappers. These he placed on a shelf in the room's only closet. His next act was to purchase fifty green Army duffel bags, stacking them on the floor of the closet. When not in use, the long fold-up table and money counters would be kept in the closet, and secured by a lock on the door handle.

Nuni hired two elderly women whom he had known for most of his life, teaching them how to use the counting machines. The two women found the work to be quite simple. A stack of bills was placed on one end of the machine and a button was pressed. The counter made a fluttering sound as it rapidly counted the bills. When the desired amount was reached, a wrapper was grabbed, and licked to secure the bills between the folds. The money was then stacked into neat piles. Counting money was all part of the game, and Nuni loved counting money.

* * *

Between the club, her apartment, and taking care of business, Peaches was exhausted. She still needed to find time out for a trip to Miami, buy two powerboats, and visit Norman's Cay. Juan, Manuel, Cheva, and Pepe needed to be reassured that everything was under control, and they would be well taken care of.

CHAPTER TWENTY
APACHE PERFORMANCE BOATS

Things were moving faster than anyone had prepared for. Every day brought new challenges to the table for Nuni to solve. The Sons of Iniquity were doing extremely well, having already sold a hundred kilos, and they were still calling in orders daily. Nuni was becoming increasing desperate and looking for alternative ways to ship larger quantities cross country. Drivers charged a thousand dollars per kilo for taking the risk of their being stopped by the highway patrol. If they were stopped, the risk of losing both the shipment and the driver's freedom was a huge risk. The question looming in Nuni's mind was which plan would be the safest and most cost effective way to ship five hundred or even a thousand kilos cross country.

Peaches stepped out of the shower, using a large fluffy towel to dry her hair. She walked from the bathroom and into the bedroom naked. From the bedroom doorway, Nuni watched her every movement. It was 9 o'clock in the morning and soon she would have to leave for the airport. Nuni had been up, showered, dressed, and watching the women count money for over an hour.

"You've gotta quit doing that," he smiled.

"What?" Peaches replied, nonchalantly wrapping the towel around her head. She sat on the edge of the bed, turned to look at Nuni, waiting for his response.

"You need to put some clothes on." Nuni answered with a grin.

"I'm more accustomed to men telling me to take them off," she laughed. "Are you going to drive me to the airport? My flight leaves at ten o'clock."

"When will you be returning?" He asked with a concerned look.

"I have to pack-up the apartment for the movers then drive my Mercedes to Orlando. I'll be back by the end of the week."

"You need to have a serious talk with Charlie while you're in Maryland.

He's still got his head stuck up his ass. It's not good for business."

"I'll see him. How many kilos have been paid for?"

"As of last Friday, four hundred. That's eight million dollars. There's four duffel bags with two million in each one, inside the storage unit. The cocaine is in my storage unit. The duffel bags are in a rented storage unit near the airport. I didn't like the idea of putting all of our eggs in one basket!"

"Is the storage unit in your name?" Nuni frowned. "Do I look stupid?"

"Who all knows about the storage units and where they're located?"

"Ramrod knows where the cocaine is stored. Nobody knows about the other unit but me." Nuni smiled.

"If something was to happen to you, what am I supposed to do, go on a fucking Easter egg hunt?"

"No, smart ass," Nuni snarled. "I intended on showing you where the storage is on our way to the airport"

Peaches laughed. "Nuni, you're not even a good liar. You didn't know that I was going to the airport until five minutes ago."

Nuni frowned, then walked away, hating the idea that she was smarter than him.

* * *

Sugar looked at Ramrod sitting at the kitchen table. He was reading the newspaper as she poured him a second cup of coffee.

"When are we getting married?" She asked slyly.

He immediately stopped reading the morning paper to look up at her with a loving smile. "When would you like for us to get hitched?"

"July fourth!" She answered quickly, clearly having given it a great deal of thought.

"I think we should have an outdoor ceremony inside of the gazebo. That's where you properly proposed to me. I think it would be a beautiful wedding."

"That's fine by me. Whatever makes you happy. There's only one king in a castle, but the queen has a lot of influence if the king has any sense," he chuckled. Sugar smiled approvingly.

"Well, good morning Sleeping Beauty." Sugar greeted her sister as she entered the kitchen and sat down at the table.

"Real cute." Peaches ignored her, reaching across the table to grab a slice of bacon from Ramrod's plate. She ate it one small bite at a time. "I'm going to be gone for most of the week." She announced.

"Where to this time?" Sugar asked.

"I have to return to Maryland to pack up our apartment and drive the Mercedes back. Unless you and Ramrod would prefer to do it. It could be your honeymoon."

"No thanks!" Sugar quickly replied.

"Are you sure you don't want to think of it as an early honeymoon?" Ramrod joined in on the teasing.

"We are going on a real honeymoon. To Hawaii, Bermuda, Cancun, or the Virgin Islands. I don't care which, somewhere romantic, just the two of us."

"How about a cruise?" Ramrod suggested.

"That's a possibility. I will consider it, depending on the destination, and how many days the cruise lasts. An overnight sensation isn't happening, that's for damn sure," she laughed. Nobody was going to cheat her!

Nuni drove to the airport, stopping to show Peaches the location of the new storage unit. It was Brokley's Storage, unit 26. He gave her the second key to the lock.

"I negotiated a reduced price by paying five years in advance. So we'll never have to worry about the unit being padlocked for non-payment of rent."

"That's good thinking." She smiled, pleased at how things were being handled.

* * *

Ten minutes after the flight landed at Baltimore International Airport, Peaches called Charlie to pick her up, but there was no answer at his house. In hindsight, she wished that she had called in advance. She browsed through her purse, saw Sergeant Hill's card and dialed his number at the Arundel County Sheriffs Department.

"Sergeant Hill speaking." He answered.

"Damn, you've got a sexy voice." She said.

"Nicole." He replied, recognizing her voice In an instant.

"I'm stranded at the airport. Can you give me a ride, or are you to busy?"

"I'll be there in twenty minutes." He promised.

"Thanks."

She walked to the gift shop, deciding to spend her time browsing through the magazines. After spending ten minutes in the gift shop, she got in a long line at a coffee shop, and when it was her turn to order, she purchased two cups of hot coffee. One with cream, plus two sugars. Then she stood outside of the terminal with her carry on luggage hanging by a strap from her left shoulder. The weather was nice, the perfect weather for a picnic in the park.

Sergeant Hill pulled up to the curb in his blue Ford Maverick. He reached across the seat to open the passenger door for her.

"Thank you." She smiled as she seated herself in the front passenger seat. She handed him a hot cup of coffee. "One cream, two sugars." She smiled, closing the door.

"You remembered!" He smiled his pleasure. It had been two years since she had made him coffee, and it had only been once. "So, how long are you here for this time?"

"Just long enough to pack up my apartment for the movers. Then I have to make the long drive to Florida."

"I had an inquiry about you and your ex-husband a few days ago. An F.B.I. Agent by the name of Moore called. He wanted to know if I had any new information. He also mentioned that you were in Pennsylvania last week on business."

She wondered if the feds were also aware of the recent trip to Bogota. "I told him that I hadn't heard anything. Technically, it was the truth."

Hill grinned. "I travel a lot. This is my second trip to Maryland this month."

"I got the impression that he was investigating illegal activity."

"Well, that asshole can investigate whatever he wants." Peaches snapped, irritated by the thought that there might be an informant working at the Pink Pussycat. Very few people knew about her trip to Bogota, or Pennsylvania.

"Will you join me for dinner?" He asked, as he pulled up to the front entrance of Regency Towers.

"Maybe Thursday night. I'll give you a call if I can make it." She promised.

Peaches walked Into the building, going through the foyer to the elevators. She shared an elevator with an elderly couple that smiled at her during the entire ride. She politely returned their smile then faced forward. Arriving on her floor, she soon opened the door to her apartment, dropping her overnight bag on the floor inside the door. She closed and locked the door behind her. Walking over to the hall closet, she grabbed a clear plastic baggy from the inside pocket of her black leather jacket. She laid out double lines of cocaine, two inches long, then snorted a line up each nostril. After wiping the residue from the glass topped table, she rode the elevator down to the underground parking garage. She uncovered her Mercedes-Benz and put the top down. Cranking the engine up, she tuned the radio to her favorite station, then headed for Charlie's house in Millersville. His situation had changed, making it where she no longer worked for him, instead he now worked for her. He needed to quickly come to the realization that his free ride was over. He was going to have to earn his money or retire.

Charlie's prized blue Corvette Stingray was parked in the driveway. She parked behind it, walked to the front door and rang the doorbell. Charlie answered the door looking tired.

"Where have you been?" She demanded. "I tried calling from the airport."

"I went to the grocery store and back. I wasn't gone for more than a half hour."

"How are you doing?" She asked in a softer tone.

"I'm okay." Charlie spoke in a flat voice.

She immediately sensed that he did not want to talk about Dee Dee. So she got right to the point. "Nuni is worried that you're not going to be able to take care of your end of the business. When he calls you with an order, it has to be delivered or shipped right away."

"That's never been my job."

"Things have changed, Charlie. I'm no longer selling fifty kilos a month for you. John Leder is no longer in charge. Neither you or I planned on this. I realize this and intend on honoring our original agreement concerning the fifty kilos, providing you're willing to earn it. Everyone has to do their part. I'm not expecting you to sell anything. Just make sure when Nuni calls in an order, it's delivered on time."

"I'm still going to collect two hundred and fifty thousand dollars a month?"

"Yes. But, if you hire someone to help you, they are your responsibility, and it's up to you to pay for them."

"I don't trust anyone." Charlie smiled. "Except you, of course."

Peaches returned his smile. "I could use some help packing up my apartment, if you don't have any plans."

"I'll help you." Charlie shrugged.

He followed her back to her apartment, parking his car beneath a light pole in front of the building.

"Why are you moving to Florida?" He asked as they entered the building.

"I own a nightclub in Orlando, and it would be difficult for me to take care of the business from Baltimore."

"I'm going to miss you."

"Miss me?" She laughed. "I'm still sore about the time you threw my ass out of your apartment."

"Aren't you ever going to get over that?" He pleaded.

"Probably not." She smiled. Her daughter Charlotte's death, and her sitting in the hallway of his apartment with tears streaming down her face, was engraved in her memory. It was not going to be forgotten anytime soon, if ever.

"Go downstairs and grab some boxes from beside the dumpster. It's where new tenants stack them when they move in."

Charlie left, returning a short time later with eight boxes. Peaches laid out a few lines of cocaine before they got started packing up the apartment. It was 10 o'clock at night when Charlie left. Tuesday morning, Peaches finished packing.

On Wednesday, she arrived at Marsha's house to find her busy packing for the movers.

"Are we going to Manny's this afternoon?" Nicole wanted to know. "It would be nice if you were to call in advance. I didn't even know that you were in town. Does Manny know?"

"He knows that today is Wednesday." Nicole laughed.

"I'm going to take a shower and dress. Call Manny and tell him that we'll be there around two thirty."

"How's Travis? Is he looking forward to the move?"

"What do you think? He thinks he's in love."

Marsha parked her white Mustang convertible in the parking lot of Manny's building. The girls made idle chit chat as they entered the building and rode the elevator to Manny's floor. He greeted them at the door to take their jackets.

"I'm packed and ready to go." Nicole reported.

"Yeah, well. She doesn't have a house with five kids. I'll be finished packing sometime this weekend." Marsha said in her defense.

After small talk, they retreated to the bedroom. The girls undressed, kissed, and made love to one another while Manny watched. Marsha kissed him while Nicole deep throated his manhood, sucking him to completion.

* * *

Thursday morning, Peaches placed a call to Sergeant Hill, apologizing because she was not going to be able to make it for dinner, asking for a rain check instead. Her plan was to leave before noon and drive straight through to Orlando. As she stepped off of the elevator and into the underground parking garage, she looked over to her left for the last time. The blood stain was still there. It was a constant reminder of her shooting Ryan 'Dollar' Porter.

Peaches kissed her beloved Bug, and said. "I'll see you in Florida next week." She unlocked the Mercedes-Benz, seated herself in the drivers seat, then started the engine. As she cruised out of the underground parking lot she turned up the radio, feeling good to be leaving some things in her rearview mirror. She stopped at the corner to remove her Ray-Ban sunglasses from the glove compartment. Making a right turn, she covered her eyes from the blinding sun, heading south on Highway 301.

Driving through the small town of Ludowici, Georgia, she was stopped for speeding and taken before a magistrate judge. The officer swore that he clocked the Mercedes-Benz at fifty-five miles an hour in a thirty-five mile an hour zone. In the blink of an eye she was found guilty and ordered to pay a hundred and twenty-five dollar fine. Nicole found the entire situation to be a complete sham, knowing that there was no way she had been speeding. She paid the fine anyway.

* * *

It felt good to be home, Peaches thought as she pulled into the driveway. At least it felt good to be back at Nuni's house. It had been a long, tiring drive. In just one more week she would have a place of her own, a place she could truly call home. She entered the house, going directly into the kitchen.

"How was your trip?" Sugar asked, hugging her sister.

"Long!" She replied. "I know I'll never drive through Ludowici, Georgia again. I don't care if I have to drive a hundred miles out of the way."

"Why? What happened." Ramrod asked.

"It cost me a hundred and twenty-five dollars for a fuckin' speeding ticket."

"Stop speeding." Sugar laughed.

"I wasn't speeding." Peaches snapped, angered by her sisters sarcastic remark.

Saturday morning Peaches called Chris Delgado, hoping to gain some much needed information from him.

"Where can I purchase two powerboats?"

"At Apache Performance Boats, in Miami. It's directly in front of Fort Apache Marina. It's owned by Don Aranow. He's the guy to talk to."

"How well do you know him?"

"I don't. I just know of him. He builds the fastest boats on the water."

"Is the business open on Sunday?"

"I believe it is. To the best of my recollection, it's closed on Monday."

"Thanks Chris. How have things been with you?"

"Great. In a couple of weeks I'll be going shopping." Peaches knew exactly what he meant by that.

"Well, be sure to give me a call." She replied. "You know I will." He assured her.

Getting the phone number from Nuni, Peaches called Tony and Raul's new apartment.

"Hello?" Tony answered. "What's up?" Peaches asked.

"Hey! We've been wondering when you were going to call."

"If you're not too busy, I'd like to take a trip to Norman's Cay tomorrow."

"Sure, whatever you want."

"Will you do me a favor?"

"Anything."

"Buy a hundred dollars worth of groceries, four fifths of Jack Daniel's whiskey, two buckets of K.F.C., and the best radio that you can find. Make sure you buy a good supply of batteries."

"No problem. The boat is fueled and ready to go."

"I'll give you a call a half hour before I'm ready to leave and meet you at the dock."

"See you there!" Tony promised.

CHAPTER TWENTY-ONE
GREAT EXUMA

Seven o'clock Sunday morning, Peaches poured herself a hot cup of black coffee, then inserted two slices of bread into the toaster. When the toast popped up, she buttered it generously, topping it with marmalade jelly that she grabbed from a cabinet. Marmalade jelly was something Nuni had introduced her to, making it a part of her morning ritual.

Peaches walked outside to the gazebo and sat down on the swing. Miss Prissy soon followed, rubbing herself against Peaches' right leg to get her attention. The fragrance of the rose garden filled the crisp morning air.

"Good morning, Miss Prissy." Peaches smiled, breaking off a piece of toast and offering it to her. Miss Prissy smelled the toast, then turned her nose up in a motion of distain.

"Well, aren't we the picky one." Peaches laughed. After she finished eating the second slice of toast, she gently picked Miss Prissy up to sit on her lap.

"Did you miss me?" She asked, scratching Miss Prissy's head and rubbing her ears. "I've been in Maryland. Next week, I'll be moving to my new apartment, but I'll come see you. Right now, I'm on my way to Miami." She cooed the cat, then gently sat her on the ground.

"Look what you've done." Peaches giggled, brushing cat hair from her black blouse. She walked inside the house to the bathroom, undressed, and stepped into the shower. Toweling dry, she walked into the bedroom and grabbed a pair of cut-off frayed jeans from her suitcase. Before going to bed, she trimmed her toenails and polished them pink. In the morning, she slid her tiny feet into her multicolored flip-flops and joined Nuni, Ramrod and Sugar, at the breakfast table. Ramrod was preoccupied reading the Orlando Sentinel's Classifieds in search of a house to rent.

Peaches paused and announced. "There's a rotten apple in our basket, a snitch. I spoke to Sergeant Hill while I was in Maryland and the F. B. I. had called him inquiring about my ex-husband Charlie, and myself. They are aware of my trip to Pennsylvania, and possibly Bogota."

"Fuck!" Ramrod snapped in disgust.

"Tighten up! Keep your eyes and ears open."

"I could have all of the employees take a polygraph." Nuni suggested.

"Absolutely not. The employees shouldn't be aware of our illegal activities. Pay closer attention to who's asking questions."

"Bowdy asked Glenda where you were?" Sugar offered.

"Put him at the top of the list!" Peaches snapped.

"Someone is going to have a very bad day if I find out who the snitch is." Ramrod swore.

"Well, I'm on my way to Miami, then to Norman's Cay. Don't expect me back before noon tomorrow."

"Don't speed!" Sugar giggled, heckling her sister.

* * *

Five miles from the City limits of Miami, Peaches stopped for gas and to ask for directions to Apache Performance Boats. Fifteen minutes later, she parked next to a white Mercedes-Benz sporting a removable hard-top. A black plaque with white letters bordered in red was attached to the wall. It read 'RESERVED FOR DON ARANOW'.

She entered the huge pole barn to the sound of power tools filling the air. Loud power tools that shrieked and grinders that whistled making irritating noises. Unfinished boats hung in huge wooden cradles with ladders leaning against them.

"Can you tell me where I can find the owner?" She asked a worker.

The worker was dressed in blue coveralls and covered in dust. Without turning off the grinder in his left hand, he pointed to an office at the rear of the building. She thanked him, following the path he pointed out to the back office. She opened the outer door and stepped inside. Closing the door behind her she heard the sound of a wolf whistle, causing her to smile. Directly in front of her was a large brown desk with a huge man sitting behind it in a high-back brown leather chair. He was talking on the phone, his eyes staring at her. The big man had dark curly hair, a baritone voice, and a friendly smile.

He gestured with a motion of his hand that he would be with her momentarily. A few minutes later he hung up the phone.

"Are you the owner, Don Aranow?"

"I am," he grinned, standing up. He stepped from behind the desk. "I would like to buy two powerboats," she announced.

Don Aranow looked at her with an appraising eye, taking in her slim body, platinum blonde hair, and tiny feet with pink painted toenails. At first glance, he was consumed with desire.

Peaches sized-up the man standing before her. He was six two, with a dark complexion, weighing an easy two hundred and twenty pounds. His eyes were a piercing brown. His brown curly hair reminded her of a Greek in ancient times she had once seen in a book. Don Aranow was wearing white shorts with a Hawaiian shirt unbuttoned at the top exposing his hairy chest. His eyebrows were thick and his arms were hairier than any she had ever seen on a man. She secretly wondered if he was Italian, or Greek. Framed photos of him with race horses taken at Tampa Bay Downs, and in huge powerboats racing across the water adorned one wall.

"That was taken when my horse won her first race at Tampa Bay Downs." Don Aranow noted with some evident pride. He pointed to another photo with Ben Kramer at the helm. "This is when my boat Blue Thunder took first place in the Miami 500."

"It's obvious that you've lived a very colorful and fast life." Peaches smiled.

"What do you know about powerboats?" He asked, grinning.

"That they're expensive." Peaches laughed.

"That they are." He continued to grin. "Boats normally sell for one thousand dollars a foot. For example, you can expect to pay thirty-two thousand dollars for a thirty-two foot boat. With powerboats, the cost doubles. My high performance boats are custom ordered, the standard size is thirty-two foot. Anything over forty foot you need a Captain's license to operate."

"Thirty-two foot will work for me, and the price is fine."

"You can afford that?" He asked, his eyebrows raised.

"Yes. And I'm interested in purchasing two powerboats." She replied smugly.

"What is your name?"

"Cash!" She snapped.

"Is that your first or last name?"

"Just call me Peaches."

"Well, Ms. Peaches. I require a ten percent deposit. Payment upon delivery. It will take six to twelve months to build the boats."

"I need the boats by the end of the week." She retorted.

"That's impossible! Nobody can build a boat that fast, and you want two boats, not one. See those two boats in the cradles." He pointed out to the work room floor. "It took a year to build those. They were special ordered. It's been six weeks since completion and I'm still waiting for my money. Those boats cost a hundred thousand dollars each."

"I'll take them, problem solved." Peaches snapped.

"I can't sell you someone else's boats."

"You would be foolish not to. What if the buyer doesn't have the money? Like you said, it's been six weeks."

"Perhaps we can come to some arrangement." Don offered, undressing her with his eyes.

"Perhaps we can." She smiled seductively.

Don Aranow stepped to his desk, pressed a button, and a panel slid back revealing a hidden room. Inside, there was a round bed with a red velvet headboard in the shape of a half-moon. The bed was covered with a red crush velvet bedspread and white satin sheets. The floor was plush white carpet. There were mirrors on the ceiling, mood lighting, and soft music.

"A hundred and fifty thousand for both boats." Peaches smiled, even more alluring.

As much as he lusted for her, he could not agree to the price. He countered. "One hundred and ninety thousand for both boats."

"One eighty, and I'll show my appreciation."

"One eighty-five cash. Payment on delivery."

"I'll take delivery in the morning. Write the contract. Then, I'll show my appreciation."

"No tricks," he replied.

Peaches laughed.

As he wrote the contract, he requested that she leave a thousand dollar down payment to make the contract legal and binding. "No problem." Peaches agreed.

As she put the contract and money receipt in her pocket, she stepped inside of the love nest and Don closed the door behind them. She sat on the edge of the bed, unzipped his shorts, pulled his half erect penis out and slowly sucked on it. Fully erect, it was huge! He pushed her back onto the round bed, unbuttoning her tight cut-off jeans and snatched them off, exposing her well trimmed patch. She pulled her white halter top over head and tossed it to the floor.

Peaches could feel her hunger for him growing. She found it amusing that he thought he was seducing her. In truth, she had wanted him from the second her eyes had fallen on his manly good looks. He ran his hands over her firm tits lightly pinching her brown nipples. She lay naked on the bed, thrilling to the power of his touch. He quickly removed his clothes and joined her, affectionately squeezing and sucking her breasts.

His right hand slid down to her moist mound as he ran his tongue down her flat stomach. Circling her belly button, he parted the lips of her pink pussy, allowing his tongue to flutter over her clit in rapid movements. She moaned her pleasure spreading her legs wider.

Don mounted her, shoving his rock hard throbbing nine inch dick deep inside of her fucking her long and hard. He was a large, strong, powerful man who knew how to please a woman. They climaxed together several times, then lay exhausted on the bed next to each other looking into each others' eyes. Neither of them knowing who had bested the other. Neither of them really cared, they were both completely satisfied.

"May I use your phone?" She asked, as they dressed.

"Of course." He replied with a smile. She had been much more than he had ever bargained for.

She looked at her watch. It was one o'clock. When they walked back into his office she picked up the phone on his desk and dialed the number to Tony and Raul's apartment.

"Hello?" Tony answered.

"Meet me at the boat in twenty minutes."

"See you there!" He replied.

Turning to face Don Aranow, she said. "I'll be here by ten tomorrow morning with the payment for both boats in cash."

"I'll be looking forward to seeing you." He smiled, pressing the button to close the panel to secret room.

When she reached Fort Apache Marina, Tony and Raul had already carried the groceries that she asked them to buy to the boat and they were standing on the dock waiting for her.

"Did you pick up a radio?" She asked.

"The best one that I could find." Tony boasted.

Within minutes, the powerful Donzi roared out of the inlet and into open water.

Juan heard the Donzi approaching and excitedly called to the other men. Manual, Cheeva and Pepe ran to join Juan at the dock. When they saw the platinum blonde hair blowing in the wind as the Donzi approached they all smiled, knowing that it could only be one person, Peaches. As she stepped off the boat, they welcomed her like she was a returning queen.

"I brought groceries, a radio with a good supply of batteries, Jack Daniel's whiskey, and two buckets of your favorite, Kentucky fried chicken." She said proudly. "Also, I just purchased two brand new bad ass high performance powerboats. In case of an emergency, a boat will be kept docked here. You will never be left stranded on the island. How does that sound?"

"Thank you, Ms. Peaches." Juan grinned, telling the news to the other men in Spanish.

Pepe said something in Spanish. Juan translated for Peaches. "Pepe wants to know if we can use the boat for fishing?"

"Of course." She replied, laughing. "Tell Pepe that he can use it for whatever he wants."

They sat on the porch of the bungalow eating fried chicken while Peaches walked around the island surveying it. Two hours later, she announced that it was time for her to leave. Before returning to Miami, she stopped at the island of Great Exuma. She had already heard that Georgetown, the Capital of the Bahamas, was there. She soon discovered there were no paved roads and the airstrip was unpaved dirt. Customs was a concrete building with a long wooden table. Visitors walked in one door, placed their luggage on the table for inspection, and exited out of a second door. Bahamian agents dressed in green Bermuda shorts with matching short sleeve shirts. Located directly across from Customs was a grass shack, Kermit's bar. There were two motels, three bars, and a marina. The favored motel was called the Peace and Plenty. The Bahamians were black, but they spoke with a thick British accent. She learned that Lord Rholes deeded two-thirds of the island to the Bahamians, that it was generation land and could never be sold.

Peaches suddenly had a brilliant idea. She wanted to purchase a house on the island of Great Exuma, and through a local realtor she purchased a small two bedroom cottage on a hilltop that had electricity and running water. The kitchen, living room, and bathroom was small, but adequate. Next, she rented two boat slips at the marina.

Returning to Miami, she drove to the Holiday Inn on Ocean drive, rented a room, and called Nuni's house.

"Hello." Sugar answered.

"Is Nuni there?" Peaches asked excitedly.

"Well, that's a fine howdy-do. I miss you too, bitch." Sugar said, then yelled. "Nuni!"

Peaches shook her head with a little smile twisting her lips. A couple seconds later Nuni came on the line. "What's up?" He asked.

"I'm at the Holiday Inn. Go somewhere, and call me back."

"Give me ten minutes."

Fifteen minutes later the phone rang. "What's up? Is everything okay." He asked.

"Everything's fine. But I didn't trust talking over the house phone, I need for you to meet me here by nine o'clock in the morning, and bring two hundred and fifty thousand dollars with you."

"No problem. Are you sure that you don't want me to drive down tonight?"

"No, I have some things that I still need to take care of. I'll see you in the morning," she said, returning the phone to its cradle. In hindsight, she had wished she packed an overnight bag. She drove to a nearby shopping center, purchased a new outfit and personal hygiene items. Returning to the motel room, she showered, shaved her legs and underarms, then dressed in her new blue Levi's and yellow blouse. She stood looking in the mirror, satisfied with her appearance. Then, she dialed Chris' number at his apartment. When she heard his voice on the other end, before he could say anything more than hello, she said. "Hi Chris. I'm in town, by myself, at the Holiday Inn. Would you like to meet somewhere for a drink?"

"Why don't you stop by my apartment? There's no one here, but me." Chris explained,

"How do I get there?"

Chris quickly gave her directions. Twenty minutes later, there was a knock on the door of his apartment. Chris opened the door, invited her inside and offered her something to drink.

"Do you have Jack Daniel's and Coca-Cola?"

"Of course." Chris smiled as he made the drinks, he asked "Did you order a boat?"

"No." She beamed. "I purchased two high performance powerboats."

"How in the hell did you do that?" He asked in disbelief.

"After I spoke to you, I called my brother. He ordered a new boat and it's going to be ten to twelve months before delivery."

"Did you buy the boats from Apache Performance?"

"I did." She smiled, batting her eyes at him. "Maybe I'm more persuasive."

"I guess so." Chris laughed, handing her a tall glass of Jack Daniel's and Coca-Cola on ice.

Peaches looked around his apartment with an approving eye. It was spacious. There was a huge television in a cabinet, a pit group, a stereo system, and a eight-person Jacuzzi with a spectacular view of the ocean from his fourth floor balcony. Chris had the ultimate bachelor pad.

"I need your help, Chris."

"What's up?"

"I just purchased two new powerboats and a house on the island of Great Exuma. I have a plan, but I need someone local whom I can trust."

Peaches explained her plan in detail, letting Chris know exactly what she needed of him.

"That's no problem. I'll take care of everything." He assured her. "Do you have any cocaine?"

"You mean, left from my hundred kilos?"

"No." Peaches laughed. "I mean lines for us to do now."

"Of course." Chris beamed, stepping behind the small wet bar located in the corner of the living room. When he returned to where she was sitting on the sectional, he reached into a plastic baggy and laid out four lines on top of the glass coffee table. Peaches gave him a little smile, then quickly made the four lines into two and snorted them. "Aren't you having any?" She giggled.

"Yeah, after you finish." He chuckled.

Chris laid out two lines for himself, which he quickly snorted up his nose.

"I hear you're pretty hot stuff." Chris said, with a leer.

"Never listen to rumors. Always find out things for yourself." She laughed. "Is the Jacuzzi hot?"

"Not nearly as hot as you are. Would you care to try it out?" He asked, staring at her with a hungry look in his eyes.

"Why not." She smiled, standing up and striping off her clothes.

His eyes were taking in her very sexy body as he striped off his clothes and followed her naked into the pool.

"This is nice." She said, running her hands across the top of the steaming water.

"It is relaxing, isn't it?"

"I've got to buy one of these for myself." She grinned her pleasure.

Out of the blue, Chris suddenly asked. "Have you ever had a threesome?" She found the question somewhat disturbing wondering what he knew.

Did he know about Manny and Marsha?

"With another girl?" Chris clarified his question. "Maybe."

"Well, I know some really hot chicks that are bisexual. Would you like for me to give one of them a call?"

"Maybe some other time." She laughed, stepping out of the hot tub. His eyes followed her as she walked naked through his apartment to the bathroom. She returned with a towel, carefully drying herself. While slipping on her clothes, she watched Chris, who was still in the Jacuzzi.

"Thanks for the drink and the help." She smiled. Then she turned, opened the door to the apartment, and left.

Chris heard a car door close, an engine start, and a car exiting the parking lot. He leaned over, and dialed a number. Laughing quietly to himself, he picked up the phone, calmly invited a bisexual chick and her girlfriend over for the night. Still, he could not stop thinking about how nice it would have been had Peaches stuck around to join them.

CHAPTER TWENTY-TWO
LITTLE MISS DANGEROUS

Nuni parked next to Peaches' Mercedes-Benz, stopping long enough at the front desk of the Holiday Inn to ask for Nicole Redman's room number. When he knocked on the room door, she answered with a big smile.

Nuni walked inside carrying a gym bag. "What's the money for?" He aksed.

"I bought two high performance boats, and a house on the island of Great Exuma."

"Where is that?"

"Fifteen miles from Norman's Cay. It's an unspoiled island. There are no roads, few amenities, but it has electricity and fresh water. It's a good investment."

"Do you think it's a good idea to be spending money when we have a forty-eight million dollar debt to pay in less than forty-five days?" Nuni barked.

"What didn't you understand about my needing a silent partner? I make the decisions, not you! I don't want to be having this discussion every time I make a decision you don't understand. Are we clear on this?"

"Crystal." Nuni snapped.

"Four hundred kilos were sold the week before last. How many were sold last week?"

"Five hundred. There's eleven duffel bags, with twenty-two million dollars in the storage unit."

"That's great. We still have a month to meet our goal and things are steadily picking up."

"I found a way to ship larger quantities cross-country. It's fairly safe and it's the cheapest way to go."

"How's that?" She questioned.

"We will use moving and storage companies. Drivers charge a

thousand dollars per kilo to drive cross country. So let's say twenty kilos cost us twenty thousand dollars. It cost me four hundred dollars to rent a house for a month. I spent five hundred dollars furnishing it with used furniture, and another two hundred dollars for clothes I bought at the Salvation Army. I boxed everything up, along with five hundred kilos of coke, and I shipped everything through a reputable moving company to a safe house I set up in California. The entire move cost less than eight thousand dollars."

"That's what I'm talking about, Nuni. That's using your head, and that's why you're my partner."

Nuni beamed. He was delighted to be praised for his work. "Here's the money you asked for," he said, setting the gym bag on the bed. There was no reason to count it, she was sure the amount was correct. Peaches removed sixty-five thousand dollars from the bag, leaving a hundred and eighty-five thousand dollars still in the bag. Including the thousand dollar deposit that would pay for the two high performance boats in full.

"Do me a favor, Nuni. Stop by Chris Delgado's apartment and give him this sixty-four thousand dollars."

"No problem." Nuni thought about asking why, but dismissed the thought just as quickly.

"I will meet you at your house later this afternoon."

"Do you need help with the boats?"

"No, I've got that handled."

One hour later, Peaches arrived at Apache Performance Boats. She found Don Aronow's white Mercedes-Benz parked in front of the reserved sign. The hard top was removed, exposing its bright red leather interior. She parked next to it. Don spotted her walking through the pole barn and opened his office door to greet her. She walked inside, then sat the opened dark blue gym bag filled with money on his desk. He hurriedly closed the door and closed the blinds covering the windows.

"You can count it if you want." She offered.

Don opened the bag, saw the cash was in money wrappers, the denominations clearly marked, and zipped the bag closed. "The bank can count it." He smiled, confident it was all there. Then he asked. "Before I register your boats, would you like to name them?"

"What color are my boats?"

"One is yellow with silver metal-flake. The other is emerald green with silver metal-flake."

"Yellow. As in lemon?"

"Pretty close."

"I'll name the yellow one Lil' Miss Dangerous."

"Lil' Miss Dangerous." Don Aranow laughed heartily. "It's fitting. What would you like to name the other one?"

"Poor Boy."

"I'll have 'Lil' Miss Dangerous' lettered in red across the stern and 'Poor Boy' lettered in silver. Of course, if that's alright with you? The boats will be registered, numbered, and lettered before noon. Where would you like for me to deliver them?"

"Fill the tanks and put them in the water at Fort Apache Marina as close to one o'clock as possible."

"Consider it done. I will see you there."

"No, you won't. Tony and Raul Rivera will be picking the boats up at my request."

"Fine by me. Stop in anytime. I'll be looking forward to seeing you again." He said this last part with a huge grin.

"Until then." She smiled.

The boats were delivered on time. Chris met Tony and Raul at the marina. The two new high performance boats and John Leder's Donzi, the Wave Runner, left the marina following each other in a close line. Their first stop was Great Exuma. Peaches had instructed Chris to pay the realtor thirty-five thousand dollars for the house. She gave him an addftional five hundred to have the utilities turned on in his name. Then the boats raced to Norman's Cay, Lil' Miss Dangerous winning the race by a large margin. Poor Boy ran a close second, and the cobalt blue Wave Runner came in last. Chris gave Juan twenty thousand dollars, with instructions from Peaches. The remaining five hundred was to cover expenses, which included gas.

Juan, Manual, and Pepe hopped aboard Poor Boy. Chris was at the helm of Wave Runner. Tony and Raul had used the boat to make many deliveries of cocaine. Now that John Leder was gone, Chris could put it to use for Peaches' purposes. Now, the two brothers were at the helm of Lil' Miss Dangerous. The two new high performance boats docked at the marina at Great Exuma. Juan and the other men went to the house for the night. Chris, Tony and Raul returned to Miami. They refueled and docked at Fort Apache marina. Chris had completed the favor Peaches had asked of him.

* * *

"Can I see you in the office?" Ramrod told Peaches the second she entered the club. Frowning, Peaches followed Ramrod directly to the office, closing the door behind them.

"I know who the snitch is." He announced.

"How do you know? Are you absolutely sure?"

"I narrowed it down to Bowdy and Glenda. Last night I invited Bowdy to the house. I confronted him and asked if he would take a polygraph? He agreed without a moment's hesitation. So, I called John Goode and asked for a favor. He came right over and gave Bowdy a polygraph. He passed with flying colors, so the snitch has to be Glenda. What do you want me to do with her?"

"Don't tell anyone. Let's feed her some information and see if the F.B.I. takes the bait."

Ramrod grinned. "You're one devious bitch. I love it! Can I be the one to feed her the info?"

"When it's time." She promised.

"This weekend Rod is driving my car to Orlando. He's bringing us some cash and flying back Monday morning."

"The movers will be loading up my apartment and Manny and Marsha's house in the morning. Manny, Marsha and her children will be flying in tomorrow night. By Friday morning everything should be delivered and we will be unpacking at our new residences. I'm looking forward to Marsha and Manny living nearby."

"They're nice people." Ramrod said.

By the end of the week everyone had settled into their new homes. Manny joined the country club, his plan was to play golf three times a week.

Marsha proudly flew the American flag in front of her home, honoring her deceased husband, Harold. The children argued over rooms, forcing Marsha to take control, assigning the rooms as she saw fit. The children fell in love with the lake and their schools; quickly making plenty of friends. Travis joined the high school football team, becoming an instant hit with the girls. Marsha thought that moving to Orlando was working out well.

* * *

More than a month had passed since Peaches' meeting with Pablo Escobar, and Nuni had surpassed their goal of selling two thousand kilos. Inside of the storage unit, there was stored twenty-four green army duffel bags, each containing two million dollars. In two days, they would go to Norman's Cay, listening to the short-wave radio in preparation for the new pilot's call sign. This time they would be meeting a 'Captain Hooch'.

Nuni rented a U-Haul van to deliver the twenty-four duffel bags of money to the Fort Apache Marina. Peaches followed in her yellow Bug, believing it would draw less attention. They met Tony and Raul Wednesday morning at the dock, loaded the money on to Wave Runner, and raced across the water to Great Exuma. Juan, Cheeva, and Pepe were living in the house. They met at the marina on Great Exuma, and the three boats raced to Norman's Cay. Juan started the generator and monitored the short-wave radio. The bunkhouse had been torn down, the front yard cleaned up, and a garden was planted where the bunkhouse once was.

"It's looking much nicer." Peaches praised Juan for their hard work.

At two o'clock they heard the call sign over the radio. "Captain Hooch to Norman's Cay."

"Norman's Cay to Captain Hooch. You are cleared for landing." Juan answered.

To expedite the unloading, the duffel bags were divided equally between the three boats. Nuni and Peaches hopped aboard Lil' Miss Dangerous and cast the ropes onto the dock.

The powerful performance boats raced across the water at fifty miles an hour. They moored the boats at the small island and carried the duffel bags on their shoulders to the landing strip, stacking them one on top of the other. The twin-engine blue and white Gruman Goose circled the island, slowly dropping down to a smooth landing.

"Peaches." Scorpio said with a grin, surprised to see her there.

"When I saw the plane, I was hoping Captain Hooch was you."

"I'm not going to use my real call sign." He laughed.

"Were you afraid that you were going to get ripped off?" She smiled.

"I was a little worried about that." He admitted, knowing the fate of the pilot before him.

"I've got Pablo's money. All of it. There's twenty-four duffel bags, each containing two million dollars." She pointed to the stack of duffel bags.

"Pablo will be pleased. I have a feeling that we will be seeing a lot of each other."

"My apologies. I forgot your name."

"That's okay. Most people can't remember it anyway. It's Michael Coffey. Just think of a cup of coffee, and replace the last 'e' with a 'y'. Why don't you give me the fifty cent tour of the island while the guys unload the cargo and load the duffel bags."

"Sure, why not. Is this your first time being here?"

"Yes, it is. But I've been to Norman's Cay once. From there, I flew inland to Miami. That's when I picked you up and flew to Columbia."

They walked through the thick brush to the far side of the island, sat beneath a palm tree, making idle conversation. Peaches talked about her growing up in Georgia and he talked about his upbringing. He talked of his strict parents, college education, and his overwhelming love for flying.

"There's no money in flying unless you're trafficking drugs."

"Have you ever been married?" She asked.

"Nope. I'm never in one place long enough to have a relationship. Have you been married?"

"Once, but that seems like a very long time ago." Peaches smiled.

"It's good to see you, again." He told her.

Peaches smiled. "Tell Pablo that I will be needing a shipment every two weeks." She said, while ignoring his comment. Their walk back to the airplane was made in comfortable silence. The two thousand kilos of coke were unloaded and carried to the boats. A thousand kilos were placed inside the cabin of Lil' Miss Dangerous, the other thousand inside the cabin of Poor Boy. Nuni and Juan were at the helm of Lil' Miss Dangerous. Tony and Raul were in Poor Boy. The two boats raced to the unloading dock at Boco Raton. After the boats were unloaded, Peaches instructed Nuni to rent a room at the Holiday Inn for the night. She promised to join him later. Tony and Raul were to return the boats to the marina at Great Exuma.

"From now on the short-wave radio would be kept at the house on Great Exuma. It will take an extra fifteen minutes for the boats to reach this island, but it will be better and safer." Peaches explained.

"Then it is better for me as well." Scorpio replied as he climbed up into the plane. With a wave and a smile he closed the door.

The airplane gathered momentum and sped down the short runway. As it gained altitude, the pilot rocked its wings to wave goodbye.

* * *

Nuni motioned for Tony to stop. Sitting dead in the water, he shouted across to the other boat. "I need to be dropped off at Fort Apache Marina so I can pickup the van and meet you at the dock in Boco Raton."

After dropping Nuni off, Juan, Tony and Raul raced to the dock at Boco Raton. They were ready to unload the boats when Nuni arrived. Nuni covered the cocaine with a brown tarp and drove to the Holiday Inn, while the two boats raced to Great Exuma to meet Peaches.

Lil Miss Dangerous and Poor Boy docked at the marina on Great Exuma for the night. Peaches, Tony and Raul took the Wave Runner and sped across the water to the marina at Fort Apache. Peaches took her Volkswagon to the Holiday Inn, parking next to the rental van and joining Nuni in bed. Within seconds they were both sound asleep.

CHAPTER TWENTY-THREE
WRAPPED UP

The following morning, Peaches followed the bright orange U-Haul from the Holiday Inn in Miami to Nuni's storage unit In Orlando. Nuni backed up the van, and opened the cargo door of the storage unit. Peaches crawled inside the van and tossed boxes to Nuni, and he stacked them. Different size boxes for different amounts. Beginning at ten kilos, ending at fifty. After unloading the van she drove to the house, while he dropped off the van at the U-Haul rental place and picked up his Lincoln. "I'm glad you're back, Nicky." Sugar declared, running across the room to hug her sister. "I worry myself sick every time you go away on a trip."

"Well then, you can stop worrying. Hopefully, I've made my last one." Peaches comforted her.

"You're getting out of the business?"

Ramrod, who was sitting at the kitchen table, lowered the newspaper in his hands. He watched and listened for Peaches' response.

"Hell no!" She laughed. "I just think it's time that I start delegating more of my responsibilities."

"The Queen Bee has a lot of workers." Ramrod smiled his approval.

"I'm taking more risks than I should, and if something happens to me, guess what happens to the business?" Peaches explained.

"I agree. Did I say that I didn't? It just struck me as being humorous." Ramrod grinned.

"Watch yourself. I'll sic my sister on you." Peaches cautioned.

"You already have." He smiled. Sugar threw a silver oven mitt at Ramrod. He ducked and it hit the wall. "Just teasing, Sugar." He laughed.

Rod suddenly appeared in the doorway of the kitchen. He grinned, looking at Peaches. "Don't I get a hug?"

"It's good to see you." She smiled and hugged him affectionately.

The last time they had seen one another was when he had dropped of her car. "I forgot you were driving Ramrod's car here this weekend. Where is it? I didn't see it in the driveway."

"It's getting a tune-up, and I didn't see any reason to keep the snow tires on it."

"Florida gets a lot of snow too. It's called cocaine." Peaches laughed.

"Florida snow." Rod chuckled.

Nuni walked through the door and Rod greeted him with a firm handshake and a slap on the back.

"How are things at the cabin." Nuni asked.

"Great. Things are going well."

Peaches started to open the refrigerator, then stopped dead in her tracks to stare at Rod. "Has there been any takers on the reward?"

"Not yet." He replied, suddenly sounding solemnly. It was as though he was reading her mind. A thousand times over he wished that he could take the fight with Bulldog back and relive that day.

"Nuni, I think everyone will agree that both the F. B. I. and D.E.A. have me in their cross hairs. It's no secret, so it's best that I take the back seat for a while. You have things running smoothly now. If you were to replace me, who do you feel trustworthy enough to take your position?"

"I like Bowdy." Ramrod suggested.

"I grew up with Bobby. If he's interested, he would be my first choice. Bowdy would be my second choice." Nuni agreed with Ramrod.

Peaches nodded. "You're calling the shots, and you will be reporting to me weekly. If there's a problem, call me anytime, day or night. The two thousand kilos we picked up today are paid for, so we now have thirty-five hundred kilos of uncut coke available. In one month we will have to pay for another shipment. That's twenty-four million dollars. Our ultimate goal should be to establish a thousand kilo reserve supply in each district."

"It's going to take five thousand kilos to accomplish that." Nuni protested.

"I think we should do it." Peaches said firmly.

"What are you going to do if you're not running the business?" Sugar questioned her sister.

"I need some down time to unwind. I've always wanted to take a cruise through Alaska. Ramrod, for the next two weeks, I want you to be Glenda's new best friend. Thanks to you, and our plans, she now thinks my source is in Amsterdam."

"That's one stupid bitch." Ramrod chuckled.

"We're going to make sure that she gets what she's got coming." Peaches promised.

* * *

By ten o'clock the Pink Pussycat was filled to capacity. Ramrod had done a superb job of hiring and firing dancers, He called it weed and seed.

Peaches seated herself at the bar.

"Hi stranger," Glenda smiled at her. "Did you get all settled into your new apartment?"

"Almost. I hate moving, having to pack and unpack boxes. I probably should have stayed in Amsterdam. It was beautiful! Prostitution and weed is legal, and they've got the best drugs. Cheap too. If you buy in quantity, you can really get some good deals."

"How would you get them into the United States?"

"That's easy." Peaches replied with a smile, but without answering the question.

"What can I get you to drink?" Glenda asked.

"Jack Daniel's and coke on ice in a tall glass."

* * *

"Daddy, I want a gun." Dee Dee demanded of her father. Anthony Caruso looked at his daughter in disbelief.

"What for, sweetheart?" He asked, coming to his feet from behind the desk in concern.

"I'm going to shoot that no good womanizing Charlie Redman!"

"You can't do that. You would go to jail. Haven't you gotten over him yet?"

"I love him. He's the only man that I've ever loved, besides you. Did I tell you that he treated me like a princess? He rented a limo and took me to the opera. I don't understand why he hurt me so much." Dee Dee said, bursting into tears.

"Dee Dee, I have always protected you. I only wanted what was best for you. I hope you can find it in your heart to forgive me for what I've done." His eyes were sad as he stared into her anguish filled face.

"What did you do, daddy? Is Charlie dead?" She cried.

"No, baby," He said quickly. "But the reason he isn't seeing you is because of an overly protective father."

"You, daddy?" She sobbed.

"Charlie was warned never to see you again."

"I love you, daddy, but I have to go to him." Dee Dee said, running out the door. Anthony Caruso watched helplessly as his only daughter rushed to another man's arms.

Dee Dee parked behind Charlie's Stingray. She heard the lawnmower mowing the backyard and hurried around to the rear of the house. Charlie was standing at the far end of the lawn. He was shirtless and drinking from a large glass. She stared at him with her heart heavy with love. Sensing that someone was watching him, he lowered the glass to look in her direction, holding up his right forearm up to block the sun.

"Dee Dee." The glass dropped from his hands to the lawn, a gasp of shock bursting from his mouth.

She ran to him, throwing her arms tightly around his stiff body. "What are you doing here? You can't be here!"

"My father told me that you were warned not to see me again. But everything is okay now!" She promised, raining kisses all over his face.

Feeling his heart racing, he suddenly grabbed her to kiss her back. He swept her off her feet, carrying her inside the house and kicked the door closed. He reasoned that it was pointless to tell her everything he had endured. After all, he would still have to ask Anthony Caruso for his daughters hand in marriage.

* * *

"I got a call from my informant this morning." Moore told Agent Sweeny.

Sweeny knew exactly what was coming next. Moore picked up the phone and dialed the number for Detective Hill.

"Hello?" Hill answered.

"I was calling to see if you had any new information?"

"Not really. I drove by Charlie Redman's house last week, and his Corvette was parked in the driveway."

"His ex-wife has been a very busy girl. I think the trip she took to Amsterdam is going to be her downfall. We're closing in on her pretty fast. If you hear anything, give me a call."

"Will do."

That night Hill called the Pink Pussycat and informed Peaches about the second call from Agent Moore. "They know about your trip to Amsterdam and Moore said they are closing in on you fast."

"Thanks sweety. If you're ever in town, stop in."

"You know I will."

* * *

Peaches woke up Wednesday morning at 10 o'clock. She climbed out of bed to look out of her bedroom window, a yawn escaping from her wide open mouth. Her little yellow Beetle was in the parking lot below, exposed to the extreme heat of the early morning day, it's headlights reminding her of a pair of pleading eyes. Suppressing another yawn she went into the bathroom to shower and dress. She slipped on a white mini skirt with a matching halter top, sliding her feet into multicolored flip-flops on her way to the kitchen. She took the time to make two pieces of toast and a cup of hot coffee, generously topping the toast with butter and a healthy spread of marmalade jelly.

When she stepped from her apartment a heat wave struck her squarely in the face. It was 80° and climbing. She stopped to crack the windows in the Volkswagon. Driving the Bug today was not a consideration. She dropped the top of her Mercedes-Benz, put on her Ray Ban sunglasses and was soon en-route to Marsha's.

Peaches parked in the driveway, walking through the front door to the kitchen. She saw Marsha at the sink washing dishes, and asked. "How are you doing, bitch?"

"It's about time you came to see me." Marsha complained. "The place looks terrific. I love the new living room set."

"Manny bought it for me."

"Speaking of Manny. We' re expected to be at his apartment in less than an hour."

"Shit! That's right, this is Wednesday. Watch the oven, don't let my cookies burn. I've got to get a shower and dress." Marsha shouted, running down the hallway.

"Yummy. I love chocolate chip cookies." Peaches said more to herself, peeking into the oven.

Manny answered the knock on his door with a smile. The girls took turns hugging and kissing him. He had a bottle of champagne on ice. He popped the cork, pouring three glasses of bubbling champagne. He was excited to see them, and anxious to show off his newly furnished condo. It was meticulously decorated, offering the best of everything that money could buy.

"How do you like it here?" Peaches asked, sipping from her glass.

"I should have moved here years ago." He laughed.

"Have you played a game of golf yet?" Marsha inquired. "I'm a regular now." He boasted.

"It's great to see you so happy." Peaches said with a smile. Manny gave them a tour, stopping at his bedroom.

"This is nice." Marsha said, admiring his enormous king size four poster bed.

"We have a second bedroom now." Manny reminded the girls as he opened the door. a round bed was centered in the room. A swing hung above the bed, and the ceiling was mirrored. In the far corner of the room there was a treasure chest filled with adult toys.

"This ought to be fun." Peaches laughed.

Manny grinned and sat down in his favorite chair, as the girls undressed each other. Marsha laid down on the bed flat on her back while Peaches hopped into the swing, spread her legs, and told Marsha that she knew what time it was. The girls stayed in the play room for three hours, taking turns in the swing, playing with toys and pleasing Manny.

On the drive back to her house, Marsha admitted that moving to Orlando had given her life new meaning. The children were adjusting well, and it was wonderful to look out the kitchen window and watch the kids swimming in the lake.

"By the way, the twins wanted me to make sure their Aunt Nicole was aware of their both wanting fishing equipment for Christmas." Marsha laughed.

* * *

Two weeks later, Peaches stopped by Nuni's house around five o'clock in the evening. She sat inside the gazebo smelling the sweetness of the roses, holding Miss. Prissy in her lap. Ramrod walked out of the house to join her.

"Are you Glenda's new best friend?" Peaches asked. "I am!" He nodded. "What's on your mind?"

"I want you to call Glenda into the office on the pretense that you want to discuss one of the barmaids' work performance. At seven o'clock tonight, I'm going to call the club. When the phone rings, I need for you to answer it and pretend you're in a heated confrontation with someone."

Peaches explained her plan in great detail. As Ramrod left the gazebo, Sugar walked up and sat down next to her sister.

"Do you ever think about Mama?" Sugar asked.

"Everyday." Peaches smiled. "I'm sure that neither mom nor dad would be very happy about some of the choices I've made. But I know they would love us despite our shortcomings."

Sugar nodded her head in agreement.

* * *

At six forty-five Ramrod called Glenda to the office. "We've got a problem." He explained.

"What's the problem?"

"One of the barmaids is stealing from the register. It's come up short five days in a row. Do you have any idea which one is stealing from us?" Before she could answer, the phone rang.

"Hello?" Ramrod answered, then held his finger on the button disconnecting Peaches. He stood up and walked to the far side of the room, as far as the cord would allow him to go.

"Don't call the club to discuss business." He spoke into the phone in pretended annoyance. He pretended to listen to the caller.

"That's correct, next Thursday. The shipment will arrive at seven in the morning. You have to be in the Bahamas on Norman's Cay to pick it up."

He pretended to listen to a voice a little longer, then responded. "Twenty- four million. Don't ever call the club again!" He ordered. Ramrod slammed the phone down, then looked at Glenda. "Well, do you have any suspects?"

"I can tell you it's not me."

"I didn't think it was, but as the head barmaid it's your responsibility to keep an eye on things."

"I'll catch whoever it is stealing from the register." Glenda promised.

* * *

Nuni had taken the reins of the drug business, hiring his friend Bobby as his second in command. With Bobby's help, things were working like a well oiled machine. Things could not get any better, at least in Nuni's mind. Every month the call sign for the pilot changed, and the new call for this month was 'Donald Duck'. Scorpio was disappointed that Peaches was not there when he landed. The plane was quickly unloaded, and four hours later, Nuni unloaded the kilos at the dock in Boco Raton. He rented a room at the same Holiday Inn on Ocean Drive, and called Peaches at the club.

"How was your day, darling." She asked.

"Business as usual. I'll see you tomorrow afternoon."

"I'll be here."

* * *

Monday night at ten o'clock, Rod called the club.

"Hello?" Peaches answered the phone from behind the desk in her office.

"I thought that you might like to know that I've located Bulldog."

Peaches felt her heart race. "Where is he?" She shouted her excitement.

"He's working as a bouncer at a bar called Fiddler's Three in Groton, Connecticut, and he's living in a small efficiency apartment behind the bar."

"Thanks!" Peaches said, jumping for joy. "I've gotta go!" She told her sister, rushing out the door. Two hours later Peaches boarded American Airlines flight 237 for Groton, Connecticut. When the airplane landed, she rented a car and drove to a nearby Holiday Inn and rented a room. She took a hot shower and dressed in clean clothes. The weather was so nice she dressed casual.

It was three o' clock in the morning when she arrived at the bar. Bulldog's Harley was parked at the rear of the building next to an older red Mustang convertible. Peaches parked, and walked to the door of the efficiency apartment. She twisted the door handle entering without knocking, stepping lively into the very small efficiency. The bed took up most of the room. She could clearly see Bulldog, passed out on the bed with a woman laying beside him. At her entrance, the woman shot up on the bed like a jack in the box, covering herself with a white sheet.

"Let's go, bitch!" Peaches ordered, moving forward to grab the red haired woman by her hair, and yanking her from the bed. "Go find your own man!"

At the commotion a startled Bulldog came awake, his eyes going wide at the sight of Peaches.

"Do you have a problem with me putting this bitch out." Peaches asked him.

Bulldog suddenly grinned. "No problem."

"Out!" She pointed for Ginger to exit out through the open door.

Ginger shot Bulldog an angry look before snatching up her clothes and leaving the apartment.

"There are some things you need to know." Peaches said.

"I'm listening." He replied calmly.

"When Rod found out that you were responsible for the clubs showing up in Orlando to support Ramrod and look for me, he offered a twenty-five hundred dollar reward for your whereabouts. All of your brothers know the truth, and we all love, miss, and want you back."

"You want me back?" He snatched her onto the bed, hugging her close in his arms.

Peaches laughed. "You've got to shower first!"

Returning the rental car, she climbed on the back of Bulldog's Harley. Adjusting her Ray-Ban sunglasses, she wrapped her arms around his waist, and they took the long ride to the cabin in the blazing sun.

Rod greeted Bulldog with a hug and a heavy pat on the back, profusely apologizing for not being willing to listen to a true brother. All was forgiven, Bulldog understanding that his loyalty would never be questioned again. Bulldog's bedroom was just as he left it, with the exception of the new black leather jacket carefully placed on his bed. Bulldog picked the jacket up and tried it on for size. Where his Sergeant of Arms patch once rested, there was a new patch that read Vice President. The club members had voted him in.

"It's damn good to have you back, bro." Rod said.

"It's good to be back."

They tapped a fresh keg, laid out lines of crystal meth and partied throughout the night.

"I've got to leave tomorrow, but in three months, we're going on an Alaskan cruise. That's if it's okay with you." Peaches inquired, asking for her man's approval.

"I'm going to need something to keep me warm."

"You've got me." She snuggled up to him in the bed. "I'll keep things heated up."

"The arctic may melt." Bulldog laughed.

* * *

Thursday evening Peaches opened the club, having Ramrod and Nuni join her in the office the second they arrived. Together they could watch the 6 o'clock news.

"Good evening, Miami. Susan Lichtman of W.T.V.J. reporting. In an early morning raid Custom, D.E.A. and F.B.I. agents raided an island in the Bahamas, Norman's Cay, taking an elderly couple by surprise."

The scene on the television filmed from a helicopter scanned across an immaculate white bungalow with a white picket fence around it, then to a vegetable garden, and a dock with a row boat secured by a line. The camera zoomed in closer on a pair of multicolored flip-flops at the end of the pier. Susan Lichtman picked back up the narrative. "No drugs were found and no arrest were made. The F.B.I. claimed to be acting on what they believed to be credible information, adding their source of information would have to be reevaluated."

Everyone sitting in Peaches office laughed heartily.

"I love the flip flops." Ramrod chuckled. "I thought it to be a nice touch."

"You're a class act!" Nuni told Peaches, grinning from ear to ear.

They raised shots of whiskey, clanging the glasses and downing the shots to celebrate the brotherhood.

* * *

"She made us look like fools." Moore said to Sweeny on the drive back from Miami. "Customs and the D.E.A. is now worried about being sued. The elderly woman complained of chest pains. We're never going to get any help from another agency, but I'm going to get that fucking bitch if it's the last thing I ever do." Moore swore.

In fifteen years it was the first time Sweeny had ever heard profanity come out of his friend's mouth.

Two weeks later, Glenda's family reported her missing.

* * *

Three months later Peaches and Bulldog boarded a cruise ship in Alaska. Ramrod and Sugar rented a house, spending their free time planning to be married under the gazebo at Nuni's house on July 4th.

Nuni and Bobby took a week's vacation to Argentina. Nuni pitched an umbrella in the white sand, sitting down in a lounge chair beside Bobby, taking time out to admire the Brazilian beauties in string bikinis. Bobby ordered two tequila sunrises, and buried his feet in the warm sand.

"It's time for us to expand." Nuni suddenly announced.

"Expand?" Bobby questioned. "We have deliveries covering the entire United States."

"We've gotta think big!" Nuni retorted. "We still have Australia, New Zealand, China, and maybe even Russia."

* * *

Peaches leaned against the ships railing. Bulldog wrapped his arms around her, and whispered in her ear.

She laughed, then replied. "You're right. Money can't buy happiness, but it will take us a long way to look for it!" Bulldog laughed, holding her tighter.

"I've got one more thing to tell you." She whispered in his ear. "I'm pregnant."

ABOUT THE AUTHOR

William Daniel Burns was born in Lakeland, Florida. His family, and those who knew him in his early years called him "Danny." At an early age, he discovered his gift for conning people to get whatever he wanted. At the age of five, he convinced his best friend that two rusty nails and a piece of wood were from George 'Washington's rocking chair and they would someday be worth a whole lot more then his old shiny silver dollar.

When he was seven, his father moved the family to Baltimore, MD. It was a much tougher neighborhood. Danny learned to fight, and hustle. His parents divorced when he was twelve. His younger sister and older brother chose to stay with his mother. Danny chose to live with his father. They returned to live in Florida., and Danny changed his name to "Bill." His father remarried when he was thirteen. Bill quit school, and left home when he was fifteen. He married, and had two beautiful daughters by the age of seventeen - Tina Marie, and Kerri Ann. He was ill-prepared to handle the responsibility, and moved back to the mean streets of Baltimore, where he turned to crime as a means to support his family. The police made a game of that by telling him they rode around in marked cars and wore uniforms, then asked what does a criminal look like. Bill purchased a yellow panel truck and wrote THIEF WAGON across the back and sides in big black bold letters. The game ended with Bill being sent to prison.

Released from prison, he found his wife remarried and his daughters calling another man "daddy." Bill felt that he had nothing left to lose and devoted his life to crime!

Bill returned to federal prison twice. He furthered his education by obtaining his G.E.D., a degree in Commercial Art, and he has the equivalent of a two-year college Associates Degree. Bill has owned a number of successful businesses.

In 1988, Bill worked as an independent contractor for O's Auto Sales in Walbridge, Ohio. In 1991, while the owner vacationed in Florida, Bill was left in charge of the business. Several other guys also used the license, but they weren't registered to buy or sell vehicles at the auctions.

On May 29, 1991 Bill left with his girlfriend on a Florida vacation, returning June 8, 1991. A fire occurred at Adrian Auto Auction May 31, 1991, and a murder occurred in Northwood, OH on June 7, 1991. When questioned in regard to the murder, Bill accounted for his whereabouts for the entire vacation.

In 1993 Bill was charged with stolen vehicles in Monroe and Adrian, Michigan.

On the advice of two attorneys Bill pled guilty. At sentencing, he told the judge there was nothing anyone could do when they are signed, sealed, and delivered. That just because he signed the titles, it did not necessarily mean the vehicles were his!

Bill served his sentence, and in 1998, he was transferred to the halfway House in Monroe, Michigan. Ten days before his release, he was charged for the arson of Adrian Auto Auction. The prosecutor contended that his motive for the arson was to destroy incriminating evidence, the titles to the stolen vehicles. Bill filed three formal motions for discovery - none were complied with! He refused plea offers of 10 years, 5 years, and 2 years with credit for six months served. Bill was convicted, and sentenced to serve LIFE. He still maintains his innocence.

Bill is a strong supporter of prison reform. He wants to let the youth of today know that crime, drugs, and violence is not a "game." Bill thanks God for his love, insight, and guidance as he journeys through life. For more information on him, please contact him via www.jpay.com. He is inmate number #189577.

ORDER MORE EXCITING NOVELS FROM W.D. BURNS!

THE WEE HOURS

Nothing could have prepared Nicole Redman for the brutal murder of her six-year old daughter. Through a cloud of shock and pain, she seeks her daughter's murderer in a world filled with sleazy strip clubs, after-hour joints, and a notorious outlaw biker gang. She is quickly drawn into a life of illicit sex, drugs, and onto the path of a sadistic hitman.

PEACHES: WEE HOURS II

Nicole Redman found herself lost in an unforgiving world of outlaws whom she had grown to love, respect, and understand. Morally bankrupt by the rules of society, the outlaw bikers lived by one rule - an eye for an eye. The brotherhood ran deep, and Nicole 'Peaches' Redman was proud to call the Argots her family. In her wildest dreams, she had never imagined herself becoming a prostitute, a dancer, a biker chick, a murderer, or a reputed drug dealer. When life handed her lemons, she made lemonade.

FLORIDA SNOW: WEE HOURS III

Hoping to escape a trail of blood and death, Peaches arrives in Florida only to discover that the death toll had just begun. The Argots and the Heathens suddenly find themselves pitted against one another in a vicious drug war, forcing Peaches to fight to save her beloved club. Now, in order to survive she must tame a powerful Columbian Druglord, and outfox an F.B.I. and D.E.A. Task Force.

ORDER THE ENTIRE BAD ASS OUTLAW PUBLICATIONS LINEUP!

Bad Ass OutlawPublications

Mail:

    Bad Ass Outlaw Publications
    4216 Riverview Lane
    Lorian, OH 44055

Name: _____

Address:_____

City/State:_____

Zip:_____

Quantity	Titles	Price	Total
_____	The Wee Hours	$12.95	____
_____	The Wee Hours II: Peaches	$12.95	____
_____	The Wee Hours III: Florida Snow	$12.95	____

Add $3.95 for shipping and handling (Via Priority Mail) for
1 book, $5.95 for 2 books , $8.95 for 3-4 books, add $1.95
for each additional book.

Total: $_____
FORMS OF ACCEPTED PAYMENT: Certified or government
 issued checks and Money Order, all mail in order takes 7-10
Business Days to be delivered.
Or, just order online at http://www.badassoutlawpublications.com!

www.ingramcontent.com/pod-product-compliance
Lightning Source LLC
Chambersburg PA
CBHW072209170626
46813CB00003B/862